# ARCTIC QUEST
## Book 4

# D.L. Narrol

# ARCTIC QUEST
# Book 4

DOUBLE DRAGON

# A DOUBLE DRAGON PAPERBACK

ISBN  978-1-78695-870-9

Double Dragon
is an imprint of
Fiction4All

This Edition Published 2024
*Fiction4All*
*www.fiction4all.com*

# Chapter One

The giant, brawny captain sat on the deck of his fishing vessel. He pulled out a small knife and began to peel an orange. Pages from a folded newspaper blew about the deck, where the captain noticed the headline: *Strange Being Sighted on University Grounds!* He then glanced at the date.

"Hmm, it's almost Christmas. Almost time to say good-bye to 1910," the captain muttered.

He was deep in his thoughts when he heard a hard crashing sound. He turned his head.

"Captain Limmerick! Get this *thing* outta the wheelhouse," Timmy demanded, while he shoved the beast onto the ladder.

The creature lunged at Timmy and threw him to the floor. Timmy stood up and kicked it in the behind. It turned to Timmy and smacked him in the face. The captain's head tilted downward and he stared at his half-peeled orange.

"Feck! I should cut me own throat with this blade, shouldn't I?"

Eddy tried to encourage the beast to climb down the ladder. "Captain, we've got loads to do, but we spend most of our time trying to tame that *thing*." Eddy paused. "Captain, what is *it*?"

Captain Colin Limmerick stood up. "Ed, yer me first mate, therefore, yer supposed to be keep everything in check on this vessel, am I correct?"

The mature first-mate's eyes widened as he glanced at the beast panting in the corner. "Captain, what's this *thing* on our ship, eh? What the hell is it?" The captain paced a bit. "It's good we're not too far from our *emerald paradise*, just now."

The captain dashed into the galley. Eddy followed. The beast sat on the deck alone. It stared at the hectic frigid waves of The Irish Sea and almost fell into a trance. Lorelei and Tara sat at the table in the galley eating crumpets and drinking wine. Lorelei appeared giddy when she noticed the captain.

"Ah, Captain Colin, yaz lookin' as if yar in the middle of some serious orgasm, huh?"

She glanced at Tara and they both giggled at the handsome captain. The captain grabbed a large bottle of whiskey.

"Surely, I'll ask the Lord to take me tonight, so I will."

Lorelei stood up and straightened her tight dress. "What's bothering yaz now? Is it that *thing?*" He popped the cap off the whiskey and stared at the bottle. "Captain, that *thing* is just awful. It reminds me of a caveman."

Lorelei snorted a few laughs with Tara. Colin raised the bottle to his lips and drank feverishly. He glanced at the two giddy prostitutes. "He's not human, in case ye didn't know."

Lorelei grinned. "I'm savin' meself up for yer love-makin'."

He tried to straighten his posture. "Love-makin'? Just tell me how much and ye'll be off to the next port."

"A handsome gent like ya, should learn to lay off the sauce, don't ya think? You could lose yar beauty some day, then what would ya do?"

He placed the bottle on the counter. "I'd relish in me new-found ugliness."

Lorelei giggled with Tara, nudging each other. "Hey, what ya gonna do about that *thing* on the deck? What is it?" Lorelei asked, while she sipped on her wine.

"Why's everyone always askin' me? Can't ye feckin' tell what *it* is?"

"It's a caveman, isn't it?" She tried to guess.

Colin grinned at her. "Uh, Right!"

Lorelei glanced at Tara. "That *thing* is a caveman? Really?"

Tara smiled at the intoxicated captain. "What's a caveman doing on *The Atlantic Mermaid*?"

Colin took a few more gulps of whiskey. "What ye think?"

Lorelei snorted with laughter as her large breasts jiggled. "I donno, is it one of yar crazy science experiments? Ya do all that research with that Russian chap, don't yaz? Ya both conjure some crazy potions in that university laboratory of yours. Tryin' to play God?"

The beast shuffled into the galley. Colin stopped drinking and noticed the creature pause and leer at him. It snatched the bottle of whiskey from his hand. Colin leaned against the counter, and tried to think what to do. He extended his arm.

"Give me that back, ye fecker, or I swear I'll throw yez overboard, ye bloody shite!"

It guzzled the whiskey. Lorelei and Tara tried to ignore what they were seeing. Eddy glanced at Colin with concern.

"Captain? Is Lorelei right? Is this monster the result of one of yar university experiments? Just never knew how ya could keep up yar fishin' trade; keep a crew, and make yar way to the university to work on a doctorate. It's not humanly possible, Captain. Now, look at ya, yar broodin' away 'cause yar pretty lass from India left yaz. Can't have it all, Captain."

Colin stared at the floor, with one eye on the beast. It continued to drink the last drop of whiskey.

"Give me that bottle! *Neanderthal!* Pass it over here!"

Eddy's eyes widened. "*Neanderthal?* Captain, ya brought a *Neanderthal* on *The Atlantic Mermaid?*"

Colin tried to look somewhere else, other than his first mate. "So, I did. I'm the bloody Captain! I can do what I want!"

Eddy stepped closer to Colin. "Captain? Ya brought a *Neanderthal* on the ship? How in the hell did ya do that? Aren't they long extinct?"

7

The *Neanderthal* yelped and raised the whiskey bottle only to smash it over the captain's head. Colin fell to the floor. The beast kicked Colin in the stomach several times. Timmy and Séamus entered the galley. Lorelei and Tara screamed and crouched in the corner with terror. The beast jumped onto Colin and tried to strangle him. Eddy, Timmy, and Séamus tried to pry the prehistoric being off the captain.

"Good Lord!" Shouted Eddy. "The poor man is knocked out cold and this *thing* is relentless enough to finish him off! It's a strong bugger, too. We have to save the captain!" Eddy shouted with a struggle in his voice.

Timmy grabbed the paring knife beside the half-peeled orange and slit the beast's shoulder, enough to draw blood. It finally released the captain. Colin lay on the floor, lifeless, drenched in whiskey and blood. Pieces of glass from the bottle surrounded him on the floor.

Eddy knelt beside him. "Captain, you've always been like a son to me. Please stay with us."

Colin's eyes opened as he continued to lie on the floor. He tried to catch his breath.

Lorelei and Tara stood beside the captain. "Drop us off at the next port. We're not coming aboard this ship with that *thing!*" Lorelei blurted.

Colin continued to lie on the floor. He stared at Lorelei in silence.

"Can't believe you'd bring that disgusting *thing* on the ship and put our lives at risk for some silly science experiment!" Lorelei blurted.

Colin laid on the floor, still silent, where he still tried to focus his eyes on Lorelei.

Eddy and Timmy helped the captain up. "Colin, speak to us, please," pleaded Eddy.

Colin tried to scoot to the wall, so he could lean his bulked physique against it. He took a few deep breaths as he wiped his bloody face with a towel. "I'm alright, Ed." Colin tried to stand straight as he noticed the beast sitting on the deck by the hold. He rubbed his head. "Awe, sweet Christ. I feel I'm gonna die right here, so I do. It near kicked the shite outta me, didn't it?"

Timmy glanced at his captain. "Captain, that *thing* ate half the fish in the hold. Now, what we gonna do, eh?"

Colin hobbled onto the deck and noticed the half empty hold. He shook his head and kissed his lips. *"Shite."*

Eddy stepped beside Colin. "Captain, I know about yar science experiments at the university. But, tell me why would ya bring this prehistoric beast on the ship? That's not like yaz, not at all."

The captain continued to stare at the hold. "'Cause I'm bloomin' arse, that's why."

"Did you time travel and find this *thing* to bring back on purpose, Captain?"

Colin's eyes widened as he lowered his head to be eye to eye with his first mate. "Shh...don't go bringin' me time travels up on the ship. Of course it wasn't me intensions to bring a prehistoric *Neanderthal* on this ship. Ye think I'm daft or somethin'?"

Eddy took a breath of relief. "Thank God, thought ya were losin' yar mind."

"I found the prehistoric creature misplaced in 1970, that's all."

"What?"

"Aye. He was misplaced. He was surely to die there. I had no choice but to bring him along."

Eddy was surprised. "But, can you mind 'im in 1910?"

Colin kept rubbing his soar head. "Surely, not."

"So, Captain, why?"

"Let me die right here. Amoli left me. Rosa's engaged to Sasha." He glanced at his first mate. "What I got to live for, Ed?"

"You're a good man, Colin. Don't go talkin' this way. Ya can't be draggin' some prehistoric extinct

9

caveman everywhere ya go. Surely, no wench will fix her eyes on yaz with that *thing* hangin' about."

Colin gave a slight chuckle. "Surely not."

"So, Rosa, that pretty wench is engaged to that Russian scientist, Dimitrikov?"

Colin stared at the half-empty hold. "Aye."

# Chapter Two

It was Monday morning. Colin and Neanderthal got off the train and plunged their way through London's hustle and bustle. Neanderthal followed Colin through the crowds, unnoticed. Colin was already dressed in his three-piece suit, ready to teach his Monday morning lecture at the university. He crossed the street with Neanderthal, trailing behind him; and made his way to the university lecture hall at the Natural History Building.

Rosa walked by Colin. "Colin! Hello!" She called out, waving her arms above her head to catch his attention.

Colin turned his head and took a few steps toward the beautiful petite figure, as he cut his way through the gaggle of university students. "Grand to see ye," he said with a smile.

"I see you still have your fine fuzzy friend by your side."

"Thankfully, he slept on the train ride to London. I was finally able to order some breakfast. It was brilliant, so it was."

"Colin, you're teaching a lecture now, and you're bringing Neanderthal with you?"

"What else can I do?"

"You can't bring Neanderthal to your lecture. Colin, he's a prehistoric prime mate. He needs to be placed back in his time."

"He's bloody-well destroyin' me life. It's eatin' me out of house and home, and it bloody feck tried to kill me on the ship, so it did."

She raised her hands to her mouth. "Oh my, Colin, I'm so sorry this is happening to you. What can I do to help?"

"Look, it's me own mess, so it is. Lorelei was right in sayin' I'm always tryin' to play God. So, this is what I get for me own wrong-doin', eh?"

Rosa lifted one eyebrow. "Lorelei said that?" She paused. "How profound."

"Why ye miffed that she said that?"

"Because she's a whore, that's why."

"So?"

"Are you sleeping with her again, Colin?"

He stepped away from Rosa. "Why should ye care? Yer off gettin' yerself married to Sasha. He's already married. Yer makin' a bloody mistake."

"We're going to get married in a Catholic church."

"Sasha's Catholic?"

"I don't really know what he is, but he said it doesn't bother him."

"Yer marryin' him and ye don't even know what denomination of Christianity he's from?"

"So, Amoli Sharma is Hindu, whatever that is. Something Asian, I suppose."

The prehistoric mammal started to grunt and poke Colin in the side.

"I've gotta dash to me lecture, now."

"By the way, Colin."

Colin turned to her. "Aye?"

"We're getting married on Christmas day."

Colin's lips were parted as he stared at Rosa in silence.

"Weren't you and Amoli to be married on Christmas day?"

Colin forced a smile and tried to nod in agreement. Neanderthal continued to poke Colin in the side. "Gotta run. Cheers."

Rosa watched Colin and Neanderthal vanish in the crowd. She continued to stand amongst the *hustle and bustle*, as she saw Colin and the beast no more.

Amoli passed by Rosa, giving a little un-intentional shove.

"Hello, Miss Emanuel," Amoli said with a partial smile.

12

"Amoli, hello. I was just speaking with Colin."

"That's nice."

"Have you spoken to him lately?"

"I think it's best that we don't see each other anymore."

"Are you sure about this?"

Amoli started to bight the ends of her book. "Are you sure you want to marry Dr. Dimitrikov?"

"Of course I'm sure."

"He smokes a lot of tobacco, Miss Emanuel."

"So?"

"Now is your chance to get Colin back."

"I don't think I can do that, Amoli." Rosa's posture demonstrated her frustration.

"I always knew you wanted him back. He's a very nice man."

"Yes, he is. Look, Amoli, it's almost 1911, times are rapidly changing and women are now allowed to do so much more than before. If you want Colin back, then, you have a chance to pursue him. You see, women can now do the pursuing."

"It was the most difficult decision that I have ever made to let go of Colin," Amoli said with a tear in her eyes.

"Me too," Rosa responded.

"You let go of Colin? I thought he let go of you?"

"Long story," Rosa said trying to focus on something else.

"You still love him, Miss Emanuel."

"I just can't live his crazy lifestyle. He works too hard. When would he ever be home? He drinks too much alcohol. When would he ever be sober? He's always time traveling. When would he ever be living in the present? He wears his hair too long. When would he ever cut his hair and look respectable?"

"I like his hair. I think it makes him look like a god."

"A god?" Rosa's eyes widened.

"When he has a beard with that long hair. Yes, I very much think he looks like a god."

"Interesting."

Amoli smiled. "Well, I suppose you have a lot of planning to do for the wedding."

"I already purchased my wedding dress," Rosa said with straight posture. "We're going to marry on Christmas day."

"I see. Colin and I were going to do that too."

Rosa fiddled with her poorly fitted engagement ring. "Do you still love Colin?"

"Of course," Amoli paused, then gazed at Rosa's over-sized engagement ring. "Don't you?"

"Of course I do."

"So, why are you marrying Dr. Dimitrikov? Isn't he already married to someone in Russia?"

Rosa shifted her eyes a bit. "He said he doesn't love her anymore and that he wants me."

"Colin thinks you're making a mistake."

"What does Colin know about relationships? He just knows about those disgusting whores on his ship."

Amoli's eyes dropped to the floor. "Well, I can't discuss Colin anymore. I'm feeling very saddened about our broken engagement."

"You were the one who broke it off in the first place."

"I don't really like that he's so popular with the women. It bothers me."

Rosa lifted one eyebrow. "Well, um, yes, that he certainly is."

"I bet if you made a pass at Colin, he would respond to you. I know he always loved you. That also bothered me."

Rosa's eyes widened and as she smiled. "Do you think so?"

"You just said it yourself that women can now do the pursuing."

Rosa fluttered her eyelashes a bit and primped her hair. "Do you think he would respond to me if I made a pass at him?"

Amoli's head hung low. "I know you want him. So, why are you so excited about your engagement to Dr. Dimitrikov?"

"Amoli, Colin and I are no more. In fact, we never were."

"I don't believe that. I can't continue this conversation, it's too painful!" Amoli blubbered, turning her head away from Rosa.

"Amoli, you made the decision to end it with him. He's very sad about that. He loves you."

"No, he loves you. I see the way he looks at you. He always calls you *love*, which makes me ill."

"All Irish men call all women *love.*"

"Too many women flock around him. I can't stand it anymore."

"He never encourages it, though."

"That's true," Amoli paused to think about what to say next. "He always gets drunk and ends up sleeping with them. "I think he encourages it."

Rosa tried to focus on something else. "Look, he has Neanderthal to worry about. I think that prehistoric creature has become a great burden to him."

"Poor Neanderthal, nobody likes him anymore."

*"Nobody ever liked Neanderthal. Neanderthal* is mean. He's always taking shots at Colin. I just saw Colin and he looked a bit banged up. Poor man."

Amoli's expression appeared somewhat surprised. "Neanderthal is misplaced and he's so very misunderstood, that's all."

"Colin is constantly in a physical confrontation with him. It was Colin's idea to bring that bipedal beast to our time period because Colin was afraid for his life."

"Colin was right. We couldn't have left Neanderthal in 1970."

Rosa rolled her eyes back and folded her arms in front of her. "Then you should mind that beast instead of Colin. Neanderthal always liked you best."

"I don't know if I can, my father wants to get me on a boat to India so I can be married off."

Rosa's eyes widened. "Don't tell that to Colin."

"I don't know what to do, Miss Emanuel, Colin loves me so much. Tell me what I should do?"

Rosa stepped back and took a breath. She focused on anything but Amoli. "Do what you want. If you want to return to India and marry your father's choice, so be it."

# Chapter Three

Colin sat at his desk in his university office with *Neanderthal* attacking the bookshelf at the same time. Colin removed his reading glasses and placed them on the desk. He glimpsed at Neanderthal as it tore away at the books in his office.

"That's enough!" Colin blurted and cracked his fist on the desk.

The beast stopped what it was doing to turn and look at Colin.

"That's enough. We don't attack books, just stop it already, ye feck!" Colin appeared rattled and a bit nervous at times: he placed his glasses back on his face and continued to read through some of his students' papers.

There was a knock at the door. Colin peered at the door, while the *Neanderthal* stormed in his way to open it. It was Chancellor Gordon. She stepped back with surprise when she saw the *Neanderthal* standing in the doorway.

She tried to see past the prehistoric beast, where she noticed Colin standing behind it. "Colin? What is this *thing?*" She asked while she tried to enter his office.

Colin stepped toward the doorway. "Sweet Jesus! Forgive me Chancellor, please come in."

She kept her arms pasted to her sides. "Oh, my, how am I going to even enter your office and walk past this *thing?* What is *it?* Good Lord."

Colin walked toward the prehistoric prime mate. "Ah, so sorry, Chancellor," he extended his hand to her and tried to reel her into the office. "This is Neanderthal. He's not from the twentieth century, in case yer not sure."

"Yes, I can see that."

Colin forced a smile as he held tightly onto her hand and drew her toward him. "Forgive me. *Neanderthal* belongs approximately twenty-eight thousand years in the past. He really shouldn't be here but we did find him roamin' about durin' our last time travel and I just didn't feel it was proper to let him be in a time that was too foreign for him, ye know?"

"Yes, but isn't our time also foreign for him?"

Colin smiled. "Aye, but I'm in the process of returnin' him to his own time just as Dr. Dimitrikov re-adjusts his time machine. It has errors, so it does."

"So, you're planning on time traveling again, Colin?"

"Aye."

"I'd really like to come with you," she said as she rubbed her body against his. *Neanderthal* continued to destroy the books.

Colin's eyes lifted. "I'd never bring ye along, it's far too dangerous."

"You've traveled with those two other females. Why is it acceptable that they come along?"

He took a deep breath and smiled. "It's a long story with Rosa and Amoli. Rosa's an archaeologist. Amoli and I were engaged to marry at one time. She's a persistent little lass. She insisted on comin' along. She's from India, ye know. Not that it changes anythin', but in some cases, it does. I just couldn't understand her ways 'n customs, ye know. Just as she couldn't with me."

Chancellor Gordon grinned at him. "You're speaking in past tense, Colin. Are you and Amoli no more?"

He paused before he responded. "Aye."

She took his hand and brought it to her lips. "I like the sound of that."

Colin kept one eye on Neanderthal. "Ye really shouldn't waste yer precious time on me, Chancellor."

"*Evelyn.* Please, address me as *Evelyn.*"

"I'm always here and there, never in one place too long. For the love of God, just think, I run me own fishin' business, I'm a PhD candidate durin' the week, not to mention, I'm also a time traveler. Jack of all trades, wouldn't ye say?"

"Yes, that will have to change, Colin. You're going to have to some day give up your fishing trade and move permanently to London and continue your life as a scholar."

He chuckled. She clutched onto his hands. "Why is this *thing* in your office? Shouldn't it be in a cage or something? Maybe it should be in a zoo?"

Colin's eyes widened. "Cage? Zoo? Oh, I try to let him roam free as much as possible. He's our close ancestor, ye know."

"I see."

"He goes with me everywhere, I'm sorry to say."

"Oh, really?"

"Aye. He's ruinin' me life, rather. He's with me on the ship. He's with me on the train to and from Fishguard. He's definitely not the best company, not a great mate, I must say."

"Oh."

"He even met me parents."

"How did that go?"

"Don't ask. A disaster, so it was. Oh good Lord, why do I always try to play God?"

"I don't know."

He took her hands and rubbed them. "Cause I thirst for the unexpected that's why. Just can't help it, if ye know what I'm sayin'?"

She paused while staring into his eyes. "Colin, is it possible for you to spend the night at my home?"

His eyes shifted a bit as he paused. "Don't think I can. I'd have to bring him along. Yer home is much too exquisite. Can't imagine a prehistoric prime mate roamin' about yer beautiful home. It's likely he'll work over yer fine servants."

"Oh."

Colin smiled at her. "It's for the best, I think."

She sighed. "Alright then, when can we spend some *alone* time together?"

"Alone time? Oh, now that I've punished me-self with this burden, just can't answer ye on that one."

"Perhaps I'd have to pay a visit to your London flat?"

"It's much too snug with a prehistoric prime mate. Three's a crowd, ye know."

"Do you own a telephone?"

"Aye. I just got me-self one. Gotta have it so I can contact me ship mates and deal with matters."

"Well, that's good, then. I'll have to contact you when I wish to visit you."

He glanced at *Neanderthal*. "Yer not serious?"

She gleamed at him. "Of course I'm serious, Colin."

"Don't think it's safe, all cramped up in me flat with Neanderthal. He's a bit temperamental these days."

Her eyes widened. "Temperamental? What do you mean by that?"

Colin glanced at Neanderthal. "He's twenty-eight thousand years old. He's misplaced. Fish outta water, one could say."

"So, what does that mean?"

Neanderthal grunted at Colin.

"Neanderthals were built much stronger than us. Ye think I'm built big and strong but *Neanderthals* have the ability to take us physically. Neanderthals have beat the shite outta me in a fight."

Her eyebrows lifted with surprise. "Really?"

"Aye, ye wouldn't wanna catch this beast tearin' me limb from limb, would yez?"

She focused on Neanderthal. The prehistoric prime mate stared back at her. "Oh, my."

She stepped closer to Colin and wrapped herself around his thick bicep. "But, I really need to spend some quality time with you, Colin. You were gone so long during your last time-travel expedition."

He smiled at her. Neanderthal slowly approached Colin and pointed to its stomach.

Colin's smile dissipated. "He's gotta eat, now."

The chancellor glanced at the prehistoric beast. "Hmm?"

"Gotta feed him. Don't wanna wait too long, 'cause then he goes berserk."

She backed up toward the wall of his office. "Oh."

"Ye should be runnin' along, I'm afraid. I really gotta find some grub for this poor beast."

She noticed Neanderthal was starting to twitch with anxiety.

"Yes, you better feed this *thing*."

Colin held her coat up, placed it around her shoulders and kissed her lips. She exited his office.

# Chapter Four

Later that day, Colin entered the lab with Neanderthal. Dr. Sasha Dimitrikov was kneeling beside his time machine.

"Sasha!" Colin called out. "Mate."

Sasha lifted his head. "Da?"

"Is that contraption of yers fixed and ready to go yet? I can't keep mindin' Neanderthal much longer. He's ruinin' me life. Terrible mate, so he is."

Sasha straightened up. "Silly contraption you say? You try make something better?"

"Not interested in yer Russian pride, mate. Bottom line, we gotta get this prehistoric creature back to the time it belongs."

"I now know problem why we go to 840 A.D. and 1487 and 1970. I know answer, da?" Sasha grinned with a slight childish giggle.

"Alright, what's the answer?"

"We have meteor strike in 1908, when we travel to your desired time of 10,000 years ago, da? Time travel went better in 1908, da?"

"Aye, so it did."

"Now, we do not have meteor strike. It is almost 1911, da?"

Colin's eyes widened. "Rosa's been sayin' this all along. Nothin' seems to be goin' right, because we're movin' farther from when the meteor strike occurred. Rosa said this a few times, I must say. Don't think ye really paid much attention to her, though."

"Rosa? Leave her out of this. She is just a woman."

"Soon, she'll be yer wife. A wife usually means she's a woman. Arse!"

"You talk like bad man. Why you say bad words?"

"Ye gotta wife in Russia, so why ye gonna marry Rosa? She's a confused wench. Why ye doin' this to her?"

"She thinks she is like man. She thinks she has brainpower like man. She is weak, frail woman. She cannot understand my time travel inventions."

"Despite how lovely she is, she's also strong-willed, not to mention brilliant. You certainly don't fancy strong women. Ye should feck off, really."

"You now with chancellor of university. She too strong, but nice legs, da?"

"She has money, lots of it, ye'd surely fancy her for that," he paused. "Nice legs? How ye know she's got nice legs? What ye do? Did ye pull up her skirt?"

Sasha laughed like a madman. "I watch her cross street one day. Wind blow skirt up. She look nice for what I could see."

"What ye doin' lookin' at her that way? She's not for ye to look at."

Sasha paced around his time machine and lit a cigarette. "Too much control over man, Rosa think this. You have big muscles that you not know how to use. You let woman control. Not me."

"Enough of this. Just tell me what's goin' on with the time machine."

Sasha sat back on a lab stool to smoke his cigarette. "I can only get power if we take boat to Arctic."

Colin's eyes widened.

"Magnetic lines converge, which create magnetic motive force to power time machine," Sasha continued. "Lines converge at pole – magnetic true north, da?"

"Ye don't say."

"You make *funny* of me? Fine, you not go on time travel expedition. I go without you."

Colin tried to pull a thread from his jacket. "*Fun*, make *fun*." He noticed from the corner of his eye that

Neanderthal wandered about the room, with a board expression on his face.

Sasha paused to blow smoke rings with his cigarette. "Fine. Make *fun*. You make *fun* of my English?"

"It's not as if I relish in yer bleedin' time travel contraptions and just fancy the idea of travelin' to some fecked up time period from the barbaric past. I've almost been killed at least a feckin' hundred times already."

"Settled!" Sasha shouted so loud his voice cracked. He held his hands above his head. "You not come!"

Colin squinted his eyes at Sasha. *"What?"*

"You not come!"

Colin glanced at Neanderthal. He took a few deep breaths. "Just calm yer-self. *Yer actin' the maggot* and it's gettin' on me nerves, I must say. I've gotta come."

"Nyet. You not come!"

"I'm fundin' all this shite! Without me, you'd be nowhere."

Sasha knelt beside the time machine with his cigarette in his mouth and continued to work. "You not come. Settled, settled. I go, you not."

Colin sat back on the lab stool and was silent.

"You stuck with beast forever. Your fishing business will dissolve."

"Now, yer talkin' like a complete arse, so ye are. Ye need me fishin' business, it funds your work."

Rosa entered the lab. She stopped when she noticed Colin and Neanderthal were present. She slowly walked toward Colin.

"Well, hello, Colin."

Colin grinned at her with one eye on Neanderthal. "Hello, love?"

Sasha straightened his torso and pulled himself from the time machine. "You not call her that word! Soon, she is my wife!"

Colin kissed his teeth. "Bigamist, so ye are."

Sasha leered at Colin. "You see how jealous he is? He call me bad names!"

Rosa smiled. "Gentlemen, please. Don't fight over me. I can only marry one of you."

Colin sighed as he balanced himself on only the two legs of the lab stool he was sitting on. "Anyways, Sasha says the time travel escapades haven't gone well 'cause we surely needed the magnetic energy from the meteor strike from 1908."

"Well, that's long gone, now, so how do we re-invent this surge of magnetic energy in order to get Neanderthal to the time period he belongs?" Rosa asked.

"Sasha seems to think we gotta get ourselves to the Arctic, where there are converging magnetic lines, which will likely create a magnetic motive force to power the time machine," Colin explained.

Rosa chuckled. "Funny, I said something of that nature a while back, but Sasha just continued to ignore me simply because I'm female."

"And ye still wanna marry this bloke?" Colin asked in a low-toned voice.

"Well, Colin, you never gave me a diamond. Sasha did."

Colin's eyes shifted. "Surely, that diamond is his mother's or his wife's. Just look at it. It doesn't fit yer finger right because it's somebody else's diamond. I would've given ye a diamond, but ye were too busy slapping me face and such."

Sasha dropped his cigarette butt into one of the laboratory sinks. "You see! I want to fight you, Mr. Limmerick! It is about time I finish you!"

Colin continued to balance his bulked body on the lab stool. His eyes followed the *Neanderthal* around the room. He ignored Sasha's surge of anger.

"Gentlemen, you've both been through hell and back together. Sasha saved your life, Colin. Please, show some order here."

Colin stood up and looked at Rosa. "If it was a diamond ye wanted, ye knew all too well, ye would've got one from me."

She appeared a bit startled by his tone. She glanced at the *Neanderthal;* then, watched disinterested Sasha continue to work on the time machine.

"We're getting married Christmas day, Colin. You can't stop it from happening, either. I think you need to accept the fact that I'm marrying someone else."

Sasha grinned at Colin.

"I need to accept this mere fact, do I? Ye best accept the fact that Sasha's got himself a wife in Russia."

"Sasha's going to leave her."

Colin sighed. "Alright, so we gotta get on me ship, so we sail the seas to the Arctic."

Sasha turned to Colin. "Da."

"*Neanderthal* needs to come with us," Colin instilled.

"Put him in zoo, where he belong," Sasha grunted.

Colin sat back on the stool. "Rosa, ye sure ye wanna marry him?"

Rosa tried to ignore Colin's comment. "So, it will be me, Colin, Sasha, and Neanderthal."

"Don't see Amoli ever comin' along again," Colin said with his head hung low.

"No, Colin, she could be back in India already. Her father is determined to match her with someone there."

Colin stared at the floor. "That hurts."

"I'm sorry, Colin. Aren't you courting the chancellor?" Rosa asked trying to change the subject.

"I suppose I am."

"Are you not interested in her?"

"She's a fine wench, but..."

Rosa stepped closer to him. "But, what?"

"She's the chancellor of the university, that's what."

Sasha placed his hands in front of his face. "Always, Mr. Limmerick in romantic turmoil."

Colin ignored Sasha. "I'm not in love with the chancellor, ye know. I fancy her and she's attractive enough, I'd say, but it's just wrong for me to be courtin' the chancellor of the university, don't ye think?"

Rosa gave Colin a blank stare. "So, don't."

Colin glanced at Neanderthal. His eyes shifted a bit. "Don't?"

Sasha sighed with frustration. "So, we go to Arctic to get energy for time machine. We go to Arctic and we bring time machine on boat, we get the energy we need from Arctic, and we travel to prehistoric past to drop off monkey man, da?"

Rosa's eyes widened as she glanced at Colin who also appeared a bit shocked.

"Monkey man? Sasha, Neanderthal is a close ancestor to us, he is definitely not a monkey man," Rosa tried to explain with distaste in her voice.

Colin took a deep breath and slumped onto one of the lab stools. "Oh, sweet Jesus, please save this man."

"I am physicist, not natural historian. Your monkey man ancestor does not have same meaning for me, da?"

Colin pulled Rosa's ring finger to his face. "So, ye sure ye wanna continue with weddin' plans with this wanker?"

She glared at Sasha. "I don't know if I could bear your idiotic comments. You're so ridiculous sometimes, Sasha. I'm not even sure if I like you anymore as a person."

"I not believe what you say, such beautiful lady. You feel more than *like* for me," he raised his eyebrows a few times with a smile.

"You are such an idiot sometimes." She crossed her arms in front of her and turned away from him.

"I am great Russian physicist, not your Mr. Limmerick, the man you know you can never marry."

Colin looked at Rosa. "Mate, stop tryin' to stir the pot. Lets just get on with gettin' Neanderthal to his time period, uh?"

"Yes, if we continue to time travel together, we should at least try to get on well," Rosa commented.

Sasha slid his arm around Rosa's delicate shoulders. "Next step. How we travel to Arctic?"

"I've never been anywhere near there. London is the highest latitude I've ever been," Rosa said.

Colin stared at Neanderthal. "So, mate, when do we sail to the Arctic? We're goin' in the *Mermaid*, no doubt."

"Colin, your *Atlantic Mermaid* is a fine vessel but I think we need something a little more dependable if we're planning on making our next venture to the Arctic," Rosa suggested.

"Dependable? Don't think ye'd find a fishin' vessel as dependable as the *Mermaid*. She's had several repairs, cost me some quid, so she has."

Rosa tried to cover her laughter with her hanky. "Colin, my dear Colin, this is not a simple procedure, we need reliability."

"Me ship is reliable, so she is."

Sasha stared at Colin. "I hate your boat. It make me sick all the time. I have been on other boats like the big one that took me from Russia to England. I did not feel sick. You're boat is not suitable. I agree with Rosa."

"It's a fishin' vessel, ye feckin' idiot. Ye came to England on an immigrant ship. Ye bloody don't know the difference."

Rosa slowly folded her arms in front of her. "Fine, we'll go to the Arctic on *The Atlantic Mermaid*, it's settled. Sasha, we've been on it before. It's best that we are familiar with this means of transportation."

Sasha was silent as he profusely lit a cigarette. "I not like all bad names I get called. I not do this to you, why you do to me?"

Colin took a deep breath. "I apologize, mate."

Rosa continued to keep herself turned away from Sasha. "I suppose I am as well."

"I'll get some of me crew mates to come along, to help us out."

"Colin, maybe that isn't such a good idea," Rosa said shifting her eyes from side to side.

Colin sighed. "Why not?"

Sasha leaned against one of the lab tables as he smoked his cigarette.

"Then, they'd find out that we're time travelers," Rosa answered.

"So?" Colin said as he lifted one eyebrow.

"Fine, then," Rosa responded, as she kept one eye on Sasha blowing a smoke ring.

"Don't ye think me crew kinda figured things out a bit? They knew somethin' was goin' on. Me first mate, Eddy, knows I'm a time traveler."

Rosa's smirk changed to a frown. "I see."

"Me parents know that I'm a time traveler. Me brother knows, me sister-in law knows. The university knows. So what?"

Sasha straightened his posture with his cigarette hanging from his lip. "You are right, Mr. Limmerick. Who cares?"

"Lets just prepare for our voyage and get *Neanderthal* to where he belongs, eh?"

Rosa tugged on Colin's arm. "I don't think Amoli will be joining us on this expedition, Colin."

"Likely she won't. Is she in India, just now?"

"She could very well be," Rosa answered as she pretended to care.

Sasha threw his arms in the air. "Fine, we will leave tomorrow! No time to waste. We must get this monkey man back to his own time. Da! Da! We leave tomorrow on Mr. Limmerick's terrible ship."

29

Colin's eyes widened. "Tomorrow? Doesn't give me much notice, does it? I'll have to ring me crew and tell them to dock at Fishguard in the mornin'."

"I'll have to pack tonight," Rosa mentioned.

Colin chuckled. "Just pack yer fur coat. We's goin' to the Arctic. How brilliant! Never been there!"

# Chapter Five

Colin awoke from a deep sleep when he forced his eyes to focus on the clock on the wall. It was 6:00 AM. He took a deep breath and fell back to sleep. He heard a faint knock on the door. He quickly sprung out of bed and stumbled his way to the door. He grinned when he saw Amoli standing in his doorway.

She smiled at him. "Hello, Colin. Forgive me. I have obviously woken you."

He took her hand and held it in his. "Forgive ye?"

"Yes, it's terribly early for me to come calling for you. I'm very sorry."

He pulled her into his flat. "Stop apologizin'."

She noticed suitcases on the floor. "Oh, am I disturbing you? You must be planning an excursion of some kind, whether it's time travel or not, you're definitely on your way somewhere."

"Aye. Time travel."

"Where?"

He led her to the sofa and sat her down. "The Arctic, no doubt."

Her eyes widened. "Oh."

"One of Sasha's concoctions, ye know. It's about Neanderthal. He can't stay in this time period. He needs to get back to his time. It's the right thing to do, so I think."

Colin noticed her twist a handkerchief in her hands with nervousness. "How is Neanderthal? I suppose he's become very much a burden for you?"

Colin's awkwardness made it difficult to answer. "Burden? Aye, so he has, it's unfortunate."

"Oh," she responded with a quiver in her voice.

He moved his bulked body to sit a little closer to her tiny, yet buxom frame. "Yer lookin' just gorgeous, I must say."

31

She giggled. "Thank-you, Colin."

He moved his body against hers. "I've been just lost without ye, lass. Are ye here to see me 'cause maybe ye might feel the same?"

"I was in India with my parents. They very much want me to marry their idea of the perfect husband."

He tried to focus on something in the room. "I see."

She smiled. "All I could think of was you. I just don't know how we could ever be a couple again. Too much has happened between us."

He clutched her hand to his chest. "Don't think I could bear to hear ye tell me it's over with us. Please don't."

"I have been trying to find a way that we could be together."

"Oh?"

She sighed. "Colin, I don't think it's possible, though."

"Then, why have ye come here?"

Her eyes filled with tears. "Because I still love you."

He kissed her hands.

"I missed you so much when I was in India."

"But, you've come here to tell me it's over?"

She trembled and her lips quivered. "Yes."

He placed her hands on her lap. "Why would ye come here so early in the mornin' to tell me somethin' I already know?"

"I just arrived from India last night. I missed you when I was there. It was too long of a time not to hear your voice or to see your face."

He sat further from her. "Yer confused, lass. Don't think I can take this anymore, maybe ye should leave."

"Are you back with Miss Emanuel yet?"

"Rosa? She's apparently gonna marry Sasha on Christmas day. What a foolish wench she is."

"So, she's going to go through with it? Do you think Dr. Dimitrikov loves and cherishes her?"

"Not in yer life."

"Are you jealous?"

He grinned at her. "Jealous? Don't think ye know me history with Sasha. He's not what ye think he is. Don't wanna see her get hurt."

"If you're not with Miss Emanuel, who are you with these days? The chancellor of the university, she's a very beautiful and classy lady. She must be older than you, though."

He stared at the floor in silence. "I'm older than yez."

"Oh, yes, I suppose."

"Is it proper in yer mind to be with a man much older?"

"In India, there are eight-year-old brides, so I don't think our age difference is a concern in my culture."

"Eight-year-old brides, ye say? Good God."

"Is the chancellor much older than you?"

"Should that matter, really?"

She sighed with glassy eyes. "I suppose, I've asked far too many questions."

He smiled at her. "Ye can ask away, anytime."

"Well, I shouldn't keep you from your Arctic quest. I'm needed at my aunt's house." She stood up and stepped toward the door. He continued to stare at the floor in silence. "Colin? Aren't you going to see me to the door?"

She waited a few seconds and saw herself out. He sat back on the sofa and took a deep breath. He noticed a small mouse run across the floor. It darted into a small crack on the wall.

"It's too early for whiskey, so it is. How I need it, though," he mumbled, and sat back on the sofa.

He scanned the room a few times, where he focused on his packed bags for the Arctic excursion. He walked to his liquor cabinet and hesitated before he poured himself a glass of whiskey. He placed the glass to his lips, when he heard another knock at the door. He swung opened the door to see the chancellor standing before him.

"Well, well, still in your long underwear?" She said with a *naughty* grin of delight. She intricately pulled each finger of her gloves off and made her way into his flat. "I must say, it looks rather sinful on you."

He watched her march into his flat. "What does? Me long underwear?"

She noticed the packed suitcases on the floor. "Going somewhere, Colin?"

"Aye, the Arctic."

"How chilly."

"I suppose."

She sprawled onto his sofa. "You look so inviting in your attire, why don't you ravish me?"

"Attire? Long underwear, I don't see how? Look, Evelyn, don't really have loads of time to chat just now, I really need to be off."

"So, I see. Are you going with that young lass from India?"

"It doesn't look like she's comin' along."

"Alright, how about that pretty PhD candidate girlfriend, whose studying archaeology?"

"Aye, Rosa so she is."

She pulled her skirt up to show her thigh off to him. "Well, what am I to do? I think I have to come along to protect you from all these women."

"From Rosa? She's engaged to Dr. Dimitrikov, they're to marry on Christmas. I apologize for rushin' ye off, but I really need to meet Sasha in the lab about now. Forgive me."

"Apologize? Whatever for? I think I'm going to come with you. It's the least I can do for such a kind gentleman such as you."

His eyes widened. "Ye can't be comin' along on one of these expeditions."

She pulled her skirt up even higher. "Yes, I can."

34

Colin put all his weight on one foot, and then he changed to the other. He glanced at the room, where he found it difficult to face her. "Well, ye just can't, 'is all."

She yanked on her guarder belt to pull it down past her knees. "I think it's the right thing to do, Colin."

He sprung up on his toes and then stood on his heels. He was silent but antsy.

"What's the matter, Colin? Aren't you ready to ravish me at this very moment?"

He walked to his liquor table and pressed the glass of whiskey to his lips. "So, it's too early in the day."

"Colin!"

He was about to drink when he focused on her call. "Aye?"

"You're going to drink that so early in the morning?"

"Aye."

"You can't be doing that, my dear! What's wrong with you, darling?"

"Everythin'."

She sprung up from the sofa, where her unfastened skirt fell to the floor. "Don't drink that now, Colin!" She took the whiskey glass from his hands.

"Yer lookin' at me as if I'm some kinda lush or somethin'. Yer tellin' me right here in me flat that yer comin' on the Arctic expedition. Ye bloody well can't be doin' that, Evelyn." He took the whiskey glass from her hands. "Ye may have power and money but ye can't be tellin' me what I can and can't do. Ye don't own me and ye never will."

She clapped her hands. "Great performance, Colin. I just don't know why you're making this more difficult than it needs to be."

He sat at the kitchen table. *"Oh, mother of God, help me."*

She stood up and stepped very close to him. "I'm intrigued by you, Colin. You're a time traveler, which is *marvelous*. Take me with you."

"I can't do that."

"Do it! I order you!"

"Ye can't."

"My, my, you are stubborn for an Irishman, aren't you?" She paced the room with her naked legs.

His eyes were fixed on her, but he pretended that he wasn't. He guzzled his whiskey and glanced at the clock on the wall.

"I'm runnin' late, so I am, please, Evelyn I really must go, now. Forgive me." He placed his hands on her shoulders and kissed her lips.

"A kiss is going to make me go away?"

"Whether I kiss yer lips or not, I'm still expectin' ye to go away at this moment."

She pressed herself against his body and ran her hands along his pectoral muscles. "You're not getting rid of me that fast, Colin."

He chuckled. "*Shite,* what's a man to do?"

# Chapter Six

Sasha sat beside the time machine in the laboratory and lit a cigarette. He watched Rosa enter the room with her heels clicking the hardwood floor, which echoed through the hallways.

"Sasha, I'm ready for anything," she said, holding her packed suitcase.

Sasha glanced at her, where his cigarette hung on his bottom lip. "What you say *ready for anything?* All will be well, you will see."

She glanced at the room. "Where's Colin?"

"He is late. I not know why. We do all this for him."

"You also get paid by him."

"I have to have bread to eat."

The door swung opened, Chancellor Gordon stormed in with Colin trailing behind. Rosa's eyes bulged in shock when she saw the chancellor.

Colin stood in front of Sasha. "Well, let's get on with it, shall we?"

"Colin, why is the chancellor of the university standing beside you?" Rosa asked.

Colin flinched a bit with nerves. "Don't know, really." He searched his jacket for something.

Sasha chuckled. "So, we go on Arctic quest with chancellor of university?"

The chancellor stepped in front of Colin. "So, you are Colin's two cohorts, I take it? I will be traveling on this Arctic expedition."

Sasha continued to chuckle as he scanned the chancellor's slender frame with his eyes. *"Da, da."*

"Wait a minute!" Rosa blurted. "What's this? Is this some kind of charade?"

"It's not. And, where's *Neanderthal?"* Colin responded, changing the subject. He pulled a small flask from his inner jacket pocket.

Sasha puffed on his cigarette. "He is in next room awaiting his departure."

"Brilliant," Colin responded, as he opened the flask to take a few quick swigs.

Rosa paced a bit. "No, Colin, not brilliant. We are not bringing outsiders on our time travel expeditions."

"Where is this written?" The chancellor asked.

Colin laid his hand over his face. "Jesus, help me." He chugged all the whiskey in the flask.

Rosa glared at the chancellor. "You see, Chancellor Gordon, it wouldn't be safe for you to come on our time travel - Arctic quest because time travel can and has been life threatening."

The chancellor folded her arms in front of her. "So tell me, young woman, why is it safe enough for you to go on this excursion?"

"Because I'm a scientist, an archaeologist. I know what I'm doing."

"And, I don't?" She blurted loudly. "I'm the chancellor of this university."

Colin sat on one of the lab stools and stared at the floor. "Evelyn, I don't know why yer insistin' on comin', it's a mistake."

"No mistake, Colin. I'm coming."

Sasha sat up and smiled at the chancellor. "It is settled. Chancellor of university comes on Arctic quest. No problem."

Rosa frowned at Sasha. "It is a great problem, Sasha. We won't be able to perform our usual life threatening escapades as we usually do."

Evelyn stepped toward Rosa. "Young woman, you are underestimating my talents. Are you in love with instructor Limmerick?"

Rosa's eyes widened with surprise. "Absolutely not so, Chancellor Gordon!"

Colin glanced at both women and paused. "Well, then, now that it's settled that ye don't give a damn 'bout

38

me, it's only proper for me to bring the woman that I'm courtin', isn't it?"

"Lets go on this expedition. Help me drag time machine to street, da?" Sasha insisted.

Rosa tugged at Colin's arm as he bent over to help Sasha lift the time machine. "Colin, I didn't mean that. You know how I feel about you."

He turned to her. "Can't really say that I do." He lifted the heavy wrought iron machine.

"Colin, please. Don't walk away like that."

He hoisted the machine in the air and grunted. "Don't ye think I'm a tad preoccupied just now?"

Evelyn sat on one of the lab stools. "Young woman, I think you should leave the instructor to attend to his own."

Rosa glanced at Evelyn. "Colin is my good friend. I know when I can and can't speak with him, Chancellor."

"It is obvious that you don't know him as well as you say. He is busy with his cohort lifting heavy machinery to another destination. It's best you leave well enough alone."

"That heavy machinery is a time machine and we're all planning on riding it once again to be put before the unthinkable."

"Yes, and I intend on participating in your endeavours."

Rosa's eyes widened with surprise. "I see."

Colin and Sasha made their exit from the laboratory, where they carried the machine down the university staircase. Sasha panted with exhaustion as he glanced at Colin.

Sasha balanced the machine on one stair. "Maybe we can get your monkey man to help us. He is strong, nyet?"

Colin squinted his eyes at Sasha. "What?"

"Why you think you must treat creature like pet?"

"Are ye wacked, man?"

"You not think I make good suggestion?"

Colin tried to catch his breath from the heavy lifting. "Ye must be seriously deranged to say what yer sayin'. We found *Neanderthal* lost in another time period and I felt compelled to bring the poor bein' here with us, so we could very well get 'im back to the time period he belongs. Why yez actin' about like yer not knowin' the whole story?"

"I not care that you pick up such strange creature as long as you take care of it. I not want any part of this."

"Ye made that clear once before, so why ye goin' about it now when we're both tryin' to drag this fecked up time machine of yers to me ship?"

"We are about to go on another prehistoric journey and I know how you are. You want to bring prehistoric creatures back with you."

Colin started to lift the machine. "Just help me with this, alright?"

# Chapter Seven

The carriage driver helped them lift the time machine to the dock. Evelyn placed some money in the man's hand and thanked him as he climbed back onto the carriage. Colin turned to her as he nudged his way to give the driver some money.

"Evelyn, please. I think I've got everythin' covered."

Sasha chuckled. Colin glanced at Sasha. "What?"

"You are with man, not woman. She has all money."

"If you'd like to pay the driver, please do," Colin responded. "After all, you're the man, aren't ye?"

Sasha continued to giggle. Rosa glanced at him.

"What's so funny?"

"This man not ever see time machine. He think we are crazy or something, da?"

Colin turned to Sasha. "So, if he does?"

"Entire world think we are nuts."

"Entire world? So the nice gent helped us with the time machine?"

"We also have pet *Neanderthal* on leash, da? He think we are crazy people, da?"

Evelyn smiled. "Well, I must say the *Neanderthal's* behavior has been quite subdued."

"Hoping he's not sick. He's been through so much," Colin commented.

Rosa took a deep breath. "Oh, Colin you've been through so much. I hope you don't get sick over this ordeal."

Evelyn clutched Colin's arm. "Everything, for now on, is going to be just fine."

Rosa stared at the chancellor with a straight face.

Colin forced a smile. "I think I see me ship in the distance. Me crewmembers seem to be right on time, eh."

Evelyn grinned at Colin. "I think this is so exciting."

Rosa sighed. "Just you wait until we travel through time, you won't think it's so exciting, when you're trying to fight for your life."

Evelyn's facial expression changed as she peered at Rosa. "I'm not frightened in the least, young woman."

"*Rosa*, my name is Rosa Emanuel."

Sasha chuckled as he slid his arm around Rosa. "Do not fight with every woman you see. There is enough space for all woman, *da?*"

***

*The Atlantic Mermaid* docked. Eddy stood by the gangway and smiled at his captain. The air was heavy with dampness, where Rosa buttoned her coat to her neck and wrapped herself in her scarf.

"Howye, Captain?" Eddy greeted. Colin smiled. "Captain, what's all this anyway, eh?" Eddy asked with some concern in his voice.

Evelyn turned to Eddy. "My good man, we are going on a scientific expedition, in fact, an Arctic quest, which you are helping us with."

Eddy stepped back and smiled at Evelyn. "Arctic quest? I understand me own captain's ways. He's always goin' about with his scientific experiments." Eddy scanned Evelyn's slender frame and smiled. "By the way, I'm the first mate. At yer service, good lady," he removed his cap and bowed forward toward the chancellor. "I've known me captain since he was a wee lad on his uncle Kevin's fishin' vessel."

Evelyn grinned at him. "Really?"

Colin slid his arm around Evelyn. "Come along everyone, we've got work to do."

"So, Captain, you said ya wanna get the *Mermaid* to the Arctic waters? Whatever happened to the Azores?"

"Sorry, Ed, the Azores just aren't in the picture just now. We've gotta get ourselves to the Arctic, if ye can believe it?"

"Captain, is this ship equipped to deal with such choppy seas?"

"It shouldn't be a problem, I don't think."

"We'll definitely come across some fine orca."

Colin took a breath. "Likely, in such frigid waters."

"What ya think, Captain?"

Colin paused as he took some time to scratch his head. "Think? 'Bout what?"

"Do we catch some orca? We'd make handsome quid, so we would."

Colin sighed. "Catch killer whales yer talkin'?"

"Aye, Captain."

"Well, where's me crew, Ed? We're not on me ship to catch anythin' just now."

"Aye, but we might as well if we come across them?"

Colin chuckled. "Yer not serious. This vessel isn't equipped to catch enormous marine life. Just mackerel 'n herrin' is what we specialize in, don't ye think?"

"Oh, forgive me, Captain."

"Ed, this is a scientific experiment we're doin' with the university. I brought Sasha 'n Rosa for a reason, mate."

"Whose the classy lady? I must say she's a looker, all dressed up."

Colin wore a blank expression on his face as he stared at Evelyn from a distance. "She? Aye, she's the chancellor of the university. Fine wench, so she is. I'm kinda courtin' her these days."

"Yer courtin' the chancellor of the university?" Eddy's eyes widened. "I suppose ladies are doin' men's jobs nowawdays?"

"London, is a very different town, Ed."

"Why she comin' along? Isn't she scared?"

"It was her idea, don't go lookin' at me that way."

"I know things didn't go well for your little lass from India, sorry, Captain."

Colin leaned against the gunnel. He noticed Evelyn and Rosa gaze at the sea from the deck. "Oh, Ed, feck me life's a bleedin' mess, so it is."

"Captain, ya gotta fix yar problems, man."

"Just don't know how. There's a feckin' *Neanderthal* on the ship besides the chancellor of the university. Feck!

"Aye, yar caveman is back with us. Isn't that just lovely. That *thing* is back."

Colin shook his head with distaste. "Aye, Ed, how brilliant it is, is right."

"Just don't go about tryin' to fix yar troubles with booze, 'is all."

"Haven't had a drink since last night, Ed. I'm not fetchin' any whiskey as of yet, am I?"

"Good start, I think."

"Perhaps."

"Rosa is on the ship? My, she's a beauty as well."

Colin stared at the planked floor of the deck. "Ed, she's to be married on Christmas day to Sasha, if ye can believe it?"

Eddy's eyes widened with surprise. "Surely not?"

"Surely so." Colin continued to stare at the floor. "Please, Ed, enough of me personal life. Did Timmy make it for this?"

"I'm afraid not, Captain. He wanted to be with Deidre. Ya know how Deidre gets when she's around yaz. Timmy couldn't bear it. He refused to step foot on this vessel today. Sorry, Captain."

"Shite."

"Don't ya worry, Captain. I haven't a problem drivin' the ship. I'll surely stay outta yar way."

Colin puffed out his chest to take a breath. Sasha positioned the time machine onto the deck. He glanced at Rosa, who stood next to the chancellor.

"Okay, now we go, da?"

"Where's *Neanderthal?*" Rosa asked.

Sasha stood straight and pointed to the wheelhouse. "I think he is driving boat."

Rosa folded her arms in front of her. "That's a scary thought."

"Get Mr. Limmerick and say him to get beast."

"Calm down, Sasha. I think your geography is a bit off. It will take some time before we reach the Arctic Ocean," Rosa added.

"How long it take?"

Rosa shrugged her shoulders. "I don't really know. Colin would likely know, but I don't think he's ever made this journey."

"Amateurs!"

"Well, it's not as if you know the answer to your question."

"All I do is look at map and I can say you how long it take, da?"

"Fine."

Colin entered the deck from the galley. "What yez all lookin' so serious about?"

"Colin, Sasha needs to know how long it will take us to reach the Arctic Ocean?"

"It'll take longer than a usual voyage 'cause of the ice caps, of course. Eddy has to steer the ship with care."

"Your boat cannot do this trip, I know it!" Sasha yelped.

Evelyn entered the deck. "What's all this commotion?"

Colin smiled at her. "No commotion. I reckon' we could reach the Arctic waters in a few days. Ice caps don't mean this vessel can't sail these waters. It just means we have to take extra precautions."

Rosa peered at Sasha. "Satisfied?"

Sasha sat down on one of the deck benches to light a cigarette.

"Mate, we're still sailin' the Irish Sea just now. Ye gotta be patient."

45

Sasha blew smoke rings in the air. "If we use dirigible we can transport time machine with security and safety."

Colin glanced at Rosa. "What's gotten into ye, mate? Are ye seasick? How on earth can ye think a dirigible would lead yer time machine to safety 'n security?"

Evelyn chuckled. "On the contrary, doctor, a dirigible would only promote a greater disaster when transporting a lead iron time machine like the one you brought on this ship."

"I not like this boat."

"You've been on it before without a single complaint, man. What's botherin' yez?"

"I want to push that monkey man over board. I hate him!"

Rosa's eyes widened. "Sasha, the reason we're going to the Arctic is to fuel the time machine with energy so we can deliver *Neanderthal* to his correct time period."

"I no like."

Colin stepped closer to Rosa. "And yer sure ye wanna wed this bloke?"

The chancellor smiled at Rosa. "Oh, I just love weddings!"

Rosa noticed *Neanderthal* was standing too close to the edge of the boat. "Colin, look! *Neanderthal* is trying to jump!"

Colin turned his head to catch a glimpse of the *Neanderthal* diving into the sea. "Feck! No!" Colin dove in after the beast.

Rosa started to pant with concern. "Sasha, we need to throw them a net or something! This is frigid water!"

Sasha stood up and noticed the large spool of twine. "We can use this!"

Colin had difficulty-spotting the *Neanderthal* in the turbulent sea. The rope fell before Colin, but he resisted taking hold of it.

Rosa hung her torso over the gunnel. "Colin! Take the rope and get out of that water! You'll die of hypothermia!"

He took hold of the rope and noticed *Neanderthal* floating in a frigid state. Sasha tried to wind up the rope around an iron spool. Eddy saw Colin splashing in the water from where he stood in the wheelhouse. He flew down the ladder to help Sasha pull in Colin. Evelyn screamed and clenched her fists.

"Oh! My God! Get him out of there!"

Colin held the rope tightly in his hand as he tried to swim closer to the *Neanderthal*. The prehistoric beast plunged its fist at Colin's face. Colin noticed blood splatter into the turbulent waves of the sea and dissolve. Colin was stunned from the hard hit to his face. The *Neanderthal* hit him again. Colin fell under the water, with his blood painting the waves. He lifted his head to peer at the being. It panted and snorted with panic. Colin was semi-conscious, where he knew he had to keep his head above the waves to survive. He ignored his bloody nose, where he had to concentrate more on swimming and use as much energy as possible to keep warm. He could hear Rosa and Evelyn's screams faintly in the background. His eyelids were half shut with his dazed state. His body temperature dropped, where he felt himself in a deep freeze. Rosa and Evelyn could no longer see him. He started to sink.

Rosa lunged at Sasha. "Do something!"

Sasha tore off his shoes and dove into the water. The waves were turbulent with chunks of ice crashing together. Sasha was eye to eye with the *Neanderthal*, but he didn't see Colin. Sasha took a deep breath and swam under water. The frigid temperature was almost unbearable. Sasha swam more erratic than ever, just to keep his body temperature up. He felt somebody brush against him. He took hold of Colin's arm and immediately pulled him to the surface. Sasha took hold of the rope.

Eddy felt the tug of the rope and began to wrap it around the iron spool.

"I see Sasha!" Rosa shouted. "He has Colin!"

The chancellor sat down on the bench on the deck and sighed. He couldn't stop trembling. "Thank-God."

Sasha struggled with the rope. He created a lasso and tightened it around Colin's chest. Eddy wrapped the rope around the spool, without taking a breath.

Rosa and Evelyn pulled on Sasha's arms to let him back onto the ship.

"How's Colin?" Rosa asked with angst.

Colin fell to the planked floor of the deck. Rosa kneeled by his side. "He's not conscious! Oh! Oh God!"

Evelyn kneeled by Colin's side as well. "Somebody do something to bring this man back!"

Rosa leaned her entire body onto Colin's chest. "Oh, my God, is he beyond saving?"

Sasha kneeled beside Colin. "Ladies, move! Out of my way! I will resuscitate!" Rosa slowly stood up. "Do it!"

Sasha pressed Colin's chest with several firm thrusts, in and out. Rosa and Evelyn fixed their eyes on Colin's face. Colin's eyelids twitched a bit. Rosa smiled and glanced at Evelyn. She caressed Colin's face.

"My God, Colin Limmerick it's as if you have nine lives."

Evelyn smiled at Colin. She casually pushed Rosa's hand away from Colin. "Colin, can you hear me?"

He opened his eyes and tried to breathe. They watched his broad chest expand with air every time he took a breath. He began to cough violently.

Eddy threw a couple of heavy wool blankets over him. "This should keep the Captain warm. That sea is mighty cold."

Sasha wrapped himself in a wool blanket and lit a cigarette. "Where is monkey man, now?"

Rosa leered at Sasha. "Do you have to keep referring to him as a monkey man?

It sounds so ridiculous to hear you refer to a *Neanderthal* that way."

"Why you defend him? He almost kill Mr. Limmerick."

"Yes, but he is a misplaced prehistoric species who needs to return to his time period, due to our silly time travels. Colder temperatures are what Neanderthals were used to, we're moving toward the right location. Neanderthal needs to be placed in his own time with the proper climate. We have got to stop playing God! It's all our fault."

Evelyn snuggled up to Colin to kiss his blue-lips. "You must be just frozen."

"Feelin' much better, now, thanks."

"Don't try to talk, my love," Evelyn said with her hand over his lips. "You need to save your energy.

"Aye."

"I was so worried, Colin. You really had me terrified."

"Evelyn, ye haven't seen nothin' yet."

Her brows lowered to her eyes. "What do you mean?"

"We haven't even time traveled yet, is what I'm sayin'."

Evelyn stared at Colin with concern written on her face. "I see. Do you still have to time travel if the prehistoric creature is missing at sea?"

"He's a *Neanderthal*, built so much tougher than us. He's likely to show himself on the ship again, I suppose."

Rosa smiled at Colin. "Oh, yes, soon he'll get hungry and he'll definitely return to us. I'm not worried at all. However, *Neanderthals* weren't the finest swimmers, though. Colin you are likely the superior swimmer, that's why you survived this episode."

Evelyn placed a clean cloth over Colin's bloody nose.

Sasha helped the chancellor up. "Come glamorous lady, we should go to galley to drink Vodka. Time to celebrate!"

The chancellor smiled at him. " Celebrate? Celebrate what? You want to get me drunk with you, doctor?"

Sasha grinned.

Rosa glared at him. "Vodka with the chancellor, how nice."

Eddy helped Colin up. Colin kept the blankets wrapped around him, where he was in a continuous shiver.

Eddy gave Colin a friendly pat on the back. "Captain, keep that compress pressed against yar nose. That *thing* gave ya a swift blow."

Colin folded the compress to a cleaner side and rearranged it on his nose. "So, I should say, Ed. Hopin' he didn't drown."

"Captain, stop worrin' about that *thing*. It almost took yaz. Just let it go."

Colin made his way to his cabin. Evelyn followed. Rosa sat in the galley to make herself some tea. Sasha followed.

"Why you ignore me?" Sasha asked.

Rosa continued to make tea. Sasha pulled at her arm. "Why you ignore me?"

She slowly turned her head. "Leave me alone."

"I see creature on deck. It is back."

Rosa's eyes widened. "Really? Is he hurt? Can you tell?"

"I not know. I not care."

"When we reach the Arctic boundaries and if he's alive and well, then he will be able to withstand a journey through time," Rosa explained.

"How it not dead, I not know."

"Neither do I. It's a miracle. Colin will be pleased about this."

"You make tea for me, too?"

"No, Sasha. Just for Colin. I don't think you're worth me making you a cup."

"*Poh-che-mu?* Why? What I do?"

"Sasha, I thank you for that bit of information and I thank you for saving Colin's life. Please leave me alone, now. Please give this cup of tea to Colin. It's steaming hot. I hope it will warm him."

Rosa watched Sasha leave the galley with the tea. She sat at the table and noticed the *Neanderthal* scoot his way into the room.

Rosa smiled when she saw the prehistoric creature. "*Neanderthal*, come sit here. I want to examine you. I want to make sure you're alright."

The creature gingerly stood before her, not really understanding her request. She gestured for him to sit on the chair beside her. It sat down. She caressed his head.

"Just relax. I want to see if you're hurt. You're going to be undergoing a complicated journey, I'm afraid."

Sasha entered. "Is beast alright?"

Rosa continued to caress the creature's head and ignored Sasha's question.

"Fine, you not talk to me. I not care. We will get married, da?"

Rosa lifted her head and stared at Sasha in silence.

"What? Why you look at me with so cold eyes? What I do?"

"You were making a pass at the chancellor, that's what you did."

"Pass? *Nyet.* I am gentleman."

"No, Sasha. You're just awful. However, I am grateful that you saved Colin's life, again. I just don't understand you sometimes."

"What? What I do so terrible?"

The creature noticed a bowl of fruit on the table and started to devour it. Colin made his way down the ladder from his bedroom and entered the galley. *"Neanderthal!"*

Rosa smiled at Colin. "Yes, he seems to be just fine, thank God."

"How brilliant that is."

"How are you feeling, Colin?" Rosa asked with a smile.

"Better, thank the Lord."

The chancellor followed Colin into the room. "Oh, the prehistoric creature has returned! How splendid!"

Colin rushed by the prehistoric primate's side. "He's lookin' well, isn't he?"

Rosa continued to caress the creature's head. "I don't know how he survived, but he did, thankfully."

"Sasha searched the galley cabinets for liquor. "You not keep vodka?"

"We usually don't, mate. Sorry."

"Drunken sailors like you all don't keep vodka?" Sasha angrily slammed some of the cabinet doors.

Colin turned to Sasha. "Can ye stop takin' yer frustration out on me ship, mate?"

"I hate this place! Where can I go to be away from all people?"

"Downstairs. Go to the hull. Thanks for savin' me life, by the way."

"That is all I do. I save your life, always!"

Rosa glanced at Sasha but centered her focus on *Neanderthal*. The chancellor rubbed her hands along Colin's back.

"Why don't you get some rest until tomorrow, hmm?"

Colin took a deep breath. "It's me ship, Evelyn. I gotta make sure all is well."

Sasha slammed the last cabinet door. "Well? Nothing is well! We make big mistake bringing her on this journey!" Sasha pointed at Rosa.

"Me? Sasha, go smoke your cigarettes and be out of our sight. I can't even stand to look at you anymore."

"I not marry you! Not now, not ever! Wedding is off!"

Rosa's eyes widened. "It's like you're some kind of *Neanderthal* yourself.

"You call me names?"

Colin stood up and walked toward Rosa. "Look, this scufflin' has gotta stop. We're just north of Scotland, now. By the middle of the night we'll be in Arctic boundary waters. I think we need to work as a team."

Sasha leered at Colin and exited the galley in silence. The chancellor looked at Rosa. "If I were you, I'd re-evaluate your engagement to the doctor. He doesn't seem balanced enough for a woman like yourself."

Rosa's lips parted. "You don't have any idea what kind of woman I am, Chancellor Gordon."

"No, I don't, but what woman would agree to marry someone as eccentric as Dr. Dimitrikov?"

"Well," Rosa began. She took a breath and glanced at *Neanderthal* who appeared bothered by the bickering. "Sasha has some interesting qualities."

Colin rolled his eyes back. "Like what? Name one."

"Well, he, uh, yes, he invented a time machine."

Colin took a deep breath. "Name two."

"He's rather handsome, I think."

"Name three."

Her eyes scanned the room and focused on *Neanderthal.* The chancellor smiled at Rosa.

"Young woman, I understand your intrigue with the doctor, he is very enthralling."

Rosa's eyes widened. "You think so?"

"Most definitely."

Colin sat down. "I think I need a shot of whiskey."

"No, you don't, my dear Colin. You need to hear this," the chancellor said placing her hand in his hand. "The doctor saved your life, Colin."

"He did." Colin responded and grabbed a bottle of whiskey off the counter while he was still seated.

"I think it would be wise for you to learn and understand what women are looking for in a man."

"Rosa snickered. Colin removed the top of the whiskey bottle with his teeth.

"You see, Colin, a man who feels compelled to drink, is not of great intrigue for a woman."

He took a few gulps of whiskey. "Don't really care."

"Well, you see that's your problem."

"What's me problem?"

"You don't care what people think of you."

"Surely, I don't."

"Chancellor, please, what I find most attractive about Colin is exactly that. He's his own man. He never worries about how others perceive him," Rosa added.

Colin sat back and continued to drink. The *Neanderthal* stood up to wander the room.

"Colin, my dear Colin, I'm only too sure that you intend to find yourself a wife. I know you desire to share your life."

He grinned, only partially. "So, I do, Evelyn, so I do." He continued to drink from the whiskey bottle.

She eased herself onto his lap and nestled up to him. "Do you have anyone in mind, I wonder?"

He chuckled as she played with his hair. Rosa sat down with one eye on the *Neanderthal*.

# Chapter Eight

The days were short as the sun showed itself with a slight appearance. The *Atlantic Mermaid* made its way into harsher waters, with brisker winds and sleet crashing against the aged vessel. The boat rocked from side to side, with greater wave activity; where parts of the deck received harsher intakes of water. Eddy sat by the deck wrapped in a thick rubber waterproof coat. He was standing in ankle-deep water, however his rubber boots kept him dry. He felt his nerves jump a bit when he would feel the boat creek and bend as if it were about to snap in two.

In the Captain's chamber, Colin and Evelyn romped about on his bed. She let out a few sighs of pleasure as he pulled his erect penis out of her. She smiled at him as he lay beside her.

"Why can't you sleep here with me tonight? It's your Captain's chamber, is it not?"

"Aye, but Rosa 'n Sasha aren't gettin' on too well. I think it's best she share this room with ye. The bunks at the bottom of the hull is no place for a fine wench like Rosa, don't ye think?"

She rolled her body on top of him. "Oh!"

"Are ye alright?"

"I just heard another crashing noise. It seems like it keeps coming from the bottom of the hull."

"Hmm…I'll have to speak to Ed about it, I think."

She lay on top of Colin with an engrossed smile on her face. "I think I'm falling in love with you, Captain."

He brushed his long hair away from his face with his hand. "Don't say that. There's so many distinguished gents ye could pair yerself with, rather than with me. I know me drinkin' bothers ye 'n such. Surely, that isn't the only thing that gets ye."

"I know the more time you spend with me, you would find no need to drink."

He smiled at her. "Maybe."

He stood up from the bed, to notice his clothes were scattered about the room. She watched him dress himself.

"I'll escort Rosa up here," he said.

"Too bad, I would really cherish your company for the night. We're entering the Arctic. I need you to keep me warm."

He grinned at her as he struggled to fascine his suspenders around his bulked physique. She gleamed at him when he leaned over the bed to kiss her lips. "Sleep well."

"Colin. Has your boat ever made it this far north before?"

"Never."

She watched him exit. Colin entered the galley. Rosa sat at the table with her sewing basket by her side.

"Where's Sasha at?" Colin asked with a gentle voice.

"I don't know."

He paused. "Where's Eddy?"

"He's likely in the wheelhouse steering the boat. Who knows?"

"Where's Neanderthal?"

"Who knows?"

"Are ye feelin' alright as the afternoon slowly fades away from us?"

"Alright? That's a silly question coming from a man with your intellect."

Colin gingerly pulled a chair beside her to sit down. He paused as he watched her thread a needle. "Love, yer lookin' like yer about to cry. Please don't do that."

She put the needle down on the table. "Everyone knows there was never a spark between Sasha and me."

"I think yer just thinkin' there's a spark 'cause there's no one else at the moment."

"There was a spark and still is a spark between you and me, Colin."

He tried to force a smile, but couldn't. "Oh, God. Please, don't do this. Ye know ye haven't the tolerance for a gent like meself."

"Rubbish! You're now sleeping with the chancellor of the university. Oh, Colin, have you no shame?"

He stared at the table. "Shame? Wish ye wouldn't put it that way."

"It's what is, isn't it, Colin?"

He paused. "Supposin' so."

"You don't love the chancellor. You love me."

He lightly tapped his foot on the floor. "Look, can we discuss this at another place 'n time? Ye really should get yerself some rest. You'll be sharin' me room with Evelyn. Sasha will sleep at the bottom of the hull with me, Eddy, 'n Neanderthal."

She buried her head in his bicep and started to cry.

"Love, what ye doin'?"

"I wish I never let you go. I'm so sorry, Colin." Her crying intensified.

"I'm sorry, too."

She pulled herself away from him. "I suppose what's done is done. You still love Amoli, don't you?"

"Always."

She tried to suck back her tears with a few more sniffles. "Well, I suppose I should turn in. I think we need all the rest we can get for our next time travel quest. You need to tend to Neanderthal."

He stood up to face her and took her delicate hands. "I'll be turnin' in soon as well."

There was a sudden rumble of the ship. Hard waves crashed against the boat. Colin fell forward onto Rosa. He lay face to face with her with him on top.

"It's nice to see ye this way, love."

"Colin, get off of me! You're so huge!"

"Thought ye'd like this position."

"I can't breathe. I'm suffocating."

There was another crashing rumble to the ship. Colin stood up and helped Rosa.

"Can ye make it to me chamber?"

"Yes, but I'm concerned. What's going on?"

"I'll investigate, please get some rest. I'll take care of it."

He coaxed her to the ladder, which led to the captain's chamber. He watched her exit until he couldn't see her. He felt the ship rumble even more. He heard voices. He immediately exited the galley. He felt there was some kind of commotion on his ship. "Good God, what was that?" Two intruders had entered the ship, they scattered about the deck, hanging off the ropes and sails. Colin dashed onto the deck. Strong Arctic winds blew his long reddish hair. "Who goes there?"

A stranger stood by the gunnel with a pistol in his hand.

"Who are you?" Colin stepped toward the man and stopped. "Yer upon me ship without invitation."

Eddy made his way to the deck with Sasha.

Sasha noticed the gun. He glanced at Colin. "Who is he?"

Two more strange men entered the *Atlantic Mermaid*, armed with pistols. Colin noticed their wreck of a ship, which was parked beside the *Atlantic Mermaid*. Colin looked at Eddy as he tried to answer Sasha's question.

"Pirates, mate."

Sasha glanced at Eddy. "I not prepared for this."

"Shh." Colin gestured.

"Is this a merchant ship?" The pirate asked.

"None of yer business what kind of ship this is," Colin responded.

"We need a better boat than this," the thief griped. "I suppose it's better than nothing."

Colin's eyes widened. "What?"

The pirate leaned toward Colin. "I said, this merchant ship should suit us fine! Are ya deaf?"

The pirate's facial expression irritated Colin. "Merchant ship?" Colin stared through the pirate, as he cursed to himself.

"It's much too big to be a trawler, it has to be a merchant ship," the pirate instilled.

"Don't really care much for givin' yez a lesson on different types of commercial vessels, so I feckin' don't."

The pirate's facial smirk intensified, where Colin clenched his fists. "Leave now, or I'll have to break yer bloody bones," Colin announced.

The other pirate pointed his pistol at Colin. "Step aside. This is our vessel now."

"Yer mouthin' off to the wrong man!" Colin blurted.

"I said step aside, or we'll have to kill you."

"So, ye will, eh?" Colin snapped back. "Yer not gettin' this vessel! Beat it! Get on yer piece of junk and get lost!"

"This merchant ship is ours now!"

"You get it on one condition," Sasha interjected as he walked toward the pirate's gun.

"Mate, what ye doin'?" Colin called.

"I must say *condition* to this stupid man," Sasha snorted as he placed his hand against the pistol.

The pirate's facial expression changed, he slowly primed his pistol ready to fire.

"You not know how to steal ship because you so dumb."

Colin stepped forward, "Sasha, this is no time to play Russian roulette!"

"I not play Russian roulette, I play truth. Stupid thief will have to get past us first before he take boat, da?"

Eddy stood back in silence.

The *Neanderthal* made his way from the hull up to the deck. The pirate stepped away from Colin and backed up toward the gunnel. The *Neanderthal* hesitated to react, so he remained still. Sasha's hand remained against the pistol. The pirate took a small step back. The *Neanderthal* suddenly lunged onto the pirate. The pistol went flying over the gunnel, into the ocean. Sasha kicked one of the pistols out of the other pirate's hands and aimed the gun at the intruders. Colin stepped closer to the pirates to swing his fist in their faces. Colin punched them several times in the face, while Sasha continued to aim the gun. They found themselves on the floor bleeding.

"Great job, Captain and Doctor!" Eddy commended.

"Monkey man save our lives!" Sasha cheered with a slight chuckle.

The expression of feeling accelerated was on Colin's face. "What? Monkey man? Are ye bleedin' outta of yer mind?"

"True. Monkey man save ship. He good monkey. Give him banana! Do you have?"

Colin glanced at Eddy then at Sasha. "*Neanderthal* is our evolutionary ancestor, stop callin' 'im that, ye wanker!"

"You get mad, I not know why. Why ladies like you, I not know."

Colin leered at Sasha in silence. He recklessly took the battered pirates to their ship, which was anchored to his.

Rosa and Evelyn made their way from the Captain's chamber. "Colin? Did something happen?" Rosa asked with angst.

We heard some commotion," Evelyn paused with concern. She grimaced when she noticed Colin handle the bloody pirates onto their sip. "Good God! What on earth has happened here?"

"Can't wait to time travel again," Colin grinned with sarcasm. "No worries, though."

"We time travel, da, time machine must be positioned on deck, then we go, da?"

60

Rosa glanced at Colin. "Oh, God, every time we do this, I always feel like we'll never come back."

The chancellor turned to Rosa. "You make it sound as if you do this often."

Rosa's eyes flickered. "Well, yes."

"Haven't I always protected everyone on these expeditions?" Colin instilled.

Sasha chuckled. "Mr. Limmerick you always get in so much trouble, I protect you, da?"

"When do we time travel?" Colin tried to change the subject.

Evelyn looked at Colin with a grin.

"Morning, we go in morning," Sasha responded. "We must make magnetic lines converge. This is Arctic, so we must do."

Rosa glanced at Colin. Colin glanced at Evelyn.

# Chapter Nine

The Arctic winds blew through every crack and crevice of the *Atlantic Mermaid*. Colin tried to pull the bed cover over his head as he snoozed in his bunk at the bottom of the ship's hull. It was about 3:00 a.m., the *Neanderthal* pretended to be asleep when he perked his head up to see the others in a deep sleep. He lifted his head, focused on the sleeping men. He gingerly slid off the bunk, where he tried not to make a sound. He placed his feet on the wood-planked floor. The wood creaked a bit but didn't wake up anyone. The *Neanderthal* made his way to the ladder and climbed up to the deck. He noticed the time machine sitting in the middle of the ship's deck. He paused and grinned. The beast slowly scanned the deck only to notice that he was the only one there. He slowly paced around the machine, where he hesitated to touch it. He ran his long gnarly fingers along the wrought-iron rails, which framed the machine. He paused to take a breath or two. With every sound of the turbulent waves that crashed against the sides of the boat, he jumped a bit from fear of being caught. His intrigue grew enough to get him to step inside of it. He gingerly placed his hands over the handles. He noticed the control panel with the time indicator sitting beside it.

Colin rolled over in his bunk. He sat up. He rubbed his large rough hands over his face as he flicked his lengthy forelock. He peered at the bunk the *Neanderthal* was supposed to sleep in, only to notice that the prehistoric prime mate was gone. His eyes widened as he gasped a bit.

*"Oh, feck,"* he blurted.

He recklessly put on his boots and jacket and climbed up the ladder to the deck. He poked his head and peered out, while he still held onto the ladder. He scanned the deck, where he noticed the *Neanderthal* standing in the time machine.

"No! Get outta there!" Colin shouted as he hoisted himself onto the deck.

The control panel enamoured the beast, where he pressed the colourful buttons and pulled down the iron leaver. Colin lunged his body at the levitating contraption. The *Neanderthal* shouted with panic. The sharp sounds of the spinning clock from above, rattled the beast. Debris encircled the machine and filled the deck. The winds grew stronger.

Sasha sprung up from the ladder and got himself onto the deck as well. "What is this? You use time machine without me?"

Colin stood still as he watched the time machine continue to spin and rise with power.

"Monkey man, he steal my machine?" Sasha shouted as he stood next to Colin.

Colin and Sasha watched the *Neanderthal* spin into a vortex of time and vanish from their sight. Colin stared at nothing. He was silent.

Eddy followed. "Oh, sweet Jesus, what happened here, Captain?"

Colin took a deep breath. "Don't know, really."

Sasha noticed something had fallen onto the floor from the machine. "What this is?" Sasha asked as he picked the object up.

Colin glanced at it. "Isn't that yer time indicator? It says something on it, I think, what's it say?"

Sasha squinted his eyes to read what the time indicator said. "It say, *1970.*"

"1970? What does that mean?" Colin asked.

"It say year he travel to, da?"

"The year he traveled to is 1970… AD it says. Oh, I'm supposin' Neanderthal is on his way to 1970," Colin paused. "Oh, shite. So, he's goin' back to the time we found him in. Feck that!"

"Back to place with outside concert? Such terrible music, I remember," Sasha commented.

Colin sighed with frustration. "We failed, mates. It's all over, I suppose."

Rosa and Evelyn entered the deck, swaddled in warm coats and scarves.

"Colin?" Rosa said.

Colin turned to her. "I'm knowin' what yer about to say, love. Just don't say anythin', if ye can do that?"

Evelyn's smile dissipated. "Colin, you look very cold and exhausted. Why are we standing out here, anyway?"

Rosa stepped closer to Colin. "Where's the time machine?" She asked with her eyes shifting to Sasha.

Sasha's head hung low as he stared at the planked floor. The wind howled and sleet slapped their faces, and penetrated their bodies.

Colin glanced at Rosa. "Time machine?"

Rosa's breathing became irregular as she panted with angst. "Colin?"

"It's gone, all gone, for feck's sake. Jesus Christ!"

"I don't understand!" Rosa glanced at Sasha. "What just happened here?"

"Sasha looked at her. "I not know. Mr. Limmerick see all."

"Colin, can you please tell me what just happened?"

"I don't think I can do that, love." He stood erect and glanced at her with only his eyes. "I think I just saw *Neanderthal* leave on the time machine. He somehow got it activated. Must be this Arctic energy, so to speak."

Evelyn tried to make her way toward Colin. "Oh, Colin, I'm so sorry. I know how hard all of you have worked on trying to get your found prehistoric species back to its time period."

Rosa took a deep breath and eased her posture. "Now, what are we going to do?"

"Go home, I suppose," Colin responded.

Rosa's eyes widened. "Go home?"

Sasha held the activator in his hands. "*Neanderthal* go to future --- 1970."

Rosa pulled the activating device from him. "1970?"

"Da, we find him in future, now he back in same place we find him."

Evelyn took Colin's arm. "I'm so sorry."

Rosa grit her teeth. "He'll die in 1970! We have to find him and place him back in his time period."

Sasha's eyes widened. "Look at this crazy woman. We not go to 1970 to find monkey man. I not do. I not even have time machine."

Rosa looked up at Colin. "Well? What are we going to do, now?"

"What can we do, eh?"

"I know! I build new time machine, da?"

Rosa smiled. "Good man, Sasha!"

"Not for monkey man. I not care about him. I build time machine so we can continue to be famous time travelers."

Colin chuckled. "Famous, eh?"

Evelyn smiled at Sasha. "How about that device activator of yours, Doctor?"

"What about?"

"Well, can it take us into different dimensions of time?" She asked.

"Da. We use it before and we travel through time."

"Evelyn, it takes ye to the wrong destinations," Colin interjected.

"I wouldn't rave about the time machine either," Rosa commented.

"How lovely," Evelyn commented, sarcastically.

Eddy patted Colin on the back. "We need to get back to the Isles and don't ya worry, Captain, you'll soon be on another quest."

Colin tried to smile at his first mate, but then he glanced at Sasha. "How long will it take ye to build

65

another time machine? Didn't ye build it with those Russian 'n Swiss gents?"

"They will not participate on new time machine. I must build it all myself. Alone!"

Rosa began to pace a bit. "You don't want to build it with other scientists because you want to reap all the glory yourself. Sasha, how could you?"

"You want so bad to see 1970 again. I build time machine and we go, da?"

Rosa looked at Colin. "I think we need to return to 1970. We have to find Neanderthal. We put him in the mess he's in, after all, therefore, we need to put him back to where he belongs."

"Love, just calm yerself. Tryin' to find *Neanderthal* in London's future would be near impossible, don't ye think? London's population would've likely doubled. How would we go about this, really?" Colin said as he placed his hands on Rosa's delicate shoulders. "I understand we did this before, but for a short while. We don't know how long it would take us to locate our *Neanderthal*. We may never find him. How do we even know where in the world Neanderthal has travelled to? Is it London?"

Sasha interjected. "Or is it Moscow?"

"I think you're getting much too close to Miss Emanuel, Colin," Evelyn snorted with a sharp nudge to Colin's ribs.

Colin stepped away from Rosa.

"I will begin to write out plan on how to create new time machine. I will do fast because I do it before, da?"

Eddy glanced at Colin. "Captain, ye want me to start headin' south to the Isles?"

"Definitely, Ed. Sasha's gonna need the equipment in the lab for this project."

Rosa continued to pace. She wrapped her long scarf around her delicate, long neck, several times; she peered

66

at the turbulent Arctic waters. She stared at something that seemed to protrude out of the water.

Evelyn noticed that Rosa appeared to be in a trance. "What are you looking at?"

Rosa squinted her eyes. "What's that?" She said pointing out to the ocean.

Evelyn tried to focus, then she fiddled with her coat pocket for her glasses and she placed them on her face. "Only God knows. It doesn't look like a fish or whale of any kind, that's for sure."

"It doesn't even seem to be living. What is it?" Rosa responded almost to herself, but aloud. "Colin!"

Colin turned to Rosa. "Aye!"

"Where's your telescope?" Rosa asked Colin with concern in her voice.

"It's likely in the galley somewhere, why?"

"Colin, what is that?" She continued to point.

Colin stood beside Rosa and Evelyn. He focused on where she was pointing. "Feck, if I know."

Sasha stood beside them. "It is your *B-whale* again, da?"

"Not at all, ye wanker. It's not livin', whatever it is."

"What is it, then?" Sasha asked.

Colin hung over the gunnel. "What is it?"

"It started to enlarge, where it started rising from the ocean. Colin and Rosa's eyes widened.

Rosa tugged on Colin's arm. "Colin?"

"Shite, if I know."

Sasha watched with amazement, but didn't focus as hard as his cohorts. Evelyn watched the strange figure rise from the ocean. Her eyes were wide with astonishment. It continued to rise, until it was afloat on the ocean's surface.

Evelyn looked at Colin. "Good God, is it what I think?"

Colin's eyebrows lifted. "A submarine, is it?

"Colin, a submarine in the Arctic waters?" Rosa questioned.

Colin grinned at her. "Likely so. That's not so strange, is it?"

Evelyn looked at Colin. "It somehow isn't one of ours."

"Ye mean it's not British?" Colin asked.

"Not exactly. I mean, it looks different, somehow. What do you think?" Evelyn questioned.

"Yer meanin' like it's not appearin' to be from our time? *Oh, feck ...*"

"No, Colin, is it really from another time? I wouldn't even say that it looks British," Rosa gasped as she continued to hang onto Colin's arm.

"We're in Arctic waters, now, love. It doesn't have to be British in this neck of the woods, don't ye think?"

"It cold be French? American? Or…," Evelyn tried to confirm.

"It could be Russian!" Sasha blurted. "I think I see Russian print on it. Da, you see? It is Russian!"

"Well, that's good, I suppose," Rosa said with a partial grin.

They watched it closely, as it sprouted up to the top and floated beside them. Sasha smiled as he watched a line of men in uniforms enter the top of the vessel.

Rosa glanced at Colin. "They're dressed in uniforms I've never seen before, Colin."

"Likely, 'cause they're Russian."

"Maybe so. I don't know very much about Russia. Maybe this is the way they dress," Rosa responded.

"I not recognize crest on uniform. It should be Russia's flag colors, but it is not," Sasha commented with uneasiness in his voice. "Their flag is red with little gold pictures in corner. This is not Russian flag. I not know this."

One man who appeared to be in-charge, gestured to be let onto *The Atlantic Mermaid.* Colin stared at the man. He couldn't make out if he was carrying a weapon or not. He reluctantly lowered the gangway. The man entered Colin's ship, with several of his cohorts armed with strange-looking guns. Rosa's eyes widened. She looked at Colin with a panicked expression.

The man and his cohorts stood erect, with their arms pasted to the sides of their bodies. *"aDEEN, dvah, tree, chTIRee!"* The leader counted to four in Russian with a slight march with his cohorts behind him.

Sasha appeared delighted. *"Zdras-tvooy-tyeh!"* He greeted with glee.

The leader appeared startled by Sasha. *"Shto?"*

Sasha stepped back. *"Kak vas zovyt?"* (what is your name?)

*"Menye Misha Yeltov."*

Colin glanced at Sasha, "Who is he?"

"Ah, *da, da*, English?" The leader realized. "I will speak you in English," he said.

Colin tried to force a smile, but he couldn't. "Aye, we're British."

The leader rubbed his chin. "British boat in these waters, how interesting."

"We're just northeast of Greenland. What's so interestin'?" Colin commented.

"What is your name?" The leader asked Sasha.

"I am Dr. Sasha Dimitrikov, physicist from Saint Petersburg."

"What are you doing on British boat?"

Rosa's eye widened with fear. Evelyn stayed tucked behind Colin.

"I am scientist. I work for British university."

"You work for British?" The leader responded with surprise. "Show me your papers!" He demanded with his arm extended toward Sasha.

Sasha glanced at Colin, who stood beside him. "Papers? What papers?"

"Show me your papers! You will be repatriated if you don't have papers. Show me your papers!"

"I not have papers. I work for British university. I am scientist."

"Your boat must leave Soviet territory now, or we will have to take you to Moscow and have you sentenced to death for trespassing."

Rosa tugged on Colin's arm harder. "We are definitely not in Russian boundary waters. I think you're mistaking."

"We will have you all killed immediately. Why is this Russian man on this ship? Are you a spy, I wonder?"

"Spy?" Sasha responded. "I am Russian, from Saint Petersburg. You cannot be Russian if you speak me this way," Sasha blurted. "Besides, you no have Russian flag branded on your submarine or your uniform. If you true Russian you would have Russian flag colors."

"The leader straightened his posture even more so. His face was stern. "Russian flag? It is long gone. It was destroyed in 1917 and replaced with our communist red. What is wrong with you? You must be taken to Moscow at once for further questioning and if we don't like your answers, you run the risk of torture and death. Why are you on a British vessel? You must be a spy."

Rosa's face was white and pasty with fear. She tugged on Colin's arm enough, where he lowered his ear to her face.

"Colin, Sasha is in trouble. I've never seen ammunition like that in my life. I'm afraid," she whispered.

"Love," Colin whispered while he blinked his eyes out of nervousness.

"What is it?"

"I think they're from the future."

Rosa's eyes bulged with fear. She trembled as she watched the futuristic soldiers point their guns at Sasha. Sasha tried to converse with them in Russian. They

70

responded where a two-way conversation continued for a while, but the futuristic soldiers seemed put-off by Sasha.

"So you defected? That's a crime and you will burn in hell for this!"

Sasha's lips, parted before responding. "Defected? What you say?"

"How do you work for British?"

"I am brilliant scientist, so I work for British."

"Then you have papers. British have no business hiding you from us."

Sasha glanced at Colin. "I not know what he say. He talk crazy."

"It's not makin' a world of sense, now is it?" Colin responded with his eyes fixed on the leader.

Sasha tried to straighten his jacket. "If you Russian, why you speak so good English? Maybe you spy too and you also work for British?"

The leader firmed his grip of the gun. I have had several meetings with U.S. President Nixon. I must be able to speak good English.

Evelyn's eyes widened. "You mean U.S. president Teddy Roosevelt, don't you?"

The leader of the submarine glanced at his men, who stood behind him with their guns pointing at the time-travelers. He appeared somewhat confused. "Roosevelt? He was during Revolution."

Sasha appeared confused as well as he glanced at Colin. "What he say? He is crazy man?"

Colin lowered his head to meet Sasha's ear. "They're from the future, can't ye see that, mate?"

Sasha's eyes widened with surprise. "Oh, my God," Sasha gasped in a whisper.

Colin tried to force a partial smile. "Are ye aware of today's date, man?"

The leader kept his gun pointed at the time travelers. "It is December 25, 1970. Your silly Christmas Day, British."

"I was supposed to be married on this day," sighed Colin.

Rosa looked up at him, also with a sigh. "Me too."

Sasha stepped forward. "It is not December 25, 1970, it is December 25, 1910."

Colin nudged Sasha. "Why would ye tell 'im that, mate? Ye should've let 'im figure it out on his own, the hard way."

"Look at him, he not believe me anyway, da? He is crazy."

The leader continued to point his gun at the time travelers. "Now, you will go into submarine."

Sasha didn't move. "I will not!"

"Your friends can stay on this terrible British boat but you are to come with me."

"I will not," Sasha instilled as he turned his head away from the leader.

"Are you or are you not Soviet?" The leader asked bold and abrupt. He stared at Sasha with menacing eyes.

Sasha's eyes widened. Colin glanced at Sasha, then at the leader. "What you say me?"

"Are you not Soviet?" The leader repeated with frustration in his voice.

Colin faced Sasha. "What's *Soviet,* mate? Do ye get what he's sayin' to yez?"

"I not know. I am Russian, not *Soviet.* I not hear this word before."

"You are against our country's leader?" The leader insinuated.

Sasha's eyes widened. "Nicolas? He is satisfactory for Russia, I think."

"Nicolas?" The leader's eyebrows lowered closer to his eyes. His face turned a shade of red. "You want to die right now?"

Colin stepped closer to Sasha, almost touching his side. "Mate, stop this game. He'll surely blow yer head off, if ye get 'im angry enough. Just go along with it."

"I not know who leader will be in 1970. How can I know this?"

"I'll just ask 'im, then."

The leader stared at Sasha with cold eyes. "In the submarine! I will take you to KGB and they will decide your destiny."

"Maybe someday I will decide your destiny," Sasha said, facing a different direction.

The leader stopped. He leered at Sasha and turned to face him. He took out his gun and smashed Sasha on the head with the back of it. Rosa screamed as she watched Sasha fall to the ground with a gash to the side of his head. Colin's eyes widened, when he noticed Sasha's blood trickle onto the planked floor.

"Look, we'll go to yer KGB people 'n abide to whatever yer askin'. Just don't harm any of us, 'cause we's innocent. Spies? So, ye think we are? Shirley not. We're innocent people mindin' our own," Colin tried to reason. Rosa fell to the floor and tried to nurture Sasha's wound.

The leader gazed at Rosa with cold eyes and murmured something to his cohorts in Russian with his eyes fixed on her.

Colin stepped closer to Rosa and Sasha bleeding on the floor. "Love, get yerself up," he cautioned her. He gave her his hand.

"For all we know," she tried to suck back her sniffles and tears of fear. "He could be dead. He seems to be breathing, though."

Colin grabbed her arm to pull her up. "Don't fuss with our mate just now, just act obedient."

She grimaced with disgust. "Obedient? Colin, what are you saying, here?"

"Just do it, love," he cautioned her.

Rosa stood up, but noticed Sasha's eyes were opened. She smiled, but Colin nudged her. The chancellor stepped in front of Colin to face the leader.

"I don't seem to understand what seems to be the problem, gentlemen. You just struck this man. Our man at that, how dare you."

Colin shoved Evelyn. "Evelyn, please be silent. Don't agitate matters more than they are already."

"Oh, Colin, are you afraid? Your bulging with muscles, you needn't be afraid of these foreigners," The chancellor said.

The leader spoke Russian to his cohorts. They stared at Evelyn and began to laugh. Colin glanced at the Russian naval men who stood firmly behind their leader. Sasha tried to stand up with help from Rosa and Evelyn. He tried to gain his balance and focus on the situation.

Colin abruptly lunged forward to snatch the gun from the leader. There was a gunshot. The two women screamed. Colin grabbed the gun from the leader and threw him to the ground, with the gun to his head. Sasha swooped toward Colin and grabbed the gun and shot one of the naval men. The man fell overboard. Colin lifted the leader and tossed him over board as well. Rosa grabbed Evelyn and pulled her to the galley. Eddy hurried down the ladder to the bottom of the hull. One of the remaining naval men pointed his gun and fired it at Colin and shot him in the thigh. Colin bent over and pressed his hand over his wound. Sasha glanced at the ocean to notice the leader was swimming in the frigid water to stay alive. Colin winced with pain. He tore off his jacket to place it over his wound. One of the naval men pointed his gun at Sasha and grabbed his arm. He looked at Sasha and spat in his face. He mumbled something in Russian. Sasha tried to pull away, but the other man's gun was pressed against his skull.

Sasha appeared outraged, but Colin nudged him in the side, gesturing for him to remain silent.

"So, he spit in yer face, let it go, 'n keep silent, mate," Colin whispered to Sasha.

74

"I cannot. These people not Russian to me. Where is the pride? The grandeur?" Sasha whispered back.

"They's from another time in the future, mate, can't ye see that? Ye don't understand who they are. Just keep calm, don't react. Don't take it too personal, cause they've got guns that I've never seen before," Colin cautioned in a low whisper.

Sasha stepped toward the lead naval officer. "So, now what you want with us?"

"You are Russian on British ship, you must be a spy. All of you must come with us to KGB office in Moscow."

Rosa's eyes bulged with fear. "Russia? We're going to Russia?"

Colin glanced at Rosa. "Aye."

The naval officers placed handcuffs on their wrists and pulled them onto the submarine. *The Atlantic Mermaid* was vacated, however, Eddy remained at the bottom of the hull.

# Chapter Ten

They entered the top of the submarine, where the lead naval officer noticed Colin was hobbling a bit from the gunshot to his thigh. Sasha held a cold compress on the side of his wounded head.

"We will get medical doctor when we reach Moscow," the head naval officer said.

"I should hope so," Rosa responded with a sarcastic tone.

The lead naval officer grabbed Rosa by the arm and brought her face to his. "You talk like that to me again and you will be used for my officer's fun."

Rosa winched with terror on her face. She glanced at Sasha and Colin. Colin and Sasha glared at him and pulled Rosa away. They entered the interior of the submarine. Rosa and Evelyn's eyes widened with surprise, when they noticed the futuristic technology. Rosa tugged on Colin's arm.

"Colin, this vessel is not from our time, is it?"

"That's right," Colin whispered back.

"Colin, this is 1970?"

"Aye, this is. They're definitely more advanced than us, no doubt."

Sasha leered at them as he searched his pockets for cigarettes. "I not have cigarettes, you have?"

The lead naval officer kept a stern look on his face, as he passed Sasha a cigarette.

*"Spasiba,"* Sasha responded, as he noticed a photograph of Joseph Stalin on the wall. "Who is this?"

The naval officer lowered his eyebrows as he glanced at his cohorts. They broke into hysterical laughter. Sasha, Colin, Rosa and Evelyn stood in silence as they watched six Russian naval officers laugh for at least a few seconds.

Sasha puffed on his cigarette. "Why you laugh? Say us who he is and that is all."

The lead naval officer's hardy laugh almost spit in Rosa's face. "You don't know? Wait until KGB finish with you."

Rosa glanced at Colin. "Whose this KGB he keeps speaking of?" she asked in a whisper.

"Donno - really, but it sounds to me this KGB could be bigger than God himself," Colin whispered back.

The lead naval officer gave Colin a shove. "Stop your talk or I'll separate you from your women."

Colin noticed how one of the other naval officers had his gun pointed at them, but he didn't react.

Sasha kept the cold compress against the side of his head and remained seated.

"Sasha, you lost quite a bit of blood, you need to take it easy before we get to Moscow," Rosa cautioned.

"Da, I will do."

Evelyn wrapped her herself around Colin's arm. "How long will it take until we reach Moscow?"

"Not sure, really, this is a vessel from the future, it's likely a lot faster, wouldn't ye think? Gotta reach Saint Petersburg's port first, likely."

"I'm just exhausted, I wish we could cuddle up together in a nice warm bed," Evelyn commented. "It would also be nice to have a quaint fireplace in the corner. We could sip on Champagne, even."

"Dream on, wench, we won't be seein' any of that, surely for a good while, if ever."

When they reached Saint Petersburg's port, the submarine seemed to have hit something. Books and papers fell off the desk. A swivel chair fell to its side. Colin glanced at the lead naval officer who entered their cabin.

"Did we hit somethin'?" Colin asked.

"We hit the port and I don't know why," the lead naval officer responded.

Sasha leaned toward Colin. "I think I know why."

Colin's eyes widened. "I think I know as well, mate."

The lead naval officer appeared bothered. "Why did we hit the port? We did some damage to our submarine!"

Colin stepped toward him. "Um, excuse me, but ye need to understand somethin'."

He turned to Colin. "What?"

"Perhaps yer mighty submarine don't fit in the port. Likely, it's too big."

"It always fit!" The naval officer blurted.

Sasha sat back to smoke his cigarette to the bare butt.

"I'm a man of the sea 'n I can tell yez right here, yer gonna need to find another way to dock this thing."

"Impossible!" The lead naval officer smashed his fist on the table.

Colin stepped closer to him. "What year was yer submarine built?"

"New art form, 1960."

Sasha glanced at Colin as he made smoke rings in the air. Rosa sat beside Sasha.

"It should fit, it did before!" He stomped out of their cabin.

Colin slowly sat beside Sasha. "This vessel is ten years old, if we're in the year 1970. Is that a good thing or bad, so I wonder?" He paused for a few seconds. "I could surely use a shot of whiskey just now."

"Ten years could be new for Soviets!" Sasha chuckled. "I think we in trouble, da?"

Colin glanced at him. "Likely. I'll maybe shut me eyes and imagine *me-self* just about to have a shot of whiskey."

Evelyn's eyes were fixed on Colin. "I think whiskey is the last thing you should be thinking of at the moment, Colin."

"We're in the year 1970. How phenomenal. Even 1960 would be phenomenal," Evelyn commented, not really understanding the situation.

Rosa remained seated with her chin resting over her hands. "Hmm...amazing."

"We're in the future, Miss Emanuel. Do you not find this amazing?"

"Future? We haven't even time travelled, Chancellor Gordon. We're still at the end of 1910. New Years Eve is less than a week away."

"Oh, yes, that is correct. So why did that Russian naval officer say his submarine was built in 1960?

Colin placed his arm around Evelyn's shoulders. "It's rather confusin', so it is. This Russian submarine was built in 1960, but this crew of submariners are from 1970. They somehow time travelled through a time vortex and ended up in their past, 1910 – our present. They don't know it, though. They seem to be ignorin' our style of dress for some reason. Nobody ignored our clothing when we went to 1970, England."

"Colin, we had just left the year 1487. Yes, those people in London thought our clothing was definitely off from what they were used to," Rosa commented.

"Okay, I think I'm starting to understand this. We haven't traveled through time yet, have we?" Evelyn asked with a confused expression on her face.

Sasha tried to stand up. "It is because of monkey-man! This is why so much trouble and so much confusion."

Evelyn's lips parted. "Monkey man? You mean *Neanderthal*, Doctor?"

Rosa stepped in front of Colin. "Neanderthal got his hands on Sasha's time machine and must have pressed random buttons. He somehow returned to 1970. We were not passing through British waters. We were closer to Russian territory. This is why we're here."

Evelyn gasped. "Returned to 1970?"

"We found *Neanderthal* in 1970, so we took him to 1910 to be with us, because we were concerned that there was no way he could survive in 1970. He's twenty-eight thousand years old," Colin tried to explain.

"I see." Evelyn hacked on her own saliva. "This doesn't make any sense," she paused to collect herself. "So, why is there a Russian submarine from 1970 or 1960, I should say?"

"They got lost in the vortex of time, 'n now, they're in a different time period. That's why the submarine is too big for the 1910 port. The port is already out-dated."

Sasha noticed a copy of *The Communist Manifesto* sitting on the desk. "I know this book. I read it. It is good idea."

"I read it some years ago as well," Colin commented. "If it can eliminate poverty, it's a good idea, I'd say."

"What you think? You think it good for Russia?"

"I think Russia has adapted the concepts behind it, by the looks of these gents on the submarine, mate."

"What you say?"

"By their discussions of this KGB, Russia may have adapted some kind-a mutation of Marx's ideas."

"What you mean?"

Rosa began to pace the room. "Oh, yes, Colin, I was thinking the same thing as you. I don't like this one bit."

The submarine hit something else, where everything in the room either shook or fell over. Rosa screamed while Evelyn gasped. Colin leaned against the wall for balance, the submarine hit something again and again: then, all was still; it then crashed against something, where furniture and file cabinets fell and smashed to the floor. Sasha remained sitting, when he noticed some plaster from the ceiling crack off into a tuft of dust over their heads.

"Oh, God!" Rosa blurted with despair.

An unopened bottle of vodka fell out of a cabinet and rolled onto the floor. Colin picked it up and handed it to Sasha. "This is yer sauce, mate."

"You want alcohol so bad, you have."

"Don't fancy the brew, so I don't."

"Take it. It is yours."

"Who cares?" Rosa gasped.

80

Evelyn tugged on Colin's jacket. "Dear, can't we leave this submarine? They do have frightening guns, I must say."

"Well, Evelyn, I don't really know how we can do that. Ye see, *Neanderthal* left with Sasha's time machine. These naval officers have taken us as their prisoners. This is all new to me because we are sill in our own time."

Rosa started to whimper. "I hate this."

"Well, then Colin, can we not somehow send this submarine and its crew to their own time period? How will they react when they come to understand that they are no longer in 1970?" Evelyn asked while she fidgeted with Colin's jacket.

Rosa began to pace. "These futuristic Russians might even blame it all on us, since they are so convinced that we're spies."

"Well, then, we definitely need to escape, so we can warn the officials in our time period, that this alien submarine has busted the Saint Petersburg dock," Colin responded.

"It is almost New Years Eve, almost 1911. Russians are having upheaval. Not a good time to be in Russia. Also, I have wife here."

Rosa looked at Sasha. "Oh, God! Sasha, I thought you were going to end your marriage?"

"I am in Russia. She is here. What am I to do?"

Colin gave Sasha a slight shove. "Ye don't go about makin' promises to other wenches, when ye know ye can't keep them, eh?"

"I must see her. I am here."

Colin sighed out of frustration as he folded his arms in front of him. "What ye goin' on about this for? We're stuck in a Russian submarine from 1970, our future. We may not make this one alive."

Evelyn stroked Colin's bicep. "Don't talk like that Colin. Of course we'll make it out of here alive. When

81

they see we aren't spies, they'll be more than happy to release us."

"Evelyn, these blokes don't strike me as the type that would simply apologize for their mistake."

"They're obviously mistaking us for someone else. They could be looking for spies, who knows? We're not what they're looking for. Justice always wins," Evelyn gave her opinion with a smile on her face.

Rosa grinned. "Really?"

Evelyn peered at Rosa. "Yes, really."

"I wish we had the time machine, so we could somehow send them back to their time," Rosa instilled.

Sasha glanced at Rosa. "Maybe time travel device could send them away."

Rosa stepped closer to Sasha. "To 1970?"

"*Nyet*. Maybe more than one-hundred-fifty-million years ago; anywhere in time. Who cares? I want them sent away."

Rosa slapped him on the arm. "How awful of you to even think that, Sasha. These Russian naval officers from the future are innocent. They have nothing to do with the fact that we keep playing God."

Colin sat down and sighed with frustration. "Don't really know what's so terrible about a Russian being on a British ship?"

Sasha sat beside Colin. "Unless relations between British and Russia go sour. I not understand this. Some strange things happen in our future, I think Mr. Limmerick."

Sasha stood up and awkwardly paced the room. "I not see photograph of Russian Czar. Why they not care about history? Who are these people?"

"Sasha, did you bring your time travel device?" Rosa asked.

"Da."

Colin glanced at Rosa.

"Try and send this submarine to its future. Do it!" Rosa demanded, as she tugged on Sasha's collar.

"We cannot be on this submarine. We must find lifeboat and get off this huge thing," blurted Sasha.

Rosa looked at Colin with angst. "Then, we must find a lifeboat! Captain Colin, you're the man of the sea. You know what to do, don't you?"

Colin pulled back from her. "What ye doin' now, love? Yer in a panic, are yez?"

"We need to leave, Colin!"

Evelyn tried to smile. "Um, I think you better calm yourself, young woman. This submarine is crawling with marines. It wouldn't hurt to educate us on their world. It could lead us to safety," Evelyn said as she placed her hands on Rosa's shoulders.

"I just want to leave. They're going to kill us!" Rosa sat down to whimper.

The lead naval officer stormed into their cabin. "What is this I hear? Crying?"

Colin ran his hands through Rosa's hair. "Calm down, love."

"It has been decided," the lead naval officer blurted.

Colin stepped toward him and lifted his eyebrows. "Decided?"

"Something strange has happened. We think Americans are behind this."

Sasha's eyes bounced around the room. "Americans? Behind what?"

"They may have launched their nuclear missals."

Colin glanced at Sasha. "Mate? What's he goin' on about nuclear missals?"

"Nuclear, da. I have heard of this. Missals, I think I might know."

"What's the Americans to do with any of this?" Colin asked in a whisper.

"I not know. America is very nice place. I was there for scientific conference in New York. Nice simple place. I not understand connection."

Rosa lifted her head as she wiped her teary eyes. "Excuse me, but, what are you talking about? What did the Americans do?"

The lead naval officer glared at Rosa with pent-up anger. "They change size of our dock. They have much power! They think they won the Second World War. Everyone knows it was the Russians who cornered Hitler." He clenched his fists and paced the room. He walked in a few circles and left.

Colin's eyes were wide. Second World War? Oh, feck. The future isn't pretty, I'm afraid. I'm supposin' there was a First World War?"

"There's going to be two World Wars?" Rosa began to cry.

Sasha sat beside her. "Where is strong woman named Rosa? Why you fall apart like Miss Amoli?"

Evelyn tried to search for information on the desk. "Hitler, who's that? I wonder."

"These blokes really haven't a clue they're in a different time period."

"Why would they, Colin?" Rosa blurted.

Colin's eyes shifted around the room a bit. "I think it's best we locate a lifeboat but we won't be able to do it without bein' shot at."

"So, then we must take their guns and shoot them. All of them!" Sasha blurted in a fury.

"How, Sasha?" Rosa asked.

"We are experts now. We can do."

Rosa sighed with frustration. "You're such an idiot."

"We'll have to trick them with some kinda ambush, or somethin'," Colin said.

Evelyn amerced herself with the piles of papers on the desk. She tried to open the filing cabinets but they were locked. She then found a typed letter sitting on the desk.

"*Attention Soviet Officials?* At least it's in English," she read.

Colin glanced at her. "Wonder what that means? Soviet Officials?"

She continued to read: "*Attention to President Nixon, Cease your duplication of nuclear missals. China has fully occupied North Vietnam and The Viet Cong is gaining strength over the Americans. Vietnam, like Cuba, will soon be fully controlled by Communist Rule. Submarine SSR – 4 contains enough nuclear power to destroy the United States. It will enter via Cuba by The Gulf of Mexico. Pull back your army in South Vietnam or submarine SSR-4 will enter U.S. boundary waters. U.S.S.R. – Naval Unit –*"

Rosa gasped. "Oh, my God!"

"I not even understand all this. What has happened to my Russia?" Sasha asked.

Rosa pulled the letter from Evelyn. "This is not considered Russia anymore, Sasha. This is called the U.S.S.R., Russia must be gone."

Colin leaned against the wall. "This submarine contains loads of nuclear power. Sounds deadly, don't it?"

"Nuclear power! I can now build new time machine with such power. With this power there will be no errors!" Sasha blurted. "We will reach exact desired location."

"Okay, mastermind, start building a new time machine and make sure those naval officers don't see you," Rosa commented with frustration in her voice.

Colin placed his arm around Rosa. "Love, just let him do it. We'll have to keep him in the shadows, so none of the blokes find out. I'll be affective, so it would."

"Fine. Start building, Sasha," Rosa responded. "Oh, and by the way, Sasha."

"What?"

"Merry Christmas."

# Chapter Eleven

Spatters of early sunlight seeped through the tiny window. Rosa and Evelyn had slept on the floor in a tiny room, cuddled with Colin. Sasha was already up, where he desperately tried to implement nuclear power to fuel a new time machine. Colin slowly sat up; he tried not to disturb the two women.

"Mate, have ye been up all night?"

"*Nyet,* maybe just one hour earlier than you."

"At least they let us sleep the night. I'd take this tiny naval office before I'd take a dungeon floor, wouldn't ye?"

Sasha didn't pay much attention, where he continued to work on physics formulas.

Colin paused. "Well, what have ye found?"

"I must go to this nuclear power. How we ask naval officers about this without killing them?"

Colin's eyes shifted from one side to the next. "Killin' them, you're sayin'? Likely they'd be killin' us, don't ye think?"

Sasha chuckled. "They too stupid to kill us. We kill them first."

"Don't want this to be a blood bath, we'd have to act out somethin', it's the only way."

Rosa raised her head. "Maybe I could occupy them with my beauty."

"That could work, love. I'm just afraid they may go too far with yez."

Evelyn raised her head. "Maybe I could do the same."

"That would surely work, but if they found out anythin', I don't think they would fancy the idea, if ye know what I'm sayin'?"

"Good, then you two ladies will lift your skirts a bit, show some skin and I can build new time machine. This will work, da?"

Rosa stepped closer to Sasha. "And, if it doesn't?"

"It will work. I know, I am great scientist."

Rosa glared at Sasha. "Positive thinking."

Colin could hear footsteps approaching their room. "Shh, mates. Someone's comin' this way."

The door unlocked and a black-haired woman in a trench coat entered the room. "I am hearing too much chatter coming from this location. All of you must be silent at all times!" She said sternly. She glanced at all of them several times. "Which one of you is the British?"

Colin stepped forward. "Aye."

Evelyn stood behind Colin. "I'm British," she whispered. "He's Irish."

The woman in the trench coat stepped toward Colin. "So you are British?"

"Aye." Colin tried to push Evelyn behind him.

"You are Viking, no?"

"Irish, actually."

"Irish, British – all the same."

"Not really. Ireland is doin' her damnedest not to be British, does that still make me British?"

"Silence!" she shouted. "Your ship is British?"

"I suppose."

She stepped closer to him, where her face was almost touching his chest. Rosa glanced at Sasha with angst. "You!"

Colin tilted his head forward to respond.

"What is your name? Or, do you have a number instead?"

"Why yez shoutin'? I haven't a number, but I've got a name."

"No number? Maybe you are spy?"

"'Cause I've got a bleedin' name? Of course I don't have a number, what is this?"

87

"You must be further investigated by KGB."

He tried to force a smile. "Excuse me, Miss, but can ye define for us what KGB means?"

"Since you are British, I will say you: *Komityet Gosudarstvennoy Bezopasnosty!*"

Colin glanced at Sasha. "Well, now we know. God himself, I'd say."

"Silence!" She blurted at Colin.

"I want to bring you for further questioning."

"Because I'm British?"

"No, because you have a very well-proportioned and imposing appearance."

Colin glanced at Rosa, then Evelyn, and Sasha. He took a breath. "I see."

She turned toward the door. "I will return soon enough. You will be separated from your people upon my return."

"Don't separate us, we need to stay together, if ye don't mind?" Colin instilled.

"I mind." She exited the room.

Rosa walked toward Colin. "Guess who will be distracting them with their beauty? It won't be me or the chancellor."

Sasha blurted a snort of laughter. "Who cares? As long as someone does the distracting. I not care if it is Mr. Limmerick."

Evelyn began to pace the room. "Colin, I didn't like the way that woman looked at you."

"Why would ye care, Evelyn? I think we're all in big trouble. I haven't a clue how we're gonna get outta this one."

"Sleep with her and we might have good chance," Sasha snorted with a cackle.

Evelyn looked at Sasha with a stern expression on her face. "I don't think that's a good idea, Doctor."

"Well, to be honest with you, I'd rather have Colin do the dirty work than me. I don't really feel like having their

88

grubby hands all over me. It never seems to bother Colin, though. I guess because he's a man. Men don't care about those things," Rosa added.

"Oh, really?" Evelyn commented.

Colin sat down. "Don't think yer bein' fare to me at all. I've done nothin' here."

"She look good, da?" Sasha grinned. "Short skirt. Nice legs."

"Don't know what yer talkin' about, really," Colin sighed with frustration.

"Oh, Colin, you won't have any problems sharing a bed with her, I know you by now," Rosa said with her arms crossed in front of her.

"I don't like this. No, I don't. I don't like this one bit," Evelyn added.

"Evelyn, this really isn't the time or place. We're all in trouble, just now. We don't know what this KGB really is. We don't know what *Soviet* really is. And, Rosa, you're feedin' the fire. I think we need to put our heads together and come up with some strategies here," Colin slowly sat himself down at one of the swivel desk chairs. "Interestin' chair, this is."

"Strategies? I don't really see Sasha coming up with anything concrete. He is the creator of time travel," Rosa said.

Sasha peered at Rosa. "I am not to blame. It is Mr. Limmerick's monkey man."

Colin stood up. "Neanderthal, is from twenty-eight-thousand years ago, and he's one of our closest ancestors. Don't go about blamin' everythin' on an ancient prime mate's curiosity."

"I blame you, Mr. Limmerick. You could have lived your simple life catching fish, but you try to prove something. I not know what. You have big problem with your booze. You try to prove something because you have many problems like you hate your younger brother."

Colin gasped with laughter. "What the feck are ye sayin', man?"

Rosa stepped toward Sasha. "Colin doesn't hate Ethan. It's the other way around. Ethan hates Colin."

"You see? Someone hates someone. Mr. Limmerick is easy man to hate."

Evelyn stepped closer to Sasha. "Not true, Dr. Dimitrikov!"

"Sasha, you're a bigger idiot than I thought," muttered Rosa.

Sasha stood up and placed his hands over Rosa's shoulders. "Stop acting like small girl. You are making big problem when we have even bigger problem ahead, da? You stop now, da?"

She stared at the floor and slowly pulled away from him to make her way to the tiny round window. She gazed at the window to notice the peer was broken into pieces of floating debris. She placed her hand over her mouth and gasped as tears rolled down her face.

Sasha stood beside her and also looked through the window. "Peer is broken into so small pieces. These 1970 naval people have not figured out that their submarine is too big."

Evelyn wrapped herself around Colin's bicep. "I wish we could leave this horrible submarine. I'm so glad I have a big strong man like you to protect me, Colin."

"I'll be of no use to yez if they put a bullet to me head."

"Colin, please, we must remain positive at all times," the chancellor instilled.

He tightened his arms around her and tried to smile. They heard footsteps approach the door and the dark-haired woman in the trench coat reappeared. She pointed at Colin. "You! Come with me!"

Colin stepped toward the woman. Evelyn stood between them. "Wait a minute!" Evelyn blurted. "Why do you need this man? What is it you need from him?"

The woman in the trench coat laughed. " Wouldn't you like to know?"

Colin's eyes widened. *"Oh, feck."*

"That is right," the woman snorted.

Evelyn's mouth hung open with surprise. "What kind of a woman are you?"

The woman laughed. "Woman? What kind of woman are you? You wear such strange clothes."

"I'm sure you could get whatever ye want from any of the gents on this submarine, eh?" Colin said feeling uncomfortable. "Surely, ye don't need me."

"You look much too impressive to me," the woman said to Colin with a devilish grin. "My name is Olga Kovandova. I am daughter of the head naval officer of this submarine. We work for KGB."

Colin turned his head to glance at Rosa.

Evelyn stepped closer to Olga. "This man and myself are courting, I don't think it is appropriate to make these demands on him, especially when he is promised to someone else. A fine woman of stature like yourself should likely understand this."

"Yes, I am a fine woman of stature. I also always get what I want. I would like this man in my bed at once."

Colin stood straight, only looking at the petite woman with his eyes. "Aggressive little thing, aren't yez?"

"It is 1970, crazy woman in West burn their bras to show how they are same as man. In Russia we do things differently, we sleep with who we wish."

Two Russian guards entered the room with machine guns raked across their chests. Colin stood beside Rosa by the window. "Oh, *Shite.*"

Evelyn stepped closer to Olga. "Well, where I come from, I am also used to getting whatever I wish; but definitely not by use of aggressive unfeminine behavior. This man is my suitor; therefore you cannot remove him from this room! That is an order!"

Colin closed his eyes and took a deep breath. "Evelyn, please don't continue with this."

Olga raised her hand and smacked Evelyn so hard across the face, that she hit the floor with a loud thump. Evelyn's face was cut opened and bleeding. Colin ran to her and held her in his arms. He tore the sleeve of his shirt and tried to clot the bleeding by tightly pressing it against her wound.

*"Evelyn, stop actin' about as if yer the chancellor of the London university. Just stop it, or yer gonna get yerself killed. I can take care of myself. Don't worry 'bout me."* Colin whispered to her.

Rosa clutched Sasha's hand tightly in hers. "I'm so frightened."

"One guard pointed his gun at Colin and gestured for him to follow Olga. Olga, the two guards and Colin left the room.

# Chapter Twelve

Evelyn sat on a chair with a piece of Colin's torn shirt pressed against her bleeding cheek. "My word, what an awful woman she is. How boorish."

Rosa stood in front of her. "These people are from a different time, Chancellor. They're from our future. Some changes have obviously taken place. Women don't seem to act like women. These people seem to have lost a certain etiquette."

"I'm worried sick over Colin."

"Colin can handle himself. He's been in several tight situations. All he has to do is keep that woman fulfilled," Rosa commented.

"Well, I don't like it."

Rosa glanced at Sasha. Sasha sat at the desk with a pencil and paper. He jotted several formulas of how he was going to construct a new time machine. He paid little to no attention to the conversation.

"Chancellor, I don't really think we are in a situation where we can dislike something. I think survival is what we need to concentrate on."

"Are you saying I must accept that woman who desires the man I love?"

Rosa was silent as she paced the room.

"I refuse to accept this. I love him. Hopefully, someday, he will be my husband."

Rosa's eyebrows lifted. "You think so?"

"Yes, I do. I thought that the day I met him." She smiled and took a breath. "He's a wonderful man."

"So, you are saying that you would like to marry Colin?"

Sasha gave a slight snort of laughter.

"Yes, I think he would make a fine husband."

"Really?" Rosa responded.

"Yes, really. He's kind, considerate, very honest, generous, gentle, loving. He's a wonderful man."

"You think so? Really?" Rosa expressed.

"Of course, Colin is a fine man and you know it."

Sasha let out a loud cackle.

"Yes, he's kind, and he is the most honest man I know. Yes, yes, that is Colin, he could never tell a lie. Honest is him, completely."

Sasha raised his head and grinned at the ladies.

"Chancellor Gordon," Sasha blurted.

"Yes, Dr. Dimitrikov."

"Mr. Limmerick is not husband for you."

Rosa scowled at Sasha. "Sasha don't."

"Don't what?"

The chancellor's lips were parted, but she was silent. She stared into nothing, and sighed. "Oh, dear."

"Also, Colin is never one to say *no*," Rosa added.

"Yes, I can see that," the chancellor responded.

Rosa stepped closer to the chancellor. "I mean, he never says *no*, not to anyone. Do you follow me, Chancellor?"

"Well, I must say he gave me a bit of a fight at first."

"Only because you're the chancellor of the university."

"I see."

Evelyn sighed again. She stepped closer to Rosa. "I'm not sure if I like you, Miss Emanuel. There's something about you I don't trust."

"That's fine. We can't like trust everybody," Rosa replied.

Sasha grinned.

"No, most definitely. I do respect that you are close to Colin, though."

Rosa started to nod her head. "No, you don't, not at all. If you had your wish, I wouldn't be in Colin's life at all."

Evelyn stood up and walked to a tiny round window. "Enough of this silliness. Colin isn't here with us right now and I'm terribly worried."

"Don't be, Miss Chancellor," Sasha interjected. "He is big boy. He will be fine." Sasha stood up. "When will these naval people see that they are now in different time period?"

"I'm so afraid when that happens," Rosa responded.

"I think I have correct formulas to make nuclear-fuelled time machine. Only problem is, where would 1970 people keep it on submarine?"

"Good question," Rosa responded, while the chancellor continued to gaze out the window with worry.

*** 

Olga brought Colin to her cabin with two armed guards behind them. They remained outside the room by the door. Colin scanned the room, he was careful with every move he made and tried to remain silent.

"What you think?" She asked.

Colin turned to her; he hesitated before he responded. "Of your chamber?"

She paused. "My room! Of course my room! Is it not right place for you?"

Colin pretended to act interested in her questions. "Right place?"

"Yes, do you not see my bed in the center of the room? The sheets are satin with blood red color. What you think?"

"I think I need to sit down."

She pranced around the room. "Notice the swords on the wall? Do you like them?"

Colin found a chair to sit on, his head hung low as if he were to be sick. "Swords?"

"Yes, of course. I also have series of whips and chains, do you like them, too?"

"Why would a young wench like ye want all this *shite* anyways? And, why the hell would ye want it in your

95

feckin' blood red bedroom chamber? The hell I don't know."

She giggled like a fiend. "It all depends."

Colin raised his head to glance at her. He squinted his eyes a bit to deal with his sudden nausea. "Depends?"

"Of course." She stared at him with a crazed expression in her eyes. "Strip! Then, we will talk."

"What?"

"Strip! I want to see you!"

"Look, ye got every bloke known to man on this sub. Choose one of them."

"I've had them. I've had them all! I want to try British meat."

Colin's eyes widened as he stared at the floor. "Oh, good Lord. Irish, is what I am. Ye certainly don't want that."

"Strip!"

*Sweet Jesus 'n Mother of God, if I ever needed yez, it would be right now,"* he muttered to himself.

She pulled out a large bottle of vodka and two glasses. "How do you take it? You are western, you not want to drink this straight." She paused as she poured the Vodka. "Or, would you?"

"Don't care for it, so I don't."

"What?"

"Don't fancy Vodka. It's not me cup of tea, so to speak."

"I don't care, then! Strip!"

Colin stood up. "Ye strip."

"I will, but then I control whips and knives, yes?"

"Look, I don't know what ye have in mind, but it isn't ridin' well on me, I think I need to be leavin'," he blurted as he dashed for the door. He swung it opened to find the two armed-guards standing there. They placed their machine guns across his chest and pushed him back into the room. *"Oh, shite."*

96

"What is your name? You say you not have number. What is your name?"

"Limmerick."

"Strange name. You are so handsome!" She blurted with a girlish giggle and pressed herself against his body.

He didn't react to her. "Plagued, so I am."

Her smile dissipated. "What do you mean?"

"Cursed, is what I am."

"About what?"

"Nothin', forget I said it."

She pulled away from him. "Enough!" She circled around him. "You talk like fool! If you don't strip I will cut your clothes off with my sword." She got close to him and rubbed his chest.

Colin pushed her off him. "You'll what?"

"Great new game!"

"Game?"

"You act like you not know about bondage. Why you act like you are from sixty years ago or so?"

"'Cuz, that's who I am. What's this bondage, eh?"

"I have great vision of you. You lay on satin bed. I cut every piece of clothing off with my sword."

Colin's eyes widened. "What?"

"Sexy game, yes?"

"Don't really fancy yer new game. This bondage is *shite* in me own books."

"When I first saw you I wanted to tie you to my bed posts. I think you would look even more sexy."

"Do yez?" He started to pace the room where he walked near the door. He placed his hand on the doorknob, paused, and then walked from the door. Two-armed guards abruptly entered the room.

Colin quickly turned away from the guards and gazed at Olga. "What's with the guns? Why ye need guns?"

"You could be spy," she grunted at him.

"Spy? A spy I'm not. Why ye wanna tie me to the bed post so bad if I'm a spy?"

97

"You would look good, that is why."

*"Sweet Jesus."*

She snorted with laughter.

He leaned against the opposite wall from her. "Let me 'n me friends outta this sub."

"And, what if you are spies?" She stomped her feet to step closer to him. "Never!"

Colin sighed and rolled his eyes back.

"Americans are still in Vietnam, wasting their time. It is a win-win situation for Soviets!" She cackled.

"The Americans are fightin' in Vietnam? Why?"

She laughed so hard; she started to spit. "You know nothing."

"What's goin' on here? Why the Americans fightin' in Vietnam?"

"Enough talk!" She clinched her fists. "Strip!"

"Huh?" He took a few deep breaths. "What in the Lord's name are ye askin'?" He glanced at the armed men.

"Strip!"

He pressed his teeth together. "How romantic, I must say."

"Shut-up! Strip!"

"Lets say that the mood just isn't quite right. You're such a bitch!"

"What you call me?"

He tried to focus on something else in the room. He noticed drips of sweat run off the palms of his hands and wiped them on his pants. He hesitated to respond. *"Striapach! Bitseach! Díul mó bhad!"*

"What is this you speak? Translate! I want to know what you say me!" She demanded and called the guards over. She spoke to them in Russian. Colin continued to lean against the wall.

"Li–Limmerick, you will do as I ask or you will be tortured because you are spy. Is that spy code language?"

"Spy code language? How absurd. Gaelic, I speak Gaelic. It's definitely not a feckin' spy language."

98

"Spy talk! I not ever hear of such language."

"Calm yourself. Gaelic is a language. It's spoken in Ireland 'n Scotland. It's not English, not even close. Look it up. I'm tellin' yez the truth. It's Celtic."

"First I hear of this! Liar!"

"If ye never heard of it, then you've lived behind some kinda iron curtain or somethin', eh?"

She paced around the room, with her eyes fixed on him. "Iron curtain!" She continued to pace. "You speak to American spies, I know."

"American spies?"

"That is what Americans say. They make fun of us. They think we live behind iron curtain. We will someday show them who is greater!"

"So they do? Hmm, interestin'."

"Americans steal all Russian songs and give them to this Elvis Presley. They say it is American music!" She cackled with a fiendish grin. "I know better! All people know it is not American music! It is Russian!"

Colin tried to focus. *"I can't believe this."*

"What you say?"

"Oh, nothin', really. I was kiddin' yez, didn't think this was for real. Why the Americans say this anyways?"

"Say we live behind iron curtain? Because we want communism to take over world. Americans against us just for that. Such small thing."

"What are these American songs ye was sayin' are really Russian songs?"

"She peered at Colin and grinned like a devil. Her cackle intensified. "H-Hound Dog! Of course! J-Jailhouse R-Rock! Of course!" She started to howl."

"Really? Don't really know too many American songs. *By the light of the Silvery Moon?* Did Americans take that one away from Russia?"

Her facial expression changed. "What? What you speak of? I not hear of such song!"

He stared at the floor. "Sorry."

"Why you act dumb? You pretend to know nothing! You are spy that is why!"

Colin pretended to be accustomed to what she was telling him, despite how jolted he was from the information. His lips were dry and he tried to catch his breath. He noticed the machine guns were pointed at him. He started to un-button his shirt.

"Hurry up!" She demanded. He removed his shirt. She grinned with delight. "I like what I see." He continued to lean against the wall, shirtless. "Take off everything!" She ordered. His eyes were fixed on the guns. He gingerly removed his pants. "Boxer shorts!" She exclaimed. "Take them off!"

"Aye, boxers, ye got somethin' against them?"

He removed everything including all footwear. He stood straight and looked at her.

"Oh, my!" She yelped. She lunged at him to grab his penis. "Such size!"

He wanted to pull away from her but the guns were aimed at him. "Can ye ask those two blokes to leave? Just don't know how I'm gonna get it up in such a situation?"

"They must stay. You must be a spy," she panted and groaned. Colin remained standing as he watched her mouth suck onto his penis. She fondled with his testicles.

She shouted at the guards in Russian. One of them radioed to another, demanding Olga's request. Minutes later, a servant entered the room with a tray of goblets of liquid chocolate and whipped cream.

"What's that? Dessert?" Colin asked.

"Lay on the bed!" She demanded.

He walked backwards, with his eyes on the gunmen, and layed down. "What's next?" He asked.

She took a delicate spoon and poured chocolate onto his penis. It was hot in temperature, which made him jump; however, he kept his eyes on the gunmen. Then she cooled him off with the whipped cream.

"It looks so good!" She grinned. "Now, I will eat you."

Colin felt constant pangs of nausea pass through his stomach. "Oh, God."

"Does such a large instrument ever get hard?" She asked in a demanding tone.

He glanced at her, where he paused and tried to answer. "I don't usually perform sex with guns pointin' at me cock."

"I want to see it grow even bigger, if it is at all possible."

"Oh, it's very possible. Ye'd be surprised how much it can grow, but not with the guns, if ye please. Ask them to leave 'n you'll get one hell of a mass."

She shouted for the guards to leave the room. They immediately made their exit.

She giggled like a spoiled child. "You got your wish, Li-Limmerick, so now you must grow for me."

She placed her mouth over his penis and licked the whipped cream and chocolate. Colin's eyes widened. Despite his nausea and disgust, he became aroused. He sighed with relief. He noticed the expression on her face; despite she was covered in chocolate and whipped cream. She appeared very pleased at what she saw and felt. He started to relax, which eased him into more arousal. He grew to a new size. She rubbed his pectoral muscles and positioned herself on top of him.

"Fuck me!" He jolted a bit. He appeared a bit shocked at her behavior and language, but he tried to ignore it. She moaned, groaned and screamed as loud as she could. "I have not ever had man like you. You are like a bull!"

He forced himself to chuckle. "Surely, you have. By God, you're Russian, likely those Russian lads could satisfy a deservin' wench like you."

She wiped the chocolate and whipped cream from her face with his socks. "Silence! You talk too much!"

# Chapter Thirteen

Sasha scanned the room. "I not see wrought iron. I not see wood. How do these future people live?"

Rosa ran her hand along the desk. "Veneer or plastic? Cheap furniture. Is it because it's Russian or is it because this is the future?"

Sasha leered at her. "All Russian-made is only best quality. It comes from our special time of Czar. Russia have nothing but quality. But, maybe Soviet does."

Rosa glanced at Evelyn. "I see."

Evelyn faced Sasha. "Perhaps historical Russia had quality, as you remember it, Dr. Dimitrikov, but definitely this future Russia we are now seeing may have lost some of its finesse. I think you're correct in saying Soviet has something to do with it."

Sasha stared at the floor. "If so, this is great shame. What does Soviet mean for Russia, as I know it?"

"We got a glimpse of how London would look in 1970. It changed. Everything changes over time," Rosa commented.

"But, it should be for better," Sasha instilled. "How would average Soviet lifestyle be, I wonder?"

The chancellor paced the room. "I can't discuss fluffy topics any longer, I'm concerned about Colin. Where would that vile woman have taken him?"

Sasha grinned at her. "Her bed, where else?"

Evelyn's eyes widened. "Her bed?"

Rosa stepped toward her. "You don't understand, do you, Chancellor? She wants Colin's manliness. How unlady like of her." Rosa's eyes shifted from side to side.

The chancellor's lips were parted. She placed her hands over her face. "That woman doesn't even know Colin! How could she?"

"That woman is not like a woman of our time. I hope she doesn't harm him. Try and understand, Chancellor, if all they do is go to bed together, I would be thankful," Rosa tried to explain.

"But, we have a courtship? This isn't proper!"

Rosa glanced at Sasha.

"So nice lady like you wants to marry Mr. Limmerick. So nice, but you must understand he is time traveler. He sleeps with everyone he meets on time travels," Sasha gasped with a cackle.

"Sasha, please, don't be crass, Colin has been placed in situations where he hadn't the choice," Rosa said.

The chancellor sat down to whimper.

"Enough of this! I need to build time machine. Where would they keep nuclear power on submarine?" Sasha asked, while he searched the room for cigarettes.

"Dr. Dimitrikov, I think we need to find Colin," Evelyn urged.

Rosa scurried around the room. " We need to look for any kind of sturdy substance Sasha could construct a time machine with. I don't see any wrought iron, Sasha."

"Just cheap. Maybe submarine is cheap. Plastic, just plastic."

"Sasha, I think a military submarine like this would have only the best," Rosa commented. "But, any type of power for a sub like this would be in a reactor room, I would suppose," Rosa responded.

Sasha looked at her with a smile. "Da! Of course! Reactor room. We must go and find!" He nudged her in the arm. "Good idea! Mr. Limmerick always say me you are smart lady."

Rosa grabbed his arm. "Wait a minute! That door is locked. Even if you broke the lock, we can't go parading around on this submarine. We'd get shot in a matter of seconds," Rosa urged.

"We need to locate Colin. I can't take another minute of not knowing if he is safe or not," Evelyn panicked.

"Look, I'm worried about Colin as well, but we need to play our cards correctly here, or we'll jeopardize everything," Rosa cautioned with a stern tone.

"We must take machine gun and blow off everybody's head, da? Kill them all!"

"Sasha, what if some of these people are your grand children?" Rosa asked, getting a bit agitated.

"What you mean?"

"Sasha, they are from 1970 – our future."

"I not have kids, I not want. They are not my grandchildren. They not look like me."

"Did you get strongly acquainted with each person on this submarine? You're Russian and so are they. They could be relatives of yours, for all you know. You can't be shooting everyone. That's wrong, Sasha," Rosa instilled.

"Now, you sound like Mr. Limmerick. I will shoot these people for us to survive and that is all."

Evelyn sat down and sighed with frustration. "We have to do something. We aren't making any progress like this."

"I will take gun from someone and destroy this lock. We will wait until someone enters, you ladies distract them with your beauty and I will take gun. Then we sneak through submarine to find Mr. Limmerick. Then we find nuclear power, I build new time machine and we send this big thing to future where it belongs, da?"

Rosa glanced at him. "Fine. We now need to wait for someone to enter this room. We may have to wait for hours, maybe days."

"They have to feed us. They think we are spies. They not want to starve their spies."

"Really, Sasha," Rosa responded with an unconvinced expression on her face.

"Da. If they think we are spies, they will take care of us."

"That's ridiculous, Sasha!" Rosa began to pace the room. "I think if they feel we are their enemy, they will kill us."

Evelyn turned to Rosa. "We can't let that happen. We need to get this submarine back to where it belongs."

"We will wait," Sasha continued to search the room, where he pulled out drawers and dumped the contents on the floor.

***

Olga flopped beside Colin on the bed. She took a deep breath and smiled at him. "I never feel anything like this before."

Colin forced a smile back at her. He nodded his head, but kept silent.

"Tell me about you, Li-Limmerick."

"What ye wanna know?"

"How old are you? How tall are you? What is your weight? What is your favorite color?"

Colin paused before responding. "Such personal questions. Surprised ye didn't ask me if I'm married or not."

"Why would I ask you such a stupid question?"

Colin's lips were parted. He tried to think how to respond but he decided not to.

"Tell me your favorite food. Tell me, tell me all."

He chuckled. "Hmmm…alright then. Well, I'm one hundred and two years old, six four and I weigh eighteen stone. Me favorite color is black 'n I like eatin' shite."

Her eyes bulged. She stood up on her knees to get a better look at him on the bed. She slapped him across the face, which caused his nose to bleed.

He immediately sat up and grabbed her arms. "Ye do that again 'n I'll kick yer arsh, *Striapach!*"

She laughed in his face. "I will do it again. I will have you terminated, if you are ever rough with me. I will do it again and again. You think you are too smart for me, you

105

stupid British. I will finish you. Your British Prime Minister doesn't even care that you are here."

"Oh, feck! When will ye fecks gonna soon realize that yer not livin' in 1970 just now? Did it ever occur to yez that maybe me 'n me cohorts dress differently than ye? We speak a little different, maybe, despite yer Russian. Didn't me ship appear a tad outta date to yez?"

"We are communist, we are not at same par as British or Americans with fashion. We not care about it. Communist care more about equal share. You read Marx?"

"Aye, so I have, but this isn't what he proposed at all. He'd surely be rollin' in his grave, don't ye think?"

"Such stupidity! You are typical. Good for you, you look good to me or I'd have you killed this very moment."

Colin tried to scoot off the bed, she noticed, but did not say anything. "I will call my guards in here.

He lunged for her throat and pressed his body on top of her. "Ye'll do no such thing. I'm no bleedin' spy. Stop holdin' me 'n me friends hostage!"

She gasped and panicked. "I beg you!" She managed to say.

"Don't feck with me!"

He removed his hands from her throat but continued to bear his weight on top of her. She grinned at him.

He slowly lifted himself from her. She protruded her tongue at him in a sexual manner. "You so sexy when you are mad."

"Sexy?" He blurted as he slowly lifted himself from her.

"Da, you very sexy man. No woman has said to you?"

"Sexy? How's a man sexy? A woman is sexy, not a man."

She coughed and tried to clear her throat. "Da, a woman can be sexy, but you are the sexiest man I ever see."

106

He pulled away and off the bed. His eyes scanned the floor for his clothes. "No woman has ever told me I'm that. It's odd soundin' to me ears, ye know." He noticed his socks drenched in chocolate and whipped cream.

"Maybe British woman not say words like that. They only try to speak like queen, da?"

Colin found his boxers and tried to slip them on. "Queen? Ye mean king."

She cackled like a hyena. "You act like you are from different time period."

"Correction. You're from a different time period."

She sat up in bed, with her bare breasts still exposed to him. "You are. You talk like such stupid man. You not know anything."

"Ah, that's where you're wrong. I know about time travel. You're submarine is sittin' in waters from 1910.

She cackled. "It is 1970. Why you say it is not?"

"Because it isn't. The year is 1910, soon to be 1911. Don't even know if I missed New Years Eve."

"Tomorrow is New Years Eve. It will be 1911?" She started to panic. "What?

"Sorry, but I have to do this." He punched her in the face and knocked her out. She was unconscious. Blood dripped from her mouth. He noticed how her blood matched her satin bed sheets. His clothes were lying on the floor, so he got dressed.

He pulled a large sword from where it was mounted on the wall. He took a few daggers, and a ring of chains and opened the door. One of the armed guards turned to him with a sudden reaction to shoot, but Colin swatted his head with the chains and watched him fall to the floor. The other armed guard shouted something at him in Russian as he aimed his machine gun. Colin swung the dagger to slit his arm through the thick fabric coat, deep enough to draw blood. The gun dropped to the floor and Colin whipped the chains at his head to knock him out. Colin took both guns and darted down the dim narrow hallways. He noticed a door. He found it unlocked and stepped inside. It was a room that may have been forbidden, so it seemed. All the signage was in Russian. There were three men working at a control panel with their backs to him.

Colin made the sign of the cross over his chest and began to pray to Christ. He gingerly stepped behind the men and wacked their heads with the chain; they fell to the floor. He scanned the room to make sure nobody heard anything. There were control panels along the walls, all walls; see saw levers; rods for steam; gas blowers, as well as heat exchangers. There were pods that showed graphs, or pictures. He couldn't read what everything did but he could tell what kind of a room he was in. The room was well-lit, much better lighting from anything in his time. He noticed several tiny clocks all lined up on the wall, each clock represented something, but definitely not the time. Then he heard footsteps and the door swung opened. He was ready to thrust his sword until he saw Sasha, Rosa, and Evelyn step in.

"Colin! Thank God, you're well! We were all so worried!" The chancellor expressed and leaped into his arms.

"Well, Mr. Limmerick what we have here? You find nuclear reactor room, da?"

"Is that what this is? Wasn't too sure."

"Hurry up, Sasha start building the time machine. Someone could walk in any minute!" Rosa urged.

Sasha appeared a bit nervous. "I not ever use anything like nuclear power. It not fully developed yet in 1910."

"Who cares? Just build the time machine! You're the know-it-all!" Rosa shouted in his ear.

"There's nothin' like this in 1910, I'd say," Colin commented.

"Then, leave me be. Get out! I must create!" Sasha shouted back.

Colin held up the ammunition he had collected. "Well, at least we're armed."

"Colin, what happened to that Russian woman?" Rosa asked.

"Olga? Tell ye later."

Colin handed a machine gun to Sasha. "Take this. You'll likely need it."

"Can't believe Mr. Limmerick is handing me gun. And, what a gun this is," Sasha snorted with laughter.

"We really should let Sasha create," Rosa said with a sarcastic grin.

The chancellor, Rosa and Colin exited the reactor room. They sneaked along the dim narrow hallways, where Colin struggled to push his broad frame through.

"Hate to say this 'n all, but I think we need to capture as many as possible, if we need to get this submarine back to where it belongs. They're so fixed on us bein' spies. Ridiculous, so it sounds. This submarine needs to return to its time."

"I agree with you, Colin. You also look like you had a bloody nose," Rosa noticed. "What happened?"

"Me nose always bleeds when I'm under stress."

"No, it doesn't."

Evelyn hung onto Colin's arm. "Fine, we'll find these naval officers and get rid of them?"

"Not rid them, but contain them, likely," Colin corrected her.

"How, Colin? How are we going to contain them?" Rosa asked with disbelief.

"I'll have to wave this sword around, hopefully only give 'im a slight cut here 'n there. We need to lock 'im up, maybe in that office room where they locked us up."

"Colin, this submarine is from 1970, I'm sure swords aren't used, they're not even used in 1910," Rosa pointed out. "Where did you get that sword?"

"Olga had it kickin' around her chamber."

109

"What was she doing with a sword?" The chancellor asked.

"Later, I'll tell yez all later."

Suddenly, they heard footsteps. They knew someone was coming. They hid behind a stack of crates. Colin found a large cloth and placed it over himself. The head naval officer was walking with two affiliates.

Colin stepped in front of them to slash their arms with his sword. They immediately pulled out their guns, but fell to the floor in agony. He threw both men over his shoulder and hid the head naval officer under the sheet behind the crates.

"I'll have to come back for them," Colin blurted.

They hurried themselves to the office room. Colin laid the two knocked out naval officers under the desk. "I best go fetch the king officer, someone may find him 'n then we's done for."

"Colin, be careful," Evelyn urged.

Colin left the two women in the office with the two knocked-out naval officers hidden behind the desk. He gingerly crept along the narrow hallways to get back to the head naval officer, who was tucked away in the corner behind the wooden crates. He kept his ears perked for any on-coming footsteps. When he looked behind the wooden crates, he noticed that the head officer was gone. Colin gasped almost with a surge of suffocation. He tried to swallow but he couldn't. He pulled the crates apart to see if he could find the head naval officer.

*"Oh, feck!"* He murmured to himself. He returned to the office room.

Evelyn immediately took notice of Colin's return. "Thank-God, you're back!"

Rosa stepped closer to him. "Where's the head naval officer, Colin?"

Colin stared at the floor. "Donno."

"What?"

"He's no longer there."

Rosa paced the room in a panic. "Oh, my God! We're going to be killed!"

Evelyn appeared a bit confused. "We're not going to die. I suppose, that head naval officer came-to and walked off. It's likely he won't even remember being struck down."

Rosa looked at the chancellor. "It's very likely, some of his affiliates took him."

The chancellor snickered. "Took him?"

Colin turned to the chancellor. "Evelyn, I think Rosa's right. We're likely to be killed for this."

"How negative. Why would you dynamic time-travelers be so negative?"

"Because we are time travelers! We've gone to hell and back, Chancellor!" Rosa raised her voice in a panicked state.

"We're not even in a different time period. My Gosh, it's almost New Years Eve – almost 1911. How can anything be the Hell that you're describing?" The chancellor wondered.

"Evelyn, time-travel is life-threatenin' at all times, don't ye see?" Colin tried to instil.

"Yes, but we're not time traveling right at this moment."

"Aye, it's because of our past time travels, this sub from the future can't dock at this Russian port. Don't ye see, Evelyn? We's all been playin' God 'n when ye do that, ye get Frankenstein's monster."

Evelyn's eyes widened with concern. "I see."

"I think this chatter should cease and we should leave this room. Whatever happened to that head officer, we don't know, but it's likely he will return to us with a vengeance," Rosa cautioned.

"Agreed," Colin responded. "Don't know if there would be any visits in the nuclear reactor room, though."

"Sasha!" Rosa yelped.

111

"Wouldn't worry, if I was yez, 'cause he's armed. Mate's a clever warrior, I must say" Colin assured.

Colin first poked his head out of the room with his gun in hand, he gestured for Rosa and the chancellor to follow. Each was carrying a weapon. They heard a loud noise echo through the tight narrow hallway. They stopped and gingerly made their way back to the crates and tried to hide.

Colin took Evelyn and Rosa's hands. "It's no use, I'm gonna get us caught with me size 'n all. Perhaps you two wenches should go off without me. I just can't hide anywhere 'round here. This submarine is rather tight. It wasn't built for a man of me own size."

"Colin, it's a submarine, they're supposed to be tight. I'm sure people didn't change in size by 1970 or 1960 whenever this thing was built," Rosa responded.

"Colin, don't be silly," whispered Evelyn. "I think it's best we stay together."

"So, if you get caught, then what?" Asked Rosa with a slight quiver in her voice.

"Gotta do me best 'is all, love."

"I smell something rather, foul," Evelyn commented.

Rosa pinched her nose. "What is it?"

The same loud echoing noise was getting louder. Colin peaked over the stacked crates and jumped back, where he stepped on Rosa's foot. She yelped and Evelyn's hand immediately covered over Rosa's mouth.

"Good God! We mustn't make a sound!" Evelyn whispered.

Colin lowered his gun. "Don't know what to do. *Feck.*"

"What is it, Colin? You almost broke my foot," Rosa complained.

"Just saw a cave lion draggin' the head naval officer along the floor. *Shite, shite, feck!*"

Rosa's eyebrows lifted. "What?"

"There's a *feckin'* prehistoric cave lion on this sub."

Rosa tried to push herself against Colin so she could speak. Her lips were parted. "Oh, my God." How can this be?"

"Donno, really, but somethin' has gone terribly wrong, is all I can say to yez."

Evelyn tried to speak. "What is an animal doing on this vessel?"

Rosa peered at Evelyn. "Guess?"

Evelyn looked at Colin. "I'm sorry, but I haven't a clue why a wild animal would be on this submarine."

"Evelyn, take a closer look at this animal," Colin paused as he shifted his eyes to the prehistoric beast with the head naval officer lying before it. "I can't let anythin' happen to this innocent man, Rosa."

"You've confronted cave lions before, Colin, this should be easy for you," Rosa responded.

Evelyn's eyes widened. "Pardon? What is that creature? A wild feline, of some kind?"

Colin pushed his way from the crates and stepped in front of the prehistoric feline. The lion glanced at Colin and started to tear away at the naval officer's sleeve. Colin swung one of the heavy chains he had confiscated. The cave lion ignored Colin and continued to pull away at the naval officer.

He slammed the chain on the floor, which made a loud clanging sound. The cave lion perked its ears, stood away from the torn-up naval officer and hissed at Colin.

"Colin, you're drawing too much attention to us! Don't make so much noise!" Rosa shouted.

"Do I have a choice?" As Colin turned his head to face Rosa, the cave lion jumped up and leaped onto him and pushed him to the floor. The lion's ears were back as it dug its claws into Colin's chest. Colin used every bit of strength to push the beast off of him but the lion was too powerful. Rosa took one of the rifles and slammed it on the animal's head. The lion squealed and dashed off.

113

Evelyn's face was stark white with fear. "Oh, Colin, please tell me you're well. I've never encountered anything so frightening."

Colin was still lying on the floor beside the unconscious head officer. He tried to sit up and noticed his blood stained shirt. "Really, Evelyn? This is the most frightening you've ever seen? Well, ye haven't seen anythin' yet, 'cause I think our tamperin' with time vortexes has caused somethin' big."

"I agree with you, Colin," Rosa added. "Does *Neanderthal* have anything to do with this?"

Colin tried to hoist himself up with difficulty. "Most definitely," he grunted.

*"Neanderthal?* Why?" Evelyn asked.

Colin leaned his exhausted body against the wall. He took a few deep breaths, where he puffed his chest enough to pop a button on his shirt. The chancellor whimpered and leaned against him.

"You poor dear, imagine wrestling with a mountain lion on a submarine."

Colin remained in the same position but shifted his eyes onto Evelyn. "Mountain lion?"

"I knew it was a mistake bringing the chancellor of the university," Rosa huffed with her arms folded in front of her.

Colin glanced at Rosa and chuckled. "She insisted on joinin' us, didn't ye, Evelyn?" He raised his hand to run his finger along her cheek.

"I don't think it's wise of us to stand around here for chit-chat," Rosa barked.

"Most definitely," Colin responded as he pulled his hand away from Evelyn.

"I'm really worried about Sasha in that nuclear reactor room. I would really like to check on him," Rosa cautioned.

"What should I do with the head naval officer? He's Olga's father, in case ye didn't know," Colin asked.

"That cave lion is roaming a Russian submarine from the future. They claim they are no longer Russian, but they are Soviet, whatever that means," Rosa said.

Colin took Rosa and Evelyn's hands and pulled them toward the nuclear reactor room. They had to be vigilant when passing through the submarine corridors; there were several Soviet submariners in sight. Rosa tiptoed in front of Colin as she placed her hands onto the door latch of the nuclear reactor room. She shook the door latch, and tried to make little to no nose. She turned her head and glared at Colin. "The door is locked and Sasha is not bothering to open it. Has he lost his mind?"

"Aye."

Colin then placed his hands over the latch and realized it was locked. "I'll have to shoot the latch, I suppose," Colin said grudgingly.

Rosa gave Colin a look of surprise. "Well, you're turning out to be the master of weaponry."

Colin sighed with frustration. "What would ye like me to do, love?"

Rosa's eyes bounced around their surroundings. "I hate submarines. They're just awful, especially the ones from the future."

"I see," Colin responded, as he positioned the gun and aimed it at the door latch.

"Wait!" Rosa yelped.

"What?" Colin asked in a curt tone.

"What if Sasha is standing on the other side of the door?"

Colin looked at the ceiling. "Oh, mother of God." He pulled the trigger and blew off the latch. Rosa jolted a bit. Colin pushed the door opened and stepped in. Rosa followed, trailed by Evelyn.

Rosa's eyes scanned the room several times. She ran her hand along the wall, while she gingerly walked around the room.

"Colin? Where's Sasha?"

115

Colin glanced at every corner of the room. "He doesn't seem to be here."

Rosa panicked and leaped into Colin's arms. "Where is he?"

Colin tried to place her back onto her feet. "Don't know, love."

"Perhaps he needed the lavatory," Evelyn suggested.

Rosa peered at Evelyn. "He would have left a note, so we would know he will return."

Evelyn looked around the room. "I don't see anything here at all," Evelyn whimpered.

"Yes, because he's not here!" Rosa squealed in a panic. "Where is he?"

Colin searched the room continuously. "He's not here, love. He's likely been taken prisoner to these KGB people."

"Could they have left the vessel with the doctor?" Evelyn asked.

"Find that unlikely, when they can't really doc this thing."

"So, where would these KGB people be in this enormous submarine?" Rosa asked.

"Not sure, love. Just not familiar with submarines 'n not familiar at all with subs of the future."

"If we need to find Dr. Dimitrikov, then I suppose we should begin our search," Evelyn urged.

"Agreed, Evelyn, but we can't afford to get caught again, don't ye think?"

"Lets just go, give me that sword, Colin! You don't really know how to use it anyway," Rosa demanded with her hand reaching for the sword.

"Love? Do ye know how to handle a sword?"

"Better than you!" Rosa snapped back at him.

Evelyn didn't pay attention to their squabbles. "I don't think these KGB people are actually on this vessel, I think I heard one of them say their head office is in Moscow."

"Well, then, that closes that chapter, they haven't docked this thing. We's not anywhere near Moscow. Likely, they'd expect to take a train to Moscow," Colin added.

"Fine, but where's Sasha?" Rosa asked looking worried.

Each of them carried a weapon as they gingerly made their way through the narrow submarine corridors.

Colin, Rosa, and Evelyn stopped, before they passed another hallway. Colin peered down the narrow corridor; he jolted when a gunpoint pressed against the middle of his back. Colin could hear Rosa and Evelyn wince. He slowly turned his head to realize a Soviet submariner was pressing a machine gun into the middle of his back. He turned his head away to realize there was nothing he could do. The Soviet submariner called out to him in Russian. Rosa and Evelyn froze and slowly raised their arms. The Soviet submariner jabbed the gun a few times into Colin's back. Another Soviet submariner showed up, which seemed as if he appeared from nowhere. He handcuffed them. Colin, Rosa, and Evelyn were silent.

They brought them to the bottom of the submarine and locked them into another room. Sasha was tied to a chair and his mouth was gagged. The door shut, and locked.

"Sasha!" Rosa called out. She ran to him only to notice that he had been badly beaten. One of his eyes was a shade of purple and severely swollen. "Sasha? What did they do to you?"

Colin managed to untie the cloth that was tightly wrapped around his mouth. "Mate, can ye talk?" He paused and continued to focus on Sasha. "What happened?"

"I-I not know."

"Good Lord! They must have knocked ye cold before ye even saw anything."

"They ask many questions to me. I not know answers to them. They call me spy. Then, after that, I not know, I find myself here and tied up."

"They're convinced we're all spies, surely they are," Colin said as he cut the ropes from Sasha's wrists and ankles. "It's a miracle they didn't kill ye."

"I meet that terrible woman, Olga. She so bitch. I hate her. She say me she was with you. I say her, who cares. Then, her terrible men beat me like bad man. I do nothing to them."

"Colin, maybe we shouldn't ask Sasha anything else. He should rest," Rosa urged.

"When they return, they will kill us. She say me this. Bitch!"

"Called her dirty names in Gaelic, but she's never heard of it, so it don't really matter," Colin commented.

Sasha winched with pain. "It?" He took a breath. "What you mean -- *it?*"

"Gaelic. Olga, she never heard of the Gaelic language."

"Mr. Limmerick," Sasha sighed with exhaustion. "No one knows of this language you speak of. I hear it first time from you."

Colin's eyes widened. "Really? It's me Irish language, is what it is. Can't believe ye never heard of it."

Rosa kissed her teeth and tapped her foot furiously. "Colin! Have you gone mad? This is not the time and place to be chatting about your first language! Untie Sasha!"

The final rope fell to the floor. Sasha tried to bring the circulation back to his hands and wrists.

Rosa appeared nervous, "Sasha, why are they so interested in killing us?"

"They say we are spies."

"Is that a good enough reason to kill someone?" Rosa wondered.

"What I learn about this Soviet Russia? Da, it is good reason for them," Sasha said as he sat lifelessly on the chair.

"Mate, how about the nuclear energy that's supposed to fuel a new time machine? What happened to that?"

"I hide it in nuclear reactor room. They not find it. They never will, because they are stupid."

"Stupid? I must say this submarine is rather impressive," the chancellor commented.

"Aye, so it is but it is a vessel from the future."

"I think we need to get out of here. I'm not going to allow these horrible submariners to take our lives," Rosa blurted in a frenzy. "Lets get ourselves oriented here. Sasha needs to return to the nuclear reactor room, so he can finish developin' the time machine."

Sasha tried to speak. "Not good."

"What ye mean, mate?" Colin asked.

"They double bolted door of nuclear reactor room. It is impossible to enter."

Colin tried to keep his enthusiasm up. "No worries, mate. I'll shoot the bolted lock 'n I'll use me own weight. I'll kick the door down, if I have to. I'm not this size for nothin'."

"Sasha, if you do get the time machine fuelled by nuclear power, how can you send this submarine to where it belongs with the entire Soviet naval crew and leave us out?" Rosa asked.

"Yes, that is a very important question," the chancellor commented.

Sasha sat on the chair and paused for a few seconds. His eyes scanned the room; stared at the floor; and took a few breaths. "I not know. It is possible we go with them to 1970. You will see your lovely pet Monkey man. He is the cause of this, da?"

"Right, mate. We just can't, though. We've gotta locate the lifeboat and get off this vessel. We're not returnin' to 1970."

"Fine, Mr. Limmerick, you find life boat. How well do you understand submarine of 1970?"

"Not at all. I am a man of the sea, though. I've got a good idea where to find it, 'n what to look for."

Rosa tried to smile.

The chancellor sat down and appeared anxious.

They heard a cracking sound against the door. Two Soviet officers stomped into the room. Sasha remained sitting.

They looked at Sasha and smacked him to the floor. Colin stood in front of Sasha and Rosa screamed. Evelyn retreated to the corner of the room.

"Why are yez doin' this? We're not spies. Don't even know what a spy is, for God's sake! We've done nothin' to yez. Let us go!" Colin demanded.

"Don't play stupid, British!"

"Irish," Colin corrected him.

The Soviet officer paused. "What did you say?"

Colin's eyes bounced a bit with nerves. "I'm Irish."

"Who cares? You will talk! We will make you talk! What do you know about Americans?"

Colin squinted his eyes. "Americans?"

Rosa tended to Sasha on the floor.

"What are American's latest plans against Cuba?"

Colin's eyes widened. "Cuba?"

"Stop this game! You will die for this, British!"

"What did you do to head naval officer? You try to kill him?"

"Well, not exactly, ye see ---."

"Silence! Lucky for you, we cannot dock this submarine in Petersburg harbor! We are delayed. You are so lucky. KGB was expecting you."

"They weren't," Colin responded.

"You typical British spy! You think you can speak when you want?" The Soviet officer became irate, where he shot his gun beside Colin's feet. "Next time, I will aim better."

"Why don't ye, just aim better, now? C'mon, I'm an easy target, wouldn't ye say?"

"No, Colin!" The chancellor squealed.

"Don't play this game, Colin!" Rosa shouted with anguish.

"Ye think I've got information about Cuba so I can help the Americans with their plans? I don't even know what yer speakin' of." Colin blurted with frustration. "Ye beat up our friend, ye was armed 'n he wasn't. Not a fare game, I'd say. Do what ye will to me. If yez wanna believe I've got the American's next plan of action, so be it."

The other Soviet officer locked handcuffs around Colin's wrists. "You will tell us everything. Do you speak Russian?"

"I don't."

"You must speak some."

"I don't."

They led Colin away, but realized Sasha also needed to be handcuffed, and they led him away as well: leaving the chancellor and Rosa alone in the room.

"Good God! What do you think they're going to do to them?" The chancellor panicked to Rosa.

"Kill them. What else?"

"Excuse me?"

"Honorable Chancellor, we've been captured by a military submarine from the future. To us, this sub is Russian, but to them, they are Soviet. None of this makes any sense. By judging how hostile they are toward us, I would say their main intensions would be to kill Colin and Sasha."

The chancellor started to quiver. "What can we do to save them?"

"Nothing."

"Nothing?"

"That's right, we're in here and they're somewhere else in this hideous submarine. There's nothing we can do."

"Well, that can't be. We must break out of here at once and find them."

"I'm sure once they terminate them, we'll be next. It's the way it goes, Chancellor."

"We've got to do something."

"Welcome to our future generation."

122

# Chapter Fourteen

Colin and Sasha were taken to the bottom level of the submarine, where they were locked in an airtight room without windows.

"What is it they want with us, I not know?" Sasha said as he slid his backside along the wall to flop on the floor.

"C'mon, mate, think, why'd ye leave Russia in the first place?"

"Revolution was starting."

"What about?"

"Workers and peasants demand better work conditions. They want union for workers. I not know all details. They not want Czar."

"Did ye think that maybe the blokes on this sub are the result of the revolution from our time?"

Sasha lifted his head with a semi-smile. "You so smart sometimes, Mr. Limmerick."

Four submariners entered the room. They stared at Colin, who was standing up and they leered at Sasha who was sitting on the floor with his back against the wall. They were silent and they continued to stare at the two time travelers. They mumbled to each other in Russian, where they continued to glance back and forth at Colin and Sasha. They waved their guns at the time travelers. Then, they recklessly tied Colin and Sasha to their chairs with rope. Their hands were tied behind them, with the rope tied tightly around their wrists. Their feet were also tied tightly together.

They blindfolded Colin and Sasha with a dark cloth tied over their eyes. The four men left the room.

"Mr. Limmerick," Sasha said softly.

"Aye, mate."

"I not like dark."

"Tough."

"Mr. Limmerick."

"Aye?"

"I think we will die at this time, da?"

"Most definitely, mate."

"My wrists, they are bleeding."

"Mine too."

"I hate these people."

"Me too, mate."

"How we cut rope?"

"Well, if I try to stand up, I'd likely fall over. A man of me size would likely fall hard without the use of me arms. You wanna try 'n stand? We need to cut the rope before they return, wouldn't ye think?"

"What is sharp enough to cut rope?"

"Donno, we're blindfolded. We'll try somethin', so we will. Stand up, mate."

Sasha gingerly tried to balance himself on his feet, which were tied together. "I wish I can see. How can I find something sharp?"

"I'm gonna try 'n remove me blindfold. Just sit for now."

They could hear the door swing open. It appeared only one person entered the room.

"So, here you are, Li-Limmerick!"

Colin gasped when he heard Olga's voice.

"I want your huge cock for souvenir. I will take it first; then I will kill you second."

"It'll do yez no good if I'm not attached to it."

She stood in front of Sasha. "How about him? He's Russian. What's your cock like?"

Sasha remained silent.

She smacked Sasha across the face. "What is your cock like?" She circled Sasha. "Talk!"

"You talk like garbage can," Sasha responded.

She laughed. "Strip!"

"What you want?" Sasha asked.

She pulled off Sasha's blindfold. "I want to see if you are any good."

Sasha spit in her face.

She yelped as she turned away.

Colin was still blindfolded. "Mate, what did ye just do?"

"I spit in her face."

"Ye did what?"

"She deserve it. Bad girl!"

Two armed guards entered the room. They conversed with Olga in Russian.

"*Mate!*" Colin whispered to Sasha.

"*Da?*"

"*What they sayin'?*"

"*They say they will torture us and then they will kill us,*" Sasha whispered back.

Colin paused and took a few seconds to respond. "*Really, why?*"

"*They say we are spies, so we must die.*"

"*Oh.*"

"*They speak about China, and Cuba,*" he paused to think. "*North Korea, and North Vietnam I think. I not know why.*"

"*Nor do I.*"

One guard stood in front of Sasha and cracked the back of his gun across Sasha's face. Sasha hit the floor, his face dripped blood from his fresh wound.

"Look, remove me blindfold 'n give me the licks, if ye want. He's likely still tied up. This isn't fair!" Colin called out as he heard Sasha moan.

"I will tell you my fantasy, Li-Limmerick."

"Don't really care to hear it."

"You brought lion with you?"

Colin gasped. "Oh, yeah, *feck!*"

"So, yes, you have pet lion?"

"Hardly a pet."

"It is not very nice cat, I can tell."

"It's a cave lion, it's not supposed to be nice."

She stepped closer to Colin and wedged herself onto his lap and forced her tongue into his mouth. "How was that?"

He paused before answering. "Remove me blindfold."

Sasha continued to moan on the floor, drenched in blood as he wallowed in pain. She turned to glance at Sasha. "He is also nice looking, but he refuse to strip for me. You did agree to strip for me, L-Limmerick."

"At gunpoint – how romantic."

"I would like you and the Russian in my bed with lion."

Colin sighed. "Remove me blindfold."

"I want you tied to my bedpost, blindfolded, but you have so nice eyes. They are the color of the ocean, maybe forest, I cannot decide. So nice."

"Ye can't see me ocean eyes if they're covered up."

She slowly removed the blindfold.

"I can see. How brilliant!"

"You, the Russian on the floor, and pet lion, we will be a foursome."

"That pet lion, is a prehistoric cave lion. How much do ye wanna get yer tits bit off?"

"KGB will order you spies to talk. Tell us what Americans have planned for us?"

"Americans? Haven't a clue what yer talkin' about, wench."

"Why you pretend to know nothing?"

"Haven't the faintest idea what the Americans have planned for yez."

"Liar!"

"Slut!"

She took her whip and slashed him on the back. "You are bad man, L-Limmerick." She continued to whip him again and again.

"If ye want me to strip, then I will!" Sasha tried to shout.

She stopped. "Good. I will cut your clothes off and you will remain tied."

"That's no good."

"It's good!"

"It's not."

Sasha moaned and noticed the rope around his wrists had loosened from the fall. He continued to agitate the rope against the floor to loosen it more.

Olga took her dagger and cut away at Colin's shirt. His sleeve fell to the floor. "I see so nice picture on your arm."

Colin stared at the floor. He noticed Sasha in the corner of his eye, started to move more freely from the rope.

Sasha continued to moan so Olga wouldn't notice that he had freed up his hands. Colin's shirt was cut in shreds and she pulled away at it and let it fall to the floor. "You have so nice body. I want it."

"Ye go about as if you've never been with a man in yer life," Colin muttered to himself.

"What you say?" She widened her eyes almost in a rage.

"It's like ye don't even know what a man looks like."

"I have had many men," she paused and shifted her eyes a bit. "But, none like you."

"A man is what I am 'n that's all."

She grinned like a foolish teen. "You are so much more man. I can see."

Colin stared at the floor.

Sasha managed to gingerly slide his knees to his hands, where he could untie the rope around his feet. He remained on the floor. Colin noticed.

"Yer gonna have to buy me a new shirt," Colin said to her.

"You look better without."

"Ye still owe me a new shirt."

"You will get nothing."

127

Loud crashing sounds echoed through the hallways. Men's voices echoed and wailed throughout the submarine. Olga scurried to open the door to the narrow hallway. The cave lion made its appearance; it was dragging a mauled naval officer in its mouth. Olga screamed as she watched the cave lion make its way along the hallway. "Your pet kill one of our men? You will both die for this!"

Sasha leaped behind her to pull her arms back and tie her up with the same rope. "You stupid lady! It is prehistoric cave lion, not our pet! Why can't you tell difference?"

She squirmed and fought against him, but she was soon enough, tied to the chair. Colin sat and watched, still tied to a chair and shirtless. The cave lion was consumed with the dead naval officer and tore away at his flesh.

"You are spies! I know it!" Olga blurted.

Sasha tied a cloth around her mouth. "Now, you will shut up. I not ever see such terrible lady like you."

"Mate, we gotta get yez to a doctor. Yer lookin' pretty beat-up, I must say," Colin commented while Sasha untied him.

"Maybe we can take shirt from one of these submariners," Sasha suggested.

"I'll take anythin' at this point. Hopefully someone's shirt will fit."

"This is my city, Petersburg in winter. You need shirt. Too cold."

Colin and Sasha compiled as much ammunition as they could gather. Sasha gingerly opened the door and scanned the hallway. He saw no reminisce of the cave lion or any Soviet naval officers. "Coast is clear. So, now we go, da?"

Colin held the largest machine gun in his arms. He looked at Olga before they made their exit. "Ye know, a nice lookin' wench like yez should find yerself a nice gent 'n just settle down, don't ye think? Have a few kids, while yer at it."

"I am liberated woman!" She mumbled with the cloth over her mouth.

Colin glanced at Sasha. "Liberated woman?"

Sasha chuckled. "Not in my Russia."

"I do what American woman do, they burn brazier."

Colin and Sasha continued to chuckle as they made their exit. Olga was left tied to a chair.

***

Colin and Sasha vigilantly made their way through the narrow submarine hallways. They stepped over several dead submariners, who had been partially devoured by the cave lion.

"Never seen anythin' like this," Colin blurted.

"I not even see this in revolution of 1905. This is much death."

"Too much for me, I must say, mate."

They finally made their way to the room Rosa and the chancellor were held in. Sasha tried the door to notice it was locked.

"Rosa! You there?" Sasha called out.

"Sasha?" Rosa responded with a smile of relief when she glanced at the chancellor. "Sasha! We're locked in! Get us out of here!"

Colin looked at Sasha. "We're both here, 'n we're gonna get yez both out."

"Stand back everyone! I'm gonna bust the door down with me foot."

The door swung opened and gave a loud crack when it smacked against the wall. Rosa leaped into Colin's arms as she pushed Evelyn aside.

"Colin, thank God you're here!" Rosa called out.

Evelyn glanced at Sasha. "Hmm, it looks as if she never got over him."

"Da, you are right. This is why I cannot give her my heart. She will only break it in two. Mr. Limmerick, he can bust all relationships and marriages without care."

Rosa turned to Sasha as she embraced Colin. "What are you saying? You have a wife here in Russia, in which you forget to mention to me a while back. You cad!" She took a closer look at Sasha. "By the way, what happened to your face? Your head is bloody! Sasha, what happened?"

"We are on terrible submarine with terrible people. What you think happen?"

"Good God!" The chancellor panicked when she got a glimpse of Sasha's injury.

"I donno if ye know this," Colin tried to explain to the two women, "but a prehistoric cave lion is roamin' about the sub, it seems to be devourin' the naval team here."

"Cave lion?" Rosa expressed.

"Da, it is eating up crew. Good! They deserve it!" Sasha commented.

"Oh, my God!" Evelyn responded.

Colin peered at Sasha. "Mate, this means that prehistoric creature will also have us for a snack. Did ye think of that?"

"We must exit before next meal, da?" Sasha said somewhat anxious to vacate.

Rosa scanned Colin's naked chest. "Where's your shirt?"

"Cut up."

"My word, I can't believe you're without a shirt, if and when we get off this submarine, you will definitely need it," Evelyn commented.

"I'll have to swipe somethin' off the deceased, I'm afraid. It's really not me way, though. I'm so terribly sorry what a mess this has become. It's all me own fault, so it is."

130

"Correction Mr. Limmerick, it is monkey man that cause all this," Sasha blurted.

"Colin, that's not true," Rosa responded.

"Oh, but it is, when tryin' to play God, all else fails."

Rosa stroked his naked belly and played with his suspenders. "Colin, you're a thorough researcher. You like to take things to the next level. I admire that about you."

Sasha kissed his teeth. "I am the great scientist here. I discover time travel and yet you continue to give Mr. Limmerick so much credit just because he is not with shirt!"

"Look, I don't know why the four of us are stickin' around here. Sasha, we need to gather yer work on the time machine in the reactor room, locate the lifeboat and vacate," Colin cautioned.

Rosa took Colin's hand, which Evelyn noticed. The four of them crept along the tight submarine corridors. Colin could hear the low-toned moans of the cave lion. He immediately pushed Rosa and Evelyn back behind a small enclave. Sasha stopped in his tracks and positioned his gun. They watched the cave lion devour another naval officer, where the hallway intersected with another. They were getting closer to the reactor room, when they noticed several more half eaten bodies scattered about the floor. Rosa tried not to scream, where she was devastated by the damage. The chancellor cupped her hands over her mouth. She began to tense-up with anxiety and fear. The cave lion could smell someone was near, but when it looked up to scan its surroundings, it saw nothing. It continued to pull away at the flesh of the person it was devouring. It let out a few scathing roars and went off the same direction it entered from.

Evelyn took a few breaths. "I don't know how much more of this I can take."

Colin slid his arm around her shoulder. "I'm here for ye, it should be alright for now on."

They ventured off into the dim passageways and saw nothing until they made it to the reactor room.

Sasha tried the door. "It is locked."

"Stand back, I'll kick it in," Colin said. He kicked it hard enough to feel a jetting pain through his foot. "Shite!" He almost fell, but managed to hold his balance.

"What is wrong with you? You not know how to open locked door."

"Stand back, I'm gonna try somethin' else." Colin body-checked the door a few times, where the door didn't even creek. Colin paced a bit. "Really thought I could do this, ye know."

"Go away and I will pick lock," Sasha said.

"With what?"

"We must find something that can pick lock. I not know what."

Colin looked around. "I'm not seein' anything."

Sasha felt his inside jacket pocket. "I still have Rosa's hairpin. She give to me for love." Sasha shifted his eyebrows.

"Really? A pin is yer' token of love? Rather odd relationship from the both of yez, I must say," Colin commented.

"You are jealous of me, always." Sasha kneeled to the door-lock and gingerly inserted the hairpin in the hole of the lock.

"Make sure, yer careful, mate. That thing could easily break when inside the lock 'n then what?"

"Shh! Mr. Limmerick, I now concentrate," Sasha said as his eyes peered through the lock hole. The door unlocked. Sasha pushed it forward a bit. "You see?"

"Good, man," Colin responded.

They entered the reactor room and Sasha looked around and found the new time machine that was fuelled with nuclear power. He pushed it away from the wall with Colin's helped.

The chancellor smiled at Colin. "My dear Colin, I'm some how getting the feeling that you get great pleasure kicking down all these doors."

"We must find trolley with wheels, so we can push this along, da? We must be careful with it because it has nuclear energy in it."

"Oh, *feck*, where we gonna find a trolley with wheels?" Colin asked in a panic.

"Anything! Anything with wheels will do just fine!" Rosa blurted also in a panic.

"I don't see anything like that in this room. I would hate to think we have to search the entire submarine for this," Evelyn commented.

"Likely, very likely. Almost all of the crew is dead, but the cave lion is another story," Colin said staring at the floor.

They made their exit, as they stepped over a few more dead bodies, Colin grudgingly bent down to see if he could take a shirt or jacket from someone. He removed a shirt and a jacket from a dead naval officer and pulled the gold crucifix chain around his neck and began to pray.

"Colin, there's no time for prayers. I understand what a good Catholic you are, but this really isn't the time," Rosa cautioned.

Sasha chuckled.

Colin stood up and struggled to try on the dead man's shirt. "It's rather tight-fitting."

"As long as you're protected from the cold when we exit this disgusting submarine, that's all that matters," Rosa cautioned again.

"We need to find something with wheels," urged the chancellor, almost in frenzy.

Sasha lagged behind everyone as he struggled to push the new time machine along the floor.

"Let me help ye with that, mate," Colin offered.

133

"Don't!" Sasha yelped with his hand hovering over the time machine. "You go with our ladies and use gun, if needed. I not want you to touch my nuclear masterpiece."

"Fine, mate," Colin walked in front of the women.

Rosa stopped. "You know what I think?"

"What do you think?" The chancellor asked.

"We're alone on this submarine. It's just us and the prehistoric cave lion."

Colin stared at the floor. "I feel like a blunderin' fool. What an arse I am. Imagine, these people are from our future – 1970, and we allowed a prehistoric animal to finish them. Olga is locked up in a room. I tied her up to a chair."

"Colin, are we going to leave her tied to a chair, locked in a room with a prehistoric cave lion roaming the premises?" Rosa asked. "It's your choice."

"Of course we're not gonna do that to her."

"I'm surprised you feel that way," Rosa said.

"She's a human bein' who has no business bein' dragged into our silly time travel experiments."

"She's a horrible woman. Maybe we'll some day regret saving her," Rosa said.

"I think we gotta take her with us. When Sasha gets the time machine operatin', she needs to return to 1970, don't ye think?"

"Fine, we'll rescue her," Rosa grudgingly replied.

"I wasn't very impressed with her, I must say," the chancellor added. "Terrible woman. Dreadful."

"She was the worst wench I ever came across in me whole life," Colin blurted. "Yez wouldn't believe what she did to me socks. I had to snatch someone else's as well."

"Well, then, do you want to leave her tied to a chair and locked in a room?" Rosa asked.

Colin took his time to respond. "Likely not."

Rosa looked away from Colin.

"The longer we spend on this, the sooner that cave lion will require its next meal," the chancellor urged.

They vigilantly made their way through the submarine corridors, tracing their steps back to the room Olga was in. Colin pushed opened the door. Olga sat in a chair still tied up with a gag over mouth.

Colin took the cloth away from her mouth. "Glad yer alright, wench."

She leered at Colin. "Untie me!" Olga demanded. "You will get yours soon enough."

Colin kneeled to Olga to quickly untie her.

She immediately stood up. "Good! Now, you all will pay for this!"

Rosa stepped closer to Olga. "If I were you, I'd count my blessings that we came back to free you up from that chair and that hungry feline that's roaming this submarine."

"Who are you?"

"My name is Rosa Emanuel and you better not get on my bad side."

Colin tugged on Olga's arm. "We need to leave, now!"

Colin led the group with a machine gun in his hands, and a dagger in his back pocket. Rosa and the chancellor each held daggers and stayed behind Colin. Olga followed. Sasha lagged behind, dragging his newly constructed time machine. They noticed cave lion droppings from time to time along the corridors. They ignored it and continued to make their way to the lifeboat, in order to make their exit.

Colin peeked around another corridor. He noticed the cave lion feasting on another naval officer. He immediately pulled his body back.

He glanced at Rosa. Lets just wait here for a bit," he urged.

"Did you see the cave lion, Colin?"

135

"Aye. It'll surely get whiff of our scent, don't ye think?"

"Not if we have machine gun," Sasha added.

Colin peeked around the corner to watch each move of the cave lion. It finished eating the carcass and scanned its surroundings. It licked its fur from the blood and went off in a different direction. Colin took a deep breath and clutched the machine gun with a harder grip.

"Why you so nervous, Mr. Limmerick? If lion confronts us, we shoot it dead. Easy as that, da?"

"That's not any of our intensions now, is it, mate?"

"If I confronted with lion? I will not take minute to shoot it dead. Dead! All done!"

Rosa glanced at Colin with an expression of disgust. They crossed into the next corridor. Colin noticed a ladder, which led to the top deck of the submarine. "It's likely there's a lifeboat somewhere about the deck. I assume that's the deck of the sub."

Colin and Sasha helped Rosa and Evelyn up the ladder. Colin tried to take Olga's hand.

Olga pulled away from him. "What you doing? I not need your help, L-L-Limmerick!"

Colin pulled away from her. "Fine, do it yer way."

The five of them made it up the ladder, where they were pleased to see daylight, despite Saint Petersburg's frigid temperatures.

Sasha kept the latch door opened. "Now, Mr. Limmerick, you must very carefully help me carry time machine through to deck."

"Definitely," Colin responded.

Evelyn appeared concerned. "Please watch that prehistoric animal, Colin. I'm very worried."

Colin whisked her cheek with his two fingers. "Gotta do it, though. The time machine is key to this operation, don't ye think?"

"I suppose," she responded as he kissed her lips and climbed down the ladder with Sasha.

Olga stared at the chancellor. "You are his lady friend?"

The chancellor grinned. "Yes I am. I feel like his lady in waiting."

Rosa rolled her eyes back and grit her teeth. "So, now Colin's royalty?"

"L-Limmerick is royal?" Olga asked feeling confused.

"Of course not. I was making a joke. It was a joke," Rosa confirmed.

The chancellor forced a delicate laugh. Olga stared at her expressionless.

"You older than him?"

Evelyn's grin dissipated. "What business is it of yours?"

Rosa kneeled down to the hole with the ladder to watch Sasha and Colin carry up the time machine.

"Woman is not supposed to be older than man. Everybody knows this!"

"What makes you think I'm older than him?"

Olga gave out an annoying cackle. "I can tell you are older than him. You cannot be with him anymore. Settled! Something must be wrong with you if you not married yet."

Evelyn crinkled her nose in a huff of rage. "How dare you speak to me this way?"

Rosa stood up and tried to brush any debris off her skirt. "Why are you wasting your time with this woman, Chancellor? It's obvious she's an idiot."

The chancellor folded her arms in front of herself. "Yes, in deed, you are an idiot fool of a woman."

"You both are stupid. I can tell. Everybody knows this," Olga blurted taking a few steps back.

"What makes us stupid in your eyes?" The chancellor asked.

"Don't waste your time, Chancellor," Rosa cautioned.

"You both dress in such stupid long dress. Where are your pants? I wear pants so I can work for KGB."

"Are you saying in 1970 all women wear trousers?" Rosa asked.

"Some ladies wear dress, but not all. I work for KGB. I look very good in pants. I think so."

Rosa glanced at Evelyn. "I wouldn't mind wearing trousers everyday. I think it would be more comfortable," Rosa commented.

"In your west, women burn braziers. How stupid."

Rosa grinned. "I would do it in a second. I absolutely hate wearing a corset."

Olga chuckled. "Corset? What is that? Why you do? You so tiny ladies."

"Yes, I would give my corset away if I could," Evelyn commented.

"You both skinny! Do it! Take it off! American woman do this! I not like them. They send man on moon, so they tell world. Liars!"

Rosa's eyes widened and she grinned. "Man on the moon? Oh, my gosh! How wonderful! Chancellor, did you hear her?"

"I don't know if I believe half the things this woman says. She's ridiculous."

"Oh, how I want to believe her. Who sent a man on the moon? The Americans?"

"They make big show of it. I not believe their news. Liars! In Soviet Union, we watch only Soviet news and we have only Soviet food, Soviet toilet paper and Soviet clothes. Some of us have cars. Our cars are very good. Lada is Russian car and not so expensive like your British cars. Everything is made by us. You know what that means?"

Evelyn looked at her with a blank expression. "What? What does that mean?"

Olga grinned like a devil. "It means they are better!"

Rosa glanced at Evelyn and rolled her eyes back with a sigh of frustration.

Evelyn pretended she was engaged with the conversation. "So, they're better than British motor roadsters?"

"Better! Much better! This is what Joseph Stalin always say to us! He was right!"

Rosa folded her arms in front of her. "And, who is Joseph Stalin? And, should I even care?"

"How about trade?" Evelyn asked, while she pushed Rosa away.

"We are Soviet. No trade with other countries! We all have work! Everyone has a job. No unemployment! We are all paid the same. Everyone studies at university. We are smart people."

"Rosa looked at Olga. "Interesting."

# Chapter Fifteen

The top half of the time machine poked through the deck opening with the ladder. Sasha was on the deck, to help pull it through, while Colin was at the bottom pushing it up onto the deck. As Colin pushed the heavy machine upward, he heard something. He quickly turned his head to notice the cave lion lunged at him.

Colin fell back with the time machine smashing onto the floor and with the cave lion on top of him. The feline swatted Colin several times, slashing the shirt he was wearing into shreds. He tried to reach for his dagger. Sasha had the machine gun with him on the deck. He peered down from above, where he viewed the fallen operation. Rosa and Evelyn's screams fuelled the prehistoric feline into an uncontrollable frenzy. Colin tried to find his dagger, stashed in his back pocket. Drenched in blood, he fought back at the animal, by slicing it's upper arm.

"Oh! God! No! Sasha, use your gun! That thing is killing Colin! For God's sake, use it!" Rosa screamed.

"You want me to use gun? I thought you no want?" Sasha tried to confirm, calmly.

"You idiot! Shoot! We're going to lose Colin!" Rosa screamed.

Sasha kneeled down to focus on the prehistoric feline. "My time machine fall down. It could now be destroyed. I am so angry at Mr. Limmerick for letting this happen."

"Shoot that thing, you idiot!" Rosa shouted.

Sasha aimed and fired. He missed the cave lion, but the alien sound of a gunshot, scared the animal enough to leave the scene. Colin lay on the floor blood-drenched. Rosa pulled up her skirt and took the ladder down. Evelyn followed. Olga remained on the deck picking her fingernails.

140

Colin looked at Rosa who was knelt beside him. "Love, here ye are again comin' to me rescue."

"Colin, don't try to talk, we've got to get off this submarine and get you to a doctor," Rosa cautioned.

Evelyn had a small bottle of perfume in her pocket. "Here, rub this on his chest wounds, it has alcohol in it," Evelyn said.

Olga had made her way down the ladder. She handed Rosa the cloth her mouth was gagged with. "I will put perfume on this and it will be good antiseptic."

Rosa gave Olga a long stare. "What we need is turpentine. Why would you even try to help this man?"

Olga cackled. "Why? Why you ask? Maybe I help him because he is so good in bed."

Evelyn glanced at Rosa, where she could no longer bare the sight of Olga.

Rosa dabbed the perfume onto the cloth, enough to saturate it and pressed it onto his chest wounds, while she applied pressure.

"I think Li-Li-Limmerick like bondage very much. He is fast learner," Olga cackled again.

The chancellor turned to her. "I think it is time for you to be silent. This man is losing blood and you're standing here speaking gibberish."

Sasha pulled away from his dis-jointed time machine, so he could tend to Colin. "I will help Mr. Limmerick up. We must vacate and find doctor. I have friend in Petersburg who is best doctor in all of Russia. We will go to him."

Sasha helped Colin stand up. "Well, mate, I'm still shirtless, how ye like that, eh? I'm going to freeze when we get outside, surely I know it."

"You so scratched up, too. You look terrible without shirt. Ladies won't like you any more."

"Thanks, mate."

Olga pranced over to Colin to apply pressure to his wounds, using a perfume- drenched cloth. "I like to touch you."

Rosa pulled Olga away from Colin. "You are a ridiculous woman, can't you see this man is hurt? All you can think of is sex! There's something wrong with you."

Evelyn stood tightly beside Colin and clutched onto his arm. "My word, what a silly woman, most definitely."

"I think we should leave," Rosa said as she started to move forward. "Wait!" She stopped walking. "What do we do with the cave lion?"

"Who knows? Maybe monkey man will return with my time machine and they can eat each other," Sasha responded.

Rosa and Colin glanced at each other.

They made their way up the ladder. Rosa found another deceased naval officer on the floor. She removed his jacket and shirt.

"Here Colin, even if this is a wrong fit, you have to wear something," she said.

"All their jackets have the same strange symbol of a hammer 'n sickle," Colin noticed as he winched in pain.

"I think it is their Soviet flag, maybe. I think they do away with Russian flag, which was so beautiful," Sasha commented poignantly.

Colin struggled in pain to put on the shirt. He also put on the snug jacket. "It's alright, I suppose, it's better than nothin'. It pains me to think of the poor men who died, due to our stupidity. Just feel awful, so I do."

"Colin, please not now. We need to get you to a doctor,' Rosa instilled.

They made their way to the deck.

"Is it ever cold here!" Rosa complained.

"Of course. It is my city, Petersburg," Sasha commented. "We are in Russia. Northern Russia."

Olga grinned at Sasha. "You are Petersburg man?"

"Da."

"I was born in Kiev."

"Ukraine?"

"Da. We together in Soviet Union. No difference between Russia, Belorussia, Ukraine as well as other countries."

"Ukraine is not Russia. Big difference," Sasha said somewhat confused.

She stepped closer to him. "Better!"

Sasha appeared disenchanted. "Better? How it better?"

"Why you act so stupid? Why you not know about Soviet Union? It is a union. We are strong this way."

Colin shoved Sasha in the arm. "Direct me to this doctor friend of yours, mate."

"We must find lifeboat and get off this thing first, da?"

Olga interjected. "We must look for capsule. It is orange. We must inflate it first."

"Really?" Colin responded.

She stepped closer to Colin and smiled. "Yes, really. Why you not know this?"

"Good question. I keep tellin' ye but ye don't seem to understand me."

"Olga spotted the orange capsule. "It is beside hatch! There! Look!"

Sasha read the labeling on it in Russian. "She is right, Mr. Limmerick, we must *inflate*, instructions say."

"Interestin'," Colin commented.

Olga gripped onto Colin's arm and laughed. "Interesting? How is this interesting?"

They took hold of the capsule and tied a rope to a cleat, pulled the pin; pulled the *inflate handle* and threw the capsule into the water. They stood back to observe it inflate.

Then, they climbed down the roped-ladder into the lifeboat. Two collapsed paddles were fascine to the outer part of the lifeboat. They untied the rope, which connected them to the submarine. Sasha and Colin paddled vigorously, as Rosa and Evelyn sat somewhat comfortably in the raft, with the relief of vacating the submarine.

Rosa pulled the collar of her coat tightly around her neck. "The closer we are to this water, the colder it feels. I can't stop shivering. Oh, God, please help us. It's so cold!"

"Help me row, love, 'n ye won't feel a thing," Colin commented.

"I'm trying to think of Mediterranean beaches," Evelyn added. "Try it, Miss Emanuel. It really does work."

"That will only make me feel more depressed because I know we're not anywhere near the Mediterranean."

"We should be near the doctor, soon enough," Olga commented as she glanced at Colin. "Tell your ladies to stop complaining."

Rosa nudged her way up to Colin. "Tell me, did you really sleep with her?"

Colin struggled in pain as managed to work with Sasha to row the lifeboat through the frigid waters. "Why ye need to know this?"

"If it's true that you slept with her, then I just don't know anymore about you."

Colin continued to row the lifeboat. He gazed ahead without turning to her. "Please, Rosa. I don't want Evelyn to hear you."

"Well, it just means that you have reached your lowest."

"What's it to ye? Ye 'n me are no longer a couple."

"Fine, Colin. Rub it in!" She raised her voice.

"Shh…please, don't do this. Not now, please."

"I think the chancellor is hurt."

"Is she, now? Why would her hurt feelings even concern ye?"

"She simply adores you, Colin, that's why."

144

"Since when ye care so much about Evelyn?" He sighed. "Sweet Jesus, what am I to do? Can we just leave this conversation?"

"Colin, why did you do it?"

"Do what?"

"Sleep with that horrible woman."

Colin turned to Rosa. "Can we just speak of this another day? Just can't go into it just yet."

"Colin, what's wrong with you? You're not yourself."

"Love, almost got eaten by a prehistoric cave lion. All these innocent Russian naval officers just lost their lives due to me own stupidity. I'm courtin' the chancellor, a wench who I fancy, but I just don't know anymore."

"Don't you love her?"

Colin looked around to make sure Evelyn wasn't listening. "Look, can't we discuss this at another place 'n time?"

"How about me, Colin? I'm your true love and you know it."

She found herself pressed against him. He continued to make sure the chancellor wasn't listening. "Please. I'm in too much pain for this type of discussion."

She kissed her teeth and pretended to look away. "I don't believe you. I know you. I know I've always been your girl."

They reached one of the service peers. Sasha tried to stand up without falling into the water. "We arrive. Good."

Sasha stepped over to the peer with Colin kneeling on the raft. They helped the three women make it safely to the peer.

Rosa leered at Colin. "I just don't know you anymore, Colin."

"What?" Colin followed the group from behind. Olga tried to eavesdrop into their conversation.

"Oh, we're in Russia! How exciting. Should we sight see?" Evelyn gestured.

Rosa's smile dissipated. "Sight-see?"

"Sight-see? I'm much too banged up 'n exhausted for that. I think some quiet time on whatever bed I'm sleepin' in, would do just fine, don't ye think?" Colin blurted with exhaustion and pain.

Evelyn stepped away from him. "Oh."

"I'm just so tired. I really do need some rest, don't ye think? These Russian waters aren't easy to be rowing an inflatable lifeboat in, don't ye think?"

"Most definitely," Rosa said. "I'm very worried about you." She slowly turned herself away from him.

"Come lets go. What we do with new time machine?" Sasha asked.

"Leave it in the submarine. I think I should somehow get it back to England. Never operated a submarine before," Colin said.

"Colin, are you thinking of taking ownership of this large vessel?" The chancellor asked.

"Haven't the choice, really. Can't let it block up the harbor here, now can I?"

"So you're going to try and drive that submarine back to England? Dover won't have a harbor big enough for that huge sub either, Colin," Evelyn tried to understand.

"Aye, I think Dover can likely manage. Dover could more than the Welsh harbor, I think."

"And, if that's not the case, then what, Colin?" Rosa asked.

"It'll just fit, somehow. No worries. It should."

"But, if it doesn't?" Rosa asked.

"It should 'n it will."

They continued to walk along the peer to the concrete pathway, which led to the city of St. Petersburg. They stopped to take another look at the submarine that was somewhat docked. The cave lion showed itself on the deck. It roared a few times. The time travelers and Olga

146

looked back at the prehistoric animal, then continued to walk.

"How did lion get to deck? Lions climb?" Sasha asked.

"Felines climb trees, Sasha," Rosa blurted. "Of course it climbed up the ladder."

"You all will pay for this. Wait until KGB finishes with you," Olga burst with conviction, as she trailed behind the time travelers.

"I can't deal with the submarine, the time machine or the cave lion just now. I need to see a doctor," Colin responded.

"We go find doctor. Very close by to Winter Palace," Sasha said.

Olga stepped in front of Sasha and shoved him in the chest. "There is a doctor close to Winter Palace?"

Sasha shoved her back. "Da."

She slapped his arm. "There is no doctor near Winter Palace! You are lair! That area is for tourists!"

Rosa glared at Olga, "Tourists? If Russia turned into the Soviet Union with no trade with the free world, how would there be tourism?"

"All people are fascinated with Soviet Union," Olga replied.

Colin shook his head. "Ye know, Olga could very well be correct on that one, the forbidden fruit may allure outsiders, one would think."

Sasha stopped. "I will bet you. I am right and you are wrong!"

She stepped closer to him and slapped his face. "You know nothing! This is a trick! You are spies!"

Sasha took her arms and bent them up past her head. She screamed and struggled.

Colin grabbed Sasha's arm. "Don't fall in her pit, mate! So she slapped ye, let it go."

"I hate her!" Sasha snorted to Colin.

"Don't we all," Rosa commented.

Colin approached Olga to touch her shoulder with ease. "Mate, over here, knows what he's talkin' about. This is no trick. We're not spies. Yer just not understandin' that this is not 1970."

"KGB headquarters not so far away from Winter Palace."

"Who cares?" Sasha snorted. "Next time, I slap your face!"

Colin looked at Olga, "Sorry, but ye won't find a KGB office here."

"How would you know? You are not Soviet, you are British!"

"Irish."

Olga glared at Sasha. "You are bad Soviet. You travel with British. You are enemy."

Colin took her hand. "Since when the British are Russia's enemy?"

Olga leered at Colin. "Since 1948, if you want exact year. Did you sleep during school? Why all of you know nothing?" She winced with frustration. "You are spies! Stop playing dumb!"

Rosa glanced at Colin. "How old will I be in 1948? Oh my! I'll be 68!"

Colin forced a slight chuckle. "The future looks bleak, I must say."

"Mr. Limmerick is bleeding to death, we must go to my doctor friend. We waste too much time on stupidity," Sasha added.

Evelyn took Colin's arm. "Yes, I'm very worried about you."

"I'm worried about me too. Just need to see a medical professional, 'is all," Colin grunted, as they continued to walk against the prevailing winds and sleet of St. Petersburg.

Two Russian coast guard officials standing at the docks noticed the lifeboat and noticed the large submarine floating in the harbour. They did not react to what they were seeing. Sasha spoke to them in Russian. The two coast guard officials were very cordial but appeared impressed with the size of the submarine.

Sasha hailed a horse and carriage. The five of them stepped inside. Olga felt awkward and almost frightened.

Rosa glanced at her. "What's troubling you?"

"Taxi should be car, shouldn't it? People on the streets are dressed like you."

Colin tried to smile. "This is not 1970, that's why."

Olga appeared anxious and somewhat nervous.

"Olga, I'm glad yer takin' notice. It does look quite a bit different than London, though," Colin said.

"First, it was known as Leningrad." She pasted her face to the glass of the window of the carriage. "What is this? Am I in a time warp?"

Rosa glanced at Sasha, then at Colin.

Sasha leered at Olga. "Leningrad? What ugly name."

"Beautiful name," Olga responded with a smile.

"Is it known as St. Petersburg in 1970 or Leningrad?" Sasha asked.

"Leningrad," she snorted with a slight whimper. "It honors Vladimier Lenin."

The chancellor forced a smile. "And, who was he?"

"The great creator of Soviet Union."

The chancellor smiled at Sasha. "Ah, Saint Petersburg in our time period, is an exquisite city. So much to do and see, the food, the people, the galleries. "

Sasha smiled at her. "Of course."

"No excitement! Communism has no excitement!" Olga blurted.

The carriage bumped and swayed over uneven roads. Rosa glanced at Colin, where he returned the gesture to her with a slight wink of his eye.

"Hermitage is something I'd like to see," Evelyn commented.

"So nice, it is," Sasha responded almost in a flirtatious manner.

Rosa leered at Sasha. "Well, Sasha, when do we get to meet your wife? What's her name again?"

Olga took a few deep breaths, where she tried to stop herself from panicking. "If you want to sight-see, you must see *Nevsky Prospekt*. There, you will see much beauty. You will also see main KGB building at central district."

Sasha looked at her in silence.

"Why you act so stupid? If you are Russian, then you are Soviet," Olga blurted.

Sasha sat back in the moving carriage. "I am not Soviet. I not even know what that is."

"Then, you too much with British. You know nothing," Olga said with her face pasted against the glass.

Sasha appeared upset, but was silent. The carriage stopped two buildings down from Winter Palace. Colin and Sasha got off the carriage first, and then helped the women to the street.

Olga scanned her surroundings. "Streetcar is here, thank-God! It looks different. Why?"

Sasha and Colin glanced at each other but were silent. Sasha led them to a medical building. They walked up four flights of stairs in order to reach the doctor's office.

"Doctor will take x-ray, first," Olga said to Colin. "Right?"

"Aye, I know of x-rays. Some doctors are usin' them," Colin said. "But, I may not get an x-ray because of the time period we're in."

"You will get x-ray," she insisted.

Colin glanced at her. "Perhaps, maybe."

Olga stared at Colin with her lips parted. "We Soviets must keep up with Americans."

"Most definitely," Colin said as he tried to be polite. "Olga, try to understand what has happened here."

She winced a bit. "What has happened?"

He placed his hands around her shoulder. "You're no longer in 1970. You're in a different time period. Your past."

She pushed herself against him. "What?" She began to whimper.

They entered the doctor's office. Sasha spoke to the secretary who sat at the front behind a desk. Sasha looked at Colin. "We must sit and wait, da?"

Colin sat down with Rosa and the chancellor on each side of him. Olga leaned against the wall, where she was much too panicked to sit.

"Why you not have radio in office?" Olga blurted to the secretary. "Your patients should be listening to a radio while waiting!"

The secretary glanced at Sasha. *"Shto?"*

"Why you speak English to her? You think it is 1970!" Sasha shouted. "It's almost 1911."

The secretary appeared put-off by Olga's behavior.

Rosa stood up. "Maybe you should sit down. You no longer have your KGB to run to," Rosa blurted.

Olga sat down in a huff of rage and pulled out a cigarette. "I need a light! You have light?" She asked Sasha.

Rosa and Evelyn's eyes widened with surprise.

"A real lady would never smoke a cigarette," Evelyn muttered with disgust.

Colin searched the office for something to read.

"I am a real lady. Lady can smoke!" Olga blurted.

Evelyn sat with her legs crossed. "No, only men smoke. A woman who smokes looks like trash."

Rosa cackled. "Tramp."

The secretary looked at Colin and said that the doctor was ready to see him. Colin didn't understand her Russian so he continued to read.

Sasha stood up. "Mr. Limmerick, it is time to see doctor."

Olga remained in the waiting room, while the four entered the doctor's office.

Sasha and the doctor gave each other a manly hug.

*"Kak de la?"* Sasha expressed.

The doctor responded in Russian. They spoke for a bit, where Sasha told him why he was no longer residing in St. Petersburg. Sasha then explained Colin's wounds to him.

The doctor looked at Colin and asked him to remove his jacket and shirt.

Sasha looked at Colin. "Show doctor your lion wounds, Mr. Limmerick."

The doctor examined Colin's wounds. He rubbed alcohol on Colin's chest and asked his nurse to bandage Colin's cut flesh. The doctor spoke to Sasha in Russian, where he felt somewhat confused over the cave lion scratches and bights. Sasha brushed off the doctor's curiosity.

Colin gazed at the doctor. "Excuse me, ye wouldn't have any penicillin, would ye?"

The doctor looked at Sasha. *"Shto?"*

Sasha forced himself to chuckle. He tried to explain in Russian to the doctor that Colin was crazy and that he had a tendency to ask ridiculous questions.

\*\*\*

They walked along Nevsky Prospect. "Wouldn't mind buyin' me-self a warm coat. It's rather chilly here," Colin commented. "I don't think what I'm wearin' is enough."

"Of course, my dear," Evelyn responded. "I wish I had my fur cape at this moment."

"London's evenings can get chilly, but it's crisper in this Russian city, don't ye think?" Colin commented as he gazed through the window of a men's clothing shop.

"Some shops along Nevsky Prospect," Sasha expressed with his hand out, as if he were doing a demonstration. "Best shopping in all of world!"

Olga peered through the shop windows. "I cannot believe these clothes I see."

"Yes, they aren't as beautiful as what London has to offer," Evelyn responded.

"What is this?" Olga started to cry. "I never walk in London. I don't know it."

"I'm sorry, we're not in London, you wouldn't be crying, I assure you," Evelyn commented.

Rosa glanced at Colin. "What do we do?"

"We need to tell her what year she's in over and over. It's just not sinking in," Colin responded.

"She already knows she's no longer in 1970, I think she has figured it out that she's in her past."

"I don't think so, love. I don't think so. How does one explain time travel?" Colin said.

They walked inside the clothing shop. Colin took Olga's hand. "Olga, I need to speak with ye."

"What? What are you going to say to me?"

"Well, it's important for ye to know that it's just days away from New Years Eve 'n the year will be 1911. You're not in the year 1970 anymore. Happy New Year."

She placed her hands over her face and let out a loud scream. "Oh my God!" She tried to control herself as she searched her trench coat.

Evelyn and Rosa glanced at each other. "What are you looking for? Did you loose something?" Rosa asked.

"I need cigarette. I am overwhelmed by this nightmare. I must smoke."

Evelyn looked at Rosa. "I suppose women will soon become smokers. Shocking thought."

"Will women look like tramps?" Rosa asked in a whisper.

Evelyn grinned. "She is definitely a tramp. I hate her."

"I hate her too," Rosa whispered back.

Colin placed his arms around Olga. "Let me explain this to ye. We're time travelers. Dr. Dimitrikov, I mean,

Sasha has invented a time machine. We somehow got yer submarine caught in a time vortex 'n it came to our time, includin' yer crew of submariners. A prehistoric cave lion, which lived thousands of years ago, also came through the vortex and landed on yer 1970 submarine. Sasha is Russian, but he don't know yer Soviet Russia. He's not familiar with the KGB at all. He only knows Russia with the Czar as the leader. Do ye follow me?"

She couldn't stop crying. "Oh, God! No! Time machine? What is that? Czar?"

Sasha stepped closer to Olga who was buried in Colin's arms. "I cannot believe you are from future and you still not have time machine. You are primitive people!"

She continued to cry. "You only know Czar?"

"Russia under Czar not so bad. Try it, you like."

"In 1911, I am nothing. In 1970, I work for KGB. I am something."

"I leave Russia when revolution begin, I not know what will happen later," Sasha said. "Bolshevik's storm into streets of Petersburg. They are so aggressive. I hate them." Sasha mumbled with seriousness in his tone.

Olga's eyes streamed with tears. "Bolsheviks?"

Sasha chuckled. "You see, Mr. Limmerick, she is not smart girl. She not know Bolsheviks. She know nothing."

"Lenin create them in 1917. Of course I know Bolsheviks. They forced communism, you stupid-ass."

Sasha appeared as if he wanted to strike her, but Colin stepped in front of him; then Colin's eyes widened. "Forced communism?"

She cackled with nervousness. "Of course, how will great ideas pass in a nation if they are not forced?"

Sasha paused, gazed at Colin, then at nothing. "That is right, I hear of Vladimir. That is right. So, he create communism? What is that?"

"It is Soviet Socialist system. You are too stupid."

Sasha appeared frustrated. "Soviet Socialist?"

"Union of Soviet Socialist Republic – U.S.S.R." She nodded her head with disgust as she tried to kick some debris under her shoe.

Colin stepped closer to Sasha. "So, ye know of this Vladimir Lenin bloke?"

"I leave Russia and flee to England because of this uprising. I think Russia try to have war with Japan. I not know why. And, with Germany, I still not know why. All I know, I could not stay in Russia; too many poor people."

She pulled away from them. "I got news for you! Your Czar will be killed!"

Sasha looked at her with his lips parted. "What you say?"

Rosa stepped closer to them. "Colin, please purchase your clothes. Let me handle this."

The chancellor was busy browsing the shop.

"Look, Sasha, the future is a very scary place. We had always ventured into the past. This time, the future came to us. You don't know what is going to happen. We don't know what will happen to England, either."

Olga gave a fiendish giggle. "England? You want to know?"

"I really don't care to know. I live in the present, which is a nice place to be," Rosa quickly responded.

Colin tried on a coat. "Fine!" he called out to Olga. "Tell us about England?"

"World wars! Two of them!"

The chancellor heard what Olga said. She stopped her browsing and stepped closer to Olga.

"Two world wars? And, England will be involved?"

"Yes it will!"

"England will have a victory, of course," Evelyn said.

"You so stupid!" Olga blurted, while nodding her head. The shopkeeper appeared distraught over their tone in his store. "England come so close to losing Second World War. London gets bombed by Germans. Almost

155

everything in London gets destroyed. People have to sleep in subways to survive. How you like your London, now?"

Rosa's expression was panicked as Colin slid his arm around her.

The chancellor stepped closer to Olga. "You don't know what you're talking about. England would never get to the point you just mentioned. Impossible!"

"Not until Soviet Union helps England and Russians save the day!"

Sasha looked at Olga. "You say Germans bomb England? Did Germans bomb Soviet Union?"

"Nothing happen to us! We are Soviet! We are strong!"

"Nothing happen to Soviet Union? I live in England, now. They strong people. You say Germans almost break England and Soviets come to England's aid? You say Soviet Union experience have no suffering?" Sasha tried to clarify.

"Soviets are stronger than British by far! And, those Americans came to war too late!"

Colin glanced at Rosa, Evelyn and Sasha. "Germany is a strong country. I can believe some of what she's sayin'. Can't fathom Londoners sleepin' in the subways, though. The London Metropolitan Rail?" Colin said. "I can't believe that."

"Believe it! Germans change into Nazi! Allies were British, Soviets and Americans! We fight German Nazis and it was Soviets who won the war because British and Americans too weak to fight!"

Colin took a deep breath. He felt sweat form on his brow. "Really?"

"She's a liar, Colin! Why don't we just leave her somewhere?" Rosa suggested.

Colin paid for his coat. "Well, I think we need to return to the Soviet submarine to its appropriate time period and tend to the cave lion, so we should."

"Why we go back there? It is not as if lion is hungry?" Sasha responded. "It ate all submarine crew. Good meal for so big cat, da?"

Colin took a deep breath as he tried to button his coat. "This cave lion, mate, is from pre-history. We pulled it outta its time of thousands of years ago, through a time vortex. It's completely on us, that this poor animal is in a submarine from our future. How can it survive if we don't get it back to its time? This will definitely disturb the evolutionary gene pool."

"Colin's right, Sasha," Rosa strongly nodded her head in agreement.

The chancellor looked at Colin. "Haven't we created a huge problem in the gene pool by allowing all those Russian submariners to die?"

Colin stared at the floor. "I wish I could take that back."

"What if you get eaten by lion? Then what?" Sasha asked.

Colin chuckled. "I'm not gonna get me-self eaten by that cave lion."

"Why not? You are big meal for it. You will make it pet, like you do with all prehistoric mammals, then when you not looking, it will make you its meal."

"It's likely I'm way too threatenin for it."

Rosa shoved Sasha in the arm. "Would you stop?"

"We gotta get ourselves to that submarine. Olga, surely, ye wanna be on this ride, so ye can get yer-self to 1970."

"Ride?" Olga expressed. "What ride?"

Rosa shoved Olga. "Time travel, Missy!"

"Just take me to 1970! I not want your primitive time. My Soviet Union 1970 is greatly advanced."

Colin smiled at her as he rubbed her shoulder. "Tell us, tell us what makes 1970 Soviet Union so advanced?"

Olga's eyes beamed with glee, when she paused to think of her own time period. "We have nuclear power."

Sasha lit a cigarette. "So?"

She continued. "We have Soviet army."

Rosa appeared board. "Continue."

"We have Nefsky Prospect in Leningrad."

Sasha blew smoke rings with his cigarette.

"We have nuclear missals."

The chancellor glanced at Olga. "Nuclear missals, for what use?"

"To blow up U.S.A."

The chancellor glanced at Colin, then at Olga. "For whatever for would your country want to blow up another country?"

"Because they say they want to blow up Soviet Union, first."

Colin stared at the floor. "I see."

"And most of all, you will never believe, we have greatest space travel in all world. *Sputnik!*"

Sasha puffed on his cigarette butt showing little interest. "Space travel?" He almost singed his thumb with the bare butt of his cigarette. You are lair!"

Rosa glanced at Olga. "Who is Sputnik?"

Olga grinned. "You mean *what?* Not *who?* The first earth satellite, of course."

Colin smiled at her. "Really?"

"The Russians came up with the first earth satellite?" The chancellor asked. "Impossible."

Olga cackled like a hyena. "Of course! It make Americans crazy with fear!"

Rosa glanced at Sasha. "This sounds outrageous."

"This is meaning of Cold War!" She grimaced.

Rosa's eyes widened with an expression of panic on her face. "Cold War? What does that mean?"

Olga's face was expressionless. "You people really not know anything, do you?"

"Surely, we don't know what ye know, 'cause yer from our future," Colin clarified.

"So this is really 1911?" she cackled again.

Colin smiled. "I think New Years Eve is today so it will be 1911 tomorrow," Colin said.

"We should at least celebrate the new year? Don't you think?" Rosa suggested.

"Celebration is waste of time. I must report back to KGB at once!" Olga murmured. "No celebrating in our Soviet world, it is for the ignorant."

"Fine, we gotta get ourselves back to that submarine 'n that's where the nuclear power is to generate some kinda time travel, eh?" Colin said walking toward the door of the store.

Evelyn followed last with her arms folded in front of her. "What is this silliness? I don't believe a word this woman has said to us, Colin."

Colin took Evelyn's hand and held it in his. "Don't mind what she says."

The chancellor appeared perturbed. "How is it that England wouldn't have been the first country to venture into space travel? I don't believe her."

"England does not space travel. They sleep in subways instead!" Olga blurted back at them with a sneer.

The chancellor stood closer to Colin. "This woman is ridiculous."

Rosa stepped closer to Olga. "Fine, but what has happened to fashion? Music? Art?"

Olga paused. "You British waste too much time on fashion, music and art. All you care about is that! I see photo of Beatles and I hear them once before. They claim to make music?"

Colin chuckled. "Look, it'll soon be 1911. We're not familiar with The Beatles. We're really not sure about anything that yer tellin' us just now.

Sasha searched for another cigarette in is jacket pocket. "If you only see photo and hear these Beatles one time before, how you know they make terrible music?"

"They steal all music from Soviets! Just like Elvis Presley!"

"Whose Elvis Presley?" Rosa asked.

"American singer. He take all music from Soviets. *You ain't nothing but hound dog! Crying all time!* All people know this song is Soviet song!" She giggled. "Even Americans know this."

"Sorry, don't know it. It's from the future, surely," Colin commented.

"This Elvis Presley is not British, he is American. He take all Russian music!

Thief!"

Rosa tugged on Colin's arm. "I'm getting a headache from listening to this woman. I think she may be crazy."

Colin grinned. "Likely, love."

# Chapter Sixteen

They made their exit from the store and strolled over to the dock. They could see beyond the cold sleet that the submarine was still afloat.

"When we get ourselves back to the submarine, we need to be mindful of the cave lion," Colin cautioned as he directed everyone to the docked lifeboat.

"Colin," Rosa said as she tugged his arm.

"Aye?"

"Sasha will need to locate that incomplete time machine, which contained the nuclear power. How is he going to send that submarine with the dead crew and that horrible woman back to 1970?" Rosa asked.

"Its gotta get done, love. We haven't the choice."

"What happens when the cave lion needs a snack?"

"Surely, it will."

"Then what?"

"We do whatever it takes."

They got themselves situated on the lifeboat. Olga lagged behind. The chancellor noticed, but didn't seem to care.

Colin took the oars of the boat and began to row. "Olga, would ye like to sit beside me? It's a much better view from here."

"I am not interested in view L–Li-Limmerick."

The chancellor sat pressed against Colin. "Why are you so concerned for that woman, Colin?"

"Cause it's me own fault she's misplaced in a different time period. She's frightened, so I can tell."

"She's absolutely horrible. Why should any of us be concerned for her?"

Colin smiled at the chancellor. He tightened his arm around her and kissed her lips. He and Sasha rowed through the frigid-choppy waters, which belonged to the Gulf of Finland. Rosa sat behind Colin and the

161

chancellor; she was wrapped in her coat with a scarf over her head. She appeared miserable with fear, and uncomfortable from the sharp cold. Olga did not appear bothered by the cold, but wanted to keep her distance from the time travelers.

Colin glanced at Sasha. "Ye know, mate, I'm not even bothered by these frigid temperatures, 'cause it' so damn difficult to row in such difficult waters. I'm feelin' rather warm or even hot from this rigorous rowin'. "

Sasha decided to take a break from rowing, where he stopped to smoke a cigarette. "Mr. Limmerick, you are Hercules, you can row this thing yourself back to England."

Colin tried to laugh, but couldn't as he continued to row. When the lifeboat got closer to the submarine, Colin extended his arms to the chancellor. She latched onto him as he hoisted her up the ladder with him to reach the top of the submarine deck. Sasha did the same with Rosa. Olga stood up on the lifeboat, where Colin offered to help her up the ladder. She pulled away from him and sat back down on the lifeboat. The Baltic winds and sleet intensified. She sat on the lifeboat and looked away from him.

"Olga, don't do this." Colin climbed up the ladder, feeling defeated. He glanced at Rosa. "She's not wantin' to come on the sub. I don't know what to do."

Rosa peered down from above. "She's being a fool, Colin. You can't make her come onto the submarine, if she refuses." Rosa responded.

"I can't leave her in the lifeboat to die, either."

"Colin, why do you consistently take on other people's burdens?" Rosa asked, as the chancellor appeared to agree.

Colin's head hung low, as he made his way back down the ladder to the lifeboat. He noticed Olga was silent and unresponsive.

"Olga! Take hold of me 'n I'll help ye onto the submarine. We're gonna get ye back to 1970, so we will!"

She sat on the lifeboat and looked away from him.

"Olga!" Colin called out.

Rosa noticed what was happening. "Colin, maybe she just wants to die here!"

"Can't let that happen!" Colin blurted in a panic as the sound of their voices were getting distorted with the howling winds and penetrating sleet. Colin bent lower, with his arms spanned out, ready to catch her and bring her onto the submarine. "Olga! Please!"

"Leave me! Go away, L-Limmerick!"

Colin lowered his body enough to climb back onto the lifeboat. Rosa turned the other way with frustration. Sasha smoked a cigarette. The chancellor stood at the edge of the submarine with angst. It started to rain, where the low temperatures created a damp sleet.

"Colin! Please! Come back here!" The chancellor called in distress.

Colin took hold of Olga and swooped her into his arms. He carefully made his way to the submarine. He held Olga with one arm and climbed onto the submarine with the other arm.

Olga placed her feet on the deck of the submarine. "Just let me die here, L-Li-Limmerick."

"I can't do that," he replied. "Yer gonna get back to yer time 'n all will be as it was."

"All will not be as it was with dead crew!" She blurted with distaste. "KGB will hold me responsible for this. They will have me killed for this."

"Most certainly not, this wasn't your fault," Colin instilled.

She stepped closer to him and buried her head in his chest. "If now I will part from you," she felt the warmth of his large frame pressed against her. "I want to say I will not forget you."

163

Colin embraced her in his arms. The relentless winds and sleet slapped their faces. He held her tight in his arms. The chancellor stood beside Rosa and Sasha as she watched Colin hold Olga tight against his body.

Rosa looked at the chancellor. "If you expect to be in Colin's life you need to understand something about him."

"I think I know what you're about to say, Miss Emanuel."

"Good."

"Well? Continue. I can take it."

"Chancellor, you see Colin has an enormous heart."

The chancellor gleamed. "Yes, he most certainly does. That's what I cherish about him."

"But!" Rosa shouted pointing her finger to the sky.

The chancellor wrapped her scarf more tightly around her long delicate neck. "But, what?"

"He is also addicted to women. Can you live with that, Chancellor?"

"Most definitely not."

Sasha stepped between the two women. "In other words, Mr. Limmerick is great big whore of man!"

The chancellor had trouble looking at Colin embraced with Olga. "She's a disgusting woman, why would he even give a damn about her?"

"Because he is Mr. Limmerick, that is why," Sasha said with fiendish grin.

"Here's the thing, Chancellor, I think you're addicted to Colin," Rosa added.

"Most definitely."

"Well, I think you need to work on that. Why do you think he's over forty and he's never married," Rosa said as if she was explaining Darwin's theory to an undergraduate student.

"Well, I'm over fifty and I have never married. I'm beautiful, so men keep telling me and I have money and power. Yet I am still a spinster." She sighed with a discreet smile.

"I don't know what your problem is, then," Rosa commented with not much thought.

"Problem?" The chancellor's grin dissipated.

Sasha slid his arm around the chancellor. "You nice looking lady. Why you not marry?"

"You're married, aren't you, Dr. Dimitrikov?"

"Da, I have wife here."

"I'm not married," Rosa said with a quiver in her voice.

"Why haven't you married, Miss Emanuel?" Evelyn asked.

"Colin and I were going to marry, then Sasha and I were going to marry and everything went down hill from there, I don't know!"

"Really?" The chancellor's lips were parted with surprise. "How could you possibly plan a wedding with Dr. Dimitrikov if he is already taken?"

Colin had his arm around Olga as they walked over to his cohorts.

"Well, mate, I think it's time we get things movin', don't ye think?" Colin instigated.

Sasha smiled. "First, we must see if cave lion is on our trail. If so, we shoot it at first sight, da?"

Rosa stepped in front of Sasha. "No, Sasha! If we see the cave lion, which is likely going to happen, we will simply scare it away with a gun shot."

"Agreed, love," Colin said with a nod.

They made their way to the hatch on the floor of the deck, but remained on the deck.

"Okay, Sasha, I don't really see why we need to venture any further on this submarine. You're the one who has to activate the time machine. We're just standing here to give you moral support, right?" Rosa tried to confirm.

"Wrong, love," Colin interjected. We're all here 'cause we need to be vigilant for Sasha while he activates

165

the time machine, which means we need to hurry back onto the lifeboat. Only Olga will remain.

"Vigilant for what?" Rosa asked.

"The cave lion is likely roamin' about 'n there could still be Soviet submariners alive. We need to do this without errors."

Olga primped herself by running her fingers through her, blunt, black hair. "I think L-Li-Limmerick likes me."

The chancellor appeared appalled by Olga's presence. "That's what you think, *tramp.*"

Olga giggled like a ghoul. Sasha and Colin kneeled beside the nuclear-powered time machine.

"I think we must be on life boat on water, away from submarine. We not want to go to 1970. Only Olga must remain on submarine if she want so bad to be in 1970 with KGB," Sasha said.

"Is there a chance the crew could come back to life, mate?" Colin asked with a hopeful expression on his face.

"I not know answer to your question, Mr. Limmerick. I am a brilliant scientist, but I cannot predict these things."

Colin stood up and turned to Olga. He took her hand and held it tightly in his. "Olga, ye need to stay here on the sub. We're gonna have to vacate so ye can go to yer own time period," he tightened his hand around hers. "Is this suitable to ye?"

She stood on her tiptoes to wrap her arms around his broad neck. "It is not. I want to be with you, always. I not ever feel like this for someone."

Colin's jaw dropped as he caught a glimpse of Rosa and the chancellor staring at him. *"Oh shite."*

The chancellor turned her head away from Colin and stared at the floor.

Sasha turned the dial of the time machine, which ignited the nuclear reactor. A heavy thump came from the machine, as well as a glow of light.

"Do not look at light! Turn away!" Sasha shouted. "We must vacate! Vacate, now!" Sasha shouted. Colin threw the chancellor over his shoulder and climbed up the ladder and Sasha did the same with Rosa. They ran to the lifeboat, which was sitting on the submarine deck. They noticed how the entire submarine started to glow and sway. Colin tossed the lifeboat into the water and pulled the chancellor with him onto the boat. Sasha did the same with Rosa. The four of them sat in the lifeboat and watched the submarine slowly transform into visible molecules. The glowing light was so intense, they kept their eyes shut with their heads down between their knees. Colin could feel that familiar jolt of nausea, he had always experienced when traveling through the time vortex. His nausea was so immense; he started to violently vomit. Frigid salty water drenched them, and bright glowing light intensified. Hard cracking sounds of loud banging barked through their ears. Rosa cupped her hands over her ears. The loud banging was so intense, that it was maddening. They felt themselves in a tailspin of centrifugal force. The chancellor screamed with terror.

# Chapter Seventeen

Sasha lifted his head from having it tucked between his knees. He noticed that he was still on the lifeboat. He noticed Colin knocked out cold on the boat, where his torso hung over the rim of the floatation device. Rosa was sprawled onto the floor of the raft. She opened her eyes to notice Sasha peering down at her.

"Sasha?" She said with little energy in her voice. She looked around to find the chancellor lying beside her. She nudged the chancellor, but there was no response. "Sasha?"

"Da?"

"I think we just went through a time vortex."

"Maybe?"

Sasha helped Rosa sit up.

"Sasha? The submarine is still here!"

"We are now with submarine, da?"

"How do you mean we're now with the submarine?"

"We entangle some how when submarine travel to future."

"Sasha, did we just time travel?"

"Da."

"Does your time indicator show that we time traveled?"

"Da."

"Oh, Sasha," she paused with a look of dread on her face. "What now?"

"Depends."

"On what?"

"If we can survive this time period that we are now in."

She sighed. "What year is that?"

"1970. Happy New Year!"

Rosa's lips were parted but she was silent. She glanced at Colin, who was still knocked out, and she noticed how the chancellor was also knocked out. "It's amazing how some people just can't endure a time vortex."

Sasha shrugged his shoulders and searched his jacket pockets for a cigarette.

Evelyn turned her head and fluttered her eyes. "Good God, where are we?"

Sasha smiled at the chancellor. "We are now in different time period but, it is good for us, I think."

"How Sasha? How is this good for us?" Rosa asked tightening her scarf around her neck.

"We travel through time vortex. It is what we do, da?"

"No Sasha, this was not supposed to happen," Rosa scowled.

"Is it ever cold on this life boat," the chancellor complained, in search for her hat.

Sasha sat back in the lifeboat and popped a cigarette in his mouth. He gazed at the submarine and lit a match. "Wake up Mr. Limmerick. I think he get very sick on this time travel. Thank God, sea water wash it away."

Rosa turned to Sasha. "Wash what away?"

"Mr. Limmerick's bile of course, what else? Bile? Is that correct word? Vomit, maybe? Or, is it barf?"

Evelyn sat up, as she placed her hat firmly on her head. "Colin was ill?"

Rosa glanced at the chancellor. "Yes, Colin never really took time vortex travel too well." Rosa placed her hand over Colin's mouth. "He is breathing, thankfully."

"We should get him to come out of this, shouldn't we?" The chancellor suggested with concern.

"I don't think it's such a good idea at this stage because he'll likely wake up with uncontrollable nausea," Rosa informed.

"How terrible! Poor man!"

169

Sasha puffed on his cigarette and looked beyond the submarine. "I see submarine is moving to port. Who driving it? Olga? She can drive submarine?"

Rosa looked at Sasha. "Does the port look any bigger? I suppose it's much more modern than it was during the time of the Czar?" Rosa commented.

Sasha stared at it in silence for almost a minute. Everyone was silent. "Nyet. It almost same as 1911. This cannot be possible. How?"

"Really?" The chancellor expressed.

"It must have changed and modernized since our time, Sasha," Rosa instilled.

"So many years, it would have to. It didn't really fit the 1911 port."

"Not what I can see. They will have to make submarine fit. Maybe this is usual for Soviet people. I not know."

Rosa's eyes widened as she glanced at the chancellor. Colin's eyes opened. With his torso hung over the lifeboat. The chancellor rubbed Colin's back. "Colin?"

Colin did not respond but he did move his head.

"Colin, are you alright?"

He pulled himself inside the boat. "Sweet Jesus, what happened?"

"Colin, brace yourself for this. We time traveled," Rosa said with a serious tone.

Colin's eyebrows lifted with a hesitated response. *"Oh, feck."*

"Colin, guess what time period we're in?"

"Really don't wanna know, love."

Sasha continued to sit back in the raft and finish his cigarette. "Who drive submarine?"

Colin turned his head to glance at the large Soviet vessel. "Olga?"

"She would not know how to operate submarine," Sasha responded.

"Why ye say that, mate? Who else? The cave lion?"

Rosa stared at nothing. "I just had an awful thought."

Colin brushed his hand along Rosa's shoulder. "What, love? Yer awful thoughts tend to always come true. What's yer awful thought?"

"This was a very turbulent time vortex journey, agreed?"

"Aye."

"Since we are now in 1970 again, so is *Neanderthal*."

Colin's jaw hung opened. "Mother of God!"

Sasha let out a loud cackle. "You say monkey-man drive submarine?" His cackle continued as small pieces of tobacco spewed from between his teeth. "Not possible!"

Colin looked at Sasha who had just flicked his cigarette butt into the turbulent water. "Anything's possible, mate. *Neanderthals* was intelligent prime mates."

"Who cares? Monkey-man cannot drive submarine. It is not possible."

Colin tried to adjust his sitting position on the lifeboat. "Number one - mate. *Neanderthal* is not a monkey-man - two, he's intelligent. The only reason *Neanderthals* didn't continue to evolve is because they couldn't adapt as well to the changin' environment as we did."

Rosa stretched her neck and gave a subtle clap with her hands. "Here! Here!"

Colin's eyes bulged a bit. "Well, mate, ye better just pay attention, there's a submarine that's makin' its way to dock at the port. The port doesn't look too different than it did in 1911, but things look as if its gonna dock. Considerin' its size, I would've expected the port to be much bigger, where a vessel of this size could likely fit. It's 1970, things don't really look too modern, not as they did when we travelled to 1970, London. Wouldn't ye think?"

"It's just mind-boggling, Colin," Rosa said.

"Maybe cave lion drive submarine, but not monkey-man!"

Rosa squinted her eyes at Sasha. "You always hated *Neanderthal*. What do you have against a poor innocent prehistoric prime mate like *Neanderthal?*"

"Monkey-man eat Mr. Limmerick out of house and home; monkey-man almost drown Mr. Limmerick; Monkey-man beat up Mr. Limmerick's crew including Mr. Limmerick, who is size of bull."

"Since when you care so much about Colin?"

The chancellor glanced at Rosa. "Maybe the Dr. Dimitrikov is correct. I don't think I could place so much value into that prehistoric link."

Colin sighed out of frustration. "Prehistoric link? Definitely not, Evelyn. Darwin counted *Neanderthal* as part of the evolutionary process leadin' to *Homo sapiens.*"

Sasha sat further back on the lifeboat and cackled. "Mr. Limmerick is such big Darwinist. His professor at university hate him for this."

"Colin, let's not waste time discussing the intelligence of an already long extinct prime mate," Evelyn said as she brushed her hand over Colin's chest and delicately ran it over his crotch.

Rosa's eyes widened with disgust, where she forced herself to look away.

The chancellor appeared empowered somehow. "I think the Dr. Dimitrikov needs to get us back to 1911. I'm terribly sorry we all didn't engage in New Years festivities. Also, I'm terribly cold out here on this life boat."

Sasha sat up. "Da, we need to return to 1911. I not like this Soviet Russia idea. The Russia I know is artistic and beautiful."

"Let me guess, mate," Colin interjected. He noticed Evelyn's wandering hands brushing along his body. His eyes shifted a bit, but he tried to continue what he was about to say. "We gotta get ourselves back on the

172

submarine, 'cause that's where the nuclear fuelled time-machine is."

Sasha cackled again. "You are right, Mr. Limmerick."

Rosa tried to ignore the chancellor's aggressive gestures with Colin. "So that would mean we would have to see Olga again, right?" Rosa asked as she turned to the chancellor with a smirk on her face. "We left it on the submarine. It fell onto that lower level floor when the cave lion pounced on Colin. I hope it's still working."

"If it is broken. I can fix," Sasha quickly responded.

Colin took the oars and rowed against the relentless current with Sasha's help as they directed the lifeboat to the landing. The four of them stood at the dock as they watched the submarine tear its way against the dock, busting any structure that stood in its way.

"I think cave lion is driving submarine," Sasha commented.

Colin brought the oars inside the small boat. "Likely not, mate."

"Who drive so terrible? Olga?"

"Perhaps it's Olga. We just don't know."

"Hopefully, a submariner is driving the submarine. Maybe the entire crew was not devoured by that lion, one can only hope," Rosa interjected.

"Lovely thought," Colin said with a semi smile.

Sasha stood up to place his foot on the landing. He extended his hand to Rosa. "Come, we will see who drive submarine so bad."

"Sasha, didn't you say you wanted to pay a visit to your wife?" Rosa inquired as Sasha brushed his hands along her delicate shoulders. "I suppose now that we're in 1970, your wife would be quite old, or she may no longer ---," she paused. "The thought of the future is frightening."

"Say it!" Sasha edged her on.

"Oh, what an awful thought, to be too old to function, or --."

Sasha brought his lips to hers. "Mr. Limmerick make me worry about monkey man. Now, I have submarine from 1970 on my hands. Now, we in 1970. We were here before and hated it, da?"

"Sasha, I can't be with you, if you're married to someone else," Rosa blurted.

"Maybe she got new man. She is beautiful lady with so nice expression. She would have new man."

"Sasha, stop your guessing. Maybe you needed to see her, when we were still in 1911?"

"You really wanted to meet her?"

Rosa's eyes shifted. She glanced at Colin as he helped the chancellor step onto the landing. Colin gave Rosa a blank stare.

"Colin?" Rosa said.

"Aye?"

"Should I do what Sasha is saying?"

Colin stepped closer to Rosa with the chancellor's hand in his. "Do what? What's the mate askin' of yez?"

"He's offering to introduce me to his wife."

Colin's eyes widened. He glanced at Rosa, then at Sasha. "How ye gonna see Sasha's wife, now? We're no longer in 1911. Would she be alive in 1970? Who knows?"

"So, you think it's a bad idea?" Rosa asked.

The chancellor stepped in front of Colin. "Of course it's a poor idea. How dreadful of an idea it is.

"Why?" Rosa appeared uncomfortable. "Why is that such a bad idea? Sasha should introduce me to his wife. I'm going to be his new wife."

Colin pressed himself against Rosa. Rosa looked up at Colin. "Go find her. We're fifty-nine years in our future. She'd be pushing her eighties, if she's alive. Time travel, especially into our future can be rough goin'. Sasha may not like what he finds."

"If she's an old lady, all the better for me."

174

Colin stood tall and straight, so he could tower over Rosa. He took a deep breath. "Now, yer gettin' tasteless."

"Colin Limmerick, I am not!"

"Why would you bother to ask for Colin's approval, if you have already made up your mind?" The chancellor commented.

"We all can meet Natasha. She is nice lady. She will cook for us, I know. She is twenty-five in 1911."

"Eighty-four? She'd be eighty-four, mate? If at all. I'd stop right there. When we was in our own time period, was when we should've met yer wife, don't ye think, mate?"

Colin peered at the submarine. "I think we should re-enter the submarine and get the time machine activated to return to 1911, don't ye think? Onward to London, in fact, not St. Petersburg, Russia, for Christ's sake."

"We should stay in Russia, Mr. Limmerick."

"Why?" Colin questioned Sasha with a frustrated sigh.

"Rosa must meet my wife."

"Why?" Colin asked with distasteful in his expression. "Mother of God, please save this man. Lets get to the time machine, get to 1911, and then we'll take a visit to St. Petersburg, when we can breathe a little easier, wouldn't ye say?"

"She would see that I am not liar, da?"

Colin shut his eyes with frustration. "Liar? Who? Ye? Feck, mate! Damn ye are a feckin' liar!"

"Why I say to Mr. Limmerick, I not know. Why not? All will be said and done," Sasha said with his arms in the air. "I not know how to lie!"

"Look, ye 'n I both know yer not plannin' on marryin' Rosa. Why ye tryin' to feck her head up? Your wife in this time, mate, will be an old wench. This is gettin' too out of focus, I think, mate. In this time, we'd all be old as well, if we wasn't time travelers."

175

Sasha stood straight and motionless. He stared at Colin and was silent. He watched Colin pull the lifeboat and oars onto the landing. The two women walked toward the submarine.

Rosa scurried herself beside Colin. "I think you hurt Sasha's feelings," she whispered to him.

Colin turned to her. "Ye think so?"

She paused. "Well, yes."

He stopped before the parked lifeboat with its oars sticking out. He took a deep sigh. "Go, then! Go meet his wife. Do what ye want, love! Fed up with this, so I am. We's all in Russia 1970. Soviet Russia, at that, whatever that means."

The Chancellor placed her hand on Colin's arm. "Soviet Russia in 1970, I think means, we will meet many more Olgas."

"Colin, I think you need to calm yourself. You're raising your voice," Rosa said, appearing as if she were frail and helpless.

"Almost sixty years of time is gonna put some age on a person, don't ye think? And I'm not raisin' me voice."

Her body language appeared meek and afraid. Colin ran his large rough hands over his face. He took another look at Rosa. "Do it! Go meet the wench. I need to see whose left in the sub, if ye don't mind?"

"Colin, why are you raising your voice at me?"

He stared at the ground. "I need to enter the sub. Go about yer own."

Sasha extended his hand to Rosa. "Come with me, beautiful lady. We will return to here soon."

"We shouldn't separate, ye know it," Colin said shaking his head with frustration. "We need to stay together."

The chancellor latched herself to Colin's arm. "Colin's right. I also think this is not the time period to be in for such a visit. D. Dimitrikovr, it would be too disturbing for you to venture through Soviet streets when you remember this city as beautiful artistic Russia."

Sasha stared at the ground. "You are right, beautiful lady. I will do what you say. We must go inside submarine now, da?"

Colin stood by the latch door to the submarine. "Lets not separate. I get the feelin' this Soviet Russia of 1970 is far from bein' a safe place to be, especially bein' British. That's a dead ringer."

Rosa took a breath. "It's settled. I'll only meet Sasha's wife when we return to our own time period."

Colin took her tiny delicate hand and kissed it. "Lovely."

Colin swung opened the top latch door of the submarine and peered down the porthole. "I don't see or hear anythin'. I'm hopeful the cave lion didn't kill Olga. Quite worried, so I am," Colin commented.

Colin started climbing down the ladder of the porthole.

"What are you doing?" The chancellor asked in a panic.

"I gotta investigate matters, don't ye think?" Colin responded as he continued down the ladder. Sasha followed. Rosa followed both men down the ladder.

"What are you doing?" The chancellor demanded.

"What does it look like I'm doing?" Rosa smugly responded. The chancellor followed as well.

Sasha stood beside his time machine. "It does not look broken. We must take it out of here."

Colin heard strange sounds, where a Soviet marine officer walked by with a walky-talky in his hand. The Soviet submariner stopped and gave Colin a deadly stare. He blurted a few harsh-sounding words at Colin in Russian and then he made a quick exit.

Colin's eyes were wide. "Sasha! That man was devoured by the cave lion!" Colin started to smile. "Thank Jesus! He's alive!"

Rosa smiled and leaped into Colin's arms at the same time. "Maybe they're all alive! In 1970, they're supposed to be alive. They weren't even born yet in 1911. Thank Goodness!"

"This is just grand! I feel so relieved!"

That same Soviet officer returned with two other armed men. They pointed their guns at the four time travelers.

The chancellor stood beside the other time travelers with her hands up. She glanced at Colin. "You're relieved?"

178

# Chapter Eighteen

Olga walked in pointing a gun at the time travelers. She blurted something in Russian to the other Soviet officers. Colin's hands were in the air. He gazed at Olga, she noticed, but turned away. She continued to speak in Russian, where she assumed the time travelers understood her.

Sasha's hands were in the air. He informed Olga that he was the only one out of the four outsiders whose first language was Russian; and that the other three were English.

She stepped in front of Colin. "So, you are English man?"

Colin stared at the floor. "Irish."

"Irish?" Her eyes shifted a bit. "Same thing!"

Colin was silent as he stared at the floor.

Olga stepped closer to him. "You? I think I see your handsome face before. I think I see you before?"

Colin continued to stare at the floor in silence.

She pressed her face against his chest. "I think I feel you before."

Colin glanced at Sasha with a confused expression on his face. Sasha glanced back and shrugged his shoulders.

Evelyn and Rosa were silent.

"Speak!" Olga ordered Colin.

"What can I say? Yer thugs are pointin' guns in our faces."

Olga smiled at Colin. "I have heard your voice. You talk like pirate."

"If ye say so," Colin responded expressionless.

"Do I know you?" She paced around Colin as she whisked her hand along his body. "How? How would I know you? You are not Russian. I was never with English man."

Colin remained silent.

179

"Talk! Who are you?"

"Captain Limmerick."

Her eyebrows lowered. "Captain?"

"Aye."

"Captain of what?"

"Of me fishin' vessel."

She stepped up to him and took his large hands in hers. "Fisherman? You are fisherman?"

"Aye, a simple man, so I am. Please lower yer guns. We are simple people."

She glared at the other three time travelers. "Who are they?"

"This is me wife," Colin gestured at Evelyn, "And, they are me friends. They are also married," Colin glanced at Rosa.

Olga kissed her lips and rolled her eyes. She paused and paced a bit. She blurted to the navel officers to lower their guns. She walked to Evelyn. "This man is your husband?"

Evelyn struggled to respond. "Yes."

Olga looked at Colin. "This lady is your wife?"

"Aye."

"How long you married to her?"

Colin's eyes shifted a bit "Twenty years!"

Olga glared at Rosa and Sasha. "You two are married?"

Sasha tried to grin. "Da."

"How you marry English lady if you are Russian?"

"I see her walking. Da, walking along Nefsky Prospect. She is tourist," Sasha responded.

Olga pursed her lips. "Tourist?" She paused. "English lady is tourist in Petersburg?"

"Sasha forced a faint chuckle. "I find many tourists along Nefsky Prospect."

Olga's eyes widened. "You do? How is this possible?" Olga stared at Rosa. "You are English lady, you leave your rose gardens to see Nefsky Prospect?"

Rosa glanced at Sasha. Her hands dripped with sweat. "Of course, who wouldn't?"

Olga looked at the Soviet naval officers. She made orders in Russian. The officers held their guns up and pressed them against the time traveler's bodies. Evelyn winched with fear. Rosa tried to keep her panicked state under control. They brought the time travelers outside the submarine and led them to a military jeep. The roads were sparse with vehicular activity.

Colin nudged Sasha in the arm. "Mate."

"Da."

"That's it, don't ye think?"

"What is it?"

"Us?"

Sasha nodded as he peered at the sparse traffic in the bumpy jeep. "Da."

Rosa nudged Colin in the shoulder. "Colin, I'm scared."

"So, ye should be, love."

"What did we say to put them off so much?" Rosa asked.

Sasha sighed with a facial expression of regret. "I turn this all bad for us. I am sorry to cost us our lives. Forgive me?"

"Never!" blurted Rosa. "I haven't a clue why they're so angry about, though."

Colin stared at the floor of the jeep. "They think we're spies. That's never gonna change. We're from Britain, and we're in Soviet Russia. I'm gettin' the feelin' this would've been unheard of in 1970. Sasha's Russian, hangin' about with a bunch of Brits, that really has them in an uproar. The cave lion? Who knows what's happened to it. Neanderthal? He could be dead for all we know. I'm just sorry, I've done this to yez."

Olga sat in the passenger seat of the jeep. She turned to the back of the jeep, where the time travelers sat. "Shut-up!"

# Chapter Nineteen

The four time travelers were led to a large *boxy-looking* building; they took the lift to the deepest level of the musty-smelling site. Colin and Sasha were taken to a dingy room with a contraption that resembled the same shape of a coffin only wider in diameter. It had a cover of class over it. Olga was accompanied with two Soviet guards. They were armed and unpleasant in their gestures. The two guards tied Colin's hair back and roughly removed their clothes. Colin and Sasha stood against the wall, naked. Their bare feet felt the dampness of the unswept linoleum floor. The two Soviet guards snorted some comments to Olga in Russian. She laughed. The two guards held their guns in front of the two time travelers.

Colin glanced at Sasha who stood beside him. Sasha spoke to the Olga in Russian. Olga approached the two men, her voice got louder and relentless in its tone. Sasha continued to speak to her, but it only made her more agitated.

She and the two guards left the room. Colin and Sasha were silent for a few seconds.

"Mate, what was said just now?" Colin asked.

"They will now torture us."

"Whatever for?"

"I am Russian and I am with three British. British is enemy to Russia, in this time," Sasha's head hung low as he stared at his naked feet. "Look," he sighed with despair. "I not know this world. We are fools for going to future."

"We can't do anythin' 'bout it now, can we?" Colin paused as he noticed the hairs on his body stand on end. "I'm scared, mate."

"Me too, Mr. Limmerick."

"What they gonna do to us?"

"That structure is called sensory deprivation tank." Sasha pointed to it.

"Huh?"

"This is our wonderful future to invent such terrible things."

"What is it?"

"They will put us in it and we will have masks on our faces so we can breathe. We will not be able to see anything. We will not be able to hear anything. We will not feel anything, or taste anything. We will be like dead men in coffin."

"We'll likely go berserk," Colin responded with lament in his tone.

"We will die first."

"Why did they leave?"

"To drink vodka."

"Celebration?"

"Da."

"Why are we naked?"

"After this, they will kick us outside in snow and watch us freeze to death. It is icing on cake, da?"

Colin and Sasha walked to the contraption; they gazed at it for a few seconds in silence, as if they were in a trance.

"They call this thing, tank. We both will go inside it at same time. We will wear masks. Olga say it will be filled with water. It will be hot, not boiling hot, but hot. Water will have salt in it. She say Epsom salt. Lots of it. We will breathe." Sasha paused in silence as he continued to gaze at the contraption. "We, we will be okay, I think."

"Don't like it, not at all. Is there another poison we can choose?" Colin asked, while he sat on the contraption to lift his feet from the cold floor.

"Da, poison."

Olga and the two guards entered the room. The guards opened the tank glass cover. It was already filled with salty water. Olga grinned like a fiend. "Get in!"

Sasha glanced at her. He then glanced at Colin and took his time to respond. "Can I have smoke first?"

Her facial expression appeared irritated. She looked at her two guards who were armed and ready to fire at any moment's notice.

"Get in!" She ordered with a more abrasive tone.

Sasha stepped on his tiptoes. "Your floor is dirty like your people, I spit on you." He spat on the floor.

"Mate! Have ye gone mad?" Colin gasped, almost choking on his own saliva.

"You not remember us, do you?" Sasha asked Olga.

"Remember you?" She responded while she narrowed her eyes. She appeared confused. "From somewhere, maybe?"

"Look at him," Sasha pointed at Colin. "Is he not your desire?"

She looked at Colin and grinned. "He is. I remember something about him but not all."

"How you not remember him? Look at his naked body, don't you want?" Sasha tried to sell.

Colin glanced at Sasha. "Mate, have ye gone mad?"

"You torture him, he will not able to be your sex slave, da?" Sasha suggested.

Her eyes widened. "Sex slave?"

One of the guards yanked on Olga's arm and pushed her into the wall. He spoke to her in Russian, with an escalating volume in his voice. Then he smacked her a few times until her nose bled. She was pasted against the wall, where she responded to the harsh treatment in Russian and also raised her voice.

Colin shut his eyes and turned away.

"I want my cigarette!" Sasha yelped.

Olga took a few unsteady steps toward Sasha. The blood from her nose dripped onto the floor. "You will get nothing! Get into the tank!"

The two guards forced the mask over Sasha's face and recklessly struggled to dip him into the tank. Colin stood on the cold cement floor, naked. He stepped toward Sasha who was partially amerced in the tank. He gasped with anguish and immediately kicked one of the guns out of guard's hands. The guard lost his balance and plunged into the tank. Olga screamed. Colin positioned the gun and aimed.

Sasha tore the mask off his face as he climbed out of the tank. He grabbed Olga by the hair. "Mr. Limmerick! Shoot her!"

Colin continued to aim the gun, but did not flinch.

"Mr. Limmerick! Shoot her! Do it!"

Olga screamed while she tried to free herself from Sasha.

"Do it!"

Colin fired the gun. The guard fell to the floor. Olga got loose of Sasha.

Sasha lunged for Olga. "We must use her for ransom! Don't let her get away!"

She ran for the exit, Sasha took the other dead guard's gun and shot her in the shoulder. She fell to the floor. Sasha picked her up and carried her to the tank.

"What ye doin'?" Colin asked.

Sasha dropped her into the tank. "Enough of this woman. She must die for good."

"No, mate! I thought ye wanted her for ransom?" Colin jumped into the tank to try to fish her out.

"What are you doing? Get out of tank, now!"

"Me head is well above it." Colin carried her out of the tank. She was gasping for oxygen.

Sasha pulled her away from Colin, where she dropped onto the floor.

"Mate, we need to escape with her."

"We are naked. This will be difficult."

There's two guards lying on the floor. We can use their clothes."

Sasha went to the exit. "This door is locked. You open it. We will now escape, da?"

She grimaced at him and was silent.

"Unlock door, now!" Sasha yelled as he rattled at the doorknob.

She was still silent.

"Mr. Limmerick, she is no good for ransom, even. We must throw her in tank."

Colin appeared a bit panicked and exhausted. "I don't think so, mate."

"Why you say this?" Sasha trembled with anger. "She is not worthy of us. She must die, da?"

"I don't think I can do that, mate."

Sasha's eyes widened with disgust. They heard Soviet guards walk the halls on the other side of the door.

"If and when they find us here, *naked –it*, they will toss us in tank without second thought. Mr. Limmerick, you just shoot down Soviet guard. You can help me throw her into tank, da?"

Sasha heard the voices of several Soviet guards. "I hear them talking, they want British spies. They are looking for Olga and us. They will find us in minutes, seconds, Mr. Limmerick."

Colin dropped the gun to the floor. "I'm a fisherman. An ordinary man. I can't go about doin' this no more. I fancy researchin' *Megaloceros giganteous*. That's all, mate."

"Mr. Limmerick, forget your life as fisherman. We are here now, in 1970 Soviet Russia. Help me throw her in tank!"

"Perhaps she can change, mate. We can bring her back to our time. She can learn to be a lady, ye think?"

Sasha shook with anger. He punched the door with his fist. "Nyet!" Sasha grabbed Olga and tossed her over his shoulder. She kicked and screamed. Her arms wrapped around his neck, and tightened her grip.

Sasha gasped as he carried her to the tank. He coughed and choked. She firmed up her grip around his neck even more.

Colin ran to her and tore her off Sasha's shoulder. He shook her up and threw her to the wall. "What ye doin'?"

She squinted her eyes at him. "I hate you!"

"I just spared yer life, ye bitch!"

She laughed. "Thank-you for sparing my life. You spared nothing. I don't need you to spare my life, I can spare my own."

The door swung opened and three Soviet guards stormed in aiming their guns. Olga stood in the middle of the two naked men. Olga was silent. Sasha blurted to the guards in Russian that they were armed and if they didn't get some clothes to wear, get reunited with their females and didn't get released that they would shoot Olga. There was silence. Colin took a few deep breaths, with a sensation of fake relief.

One of the Soviet guards glared at Olga, he turned to Sasha and expressed that he didn't care what happened to Olga. Colin appeared less tense and even wore a semi smile on his face. Sasha's smirk dissipated. He glanced at Colin.

"Mr. Limmerick," Sasha's voice was hoarse, where he could barely get the words out.

"Mr. Limmerick."

Colin tugged on Olga's arm. "Now what, wench?"

She glared at him. "Now what? You will be in that tank shortly, that's what."

"Huh?"

"Mr. Limmerick, just stop it. These men, they not care what happens to Olga. They want us in tank as soon as possible," Sasha said almost choking on his words.

The men demanded they hand Olga over to them or they would force them into the tank without masks. Colin didn't know what was being said, his heavy breathing started up again. One of the armed Soviet guards took hold of Olga. They kept their guns aimed at the two naked men. One of the guards glanced at Sasha. He demanded

Sasha in the tank. Sasha stared at the floor in silence for a few seconds.

"What's happenin'?" Colin panicked.

The guards forced a mask over Sasha's face. Sasha stepped into the tank. Colin watched Sasha appear lifeless in the tank. He felt a rush of panic run through his body but he tried not to display it. Olga looked at Colin and gestured that it was his turn.

Colin glanced at the tank. He gingerly dipped one leg into the water. One of the guards placed a mask over Colin's face and forced him to lie into the tank at gunpoint.

Colin and Sasha saw nothing, heard nothing, felt nothing. They were in a vegetative state of nothingness.

***

Rosa and Evelyn were placed in a confining room without windows. Evelyn sat on the floor as she watched Rosa pace.

"What are you thinking?" Evelyn asked.

"We've got to leave this imprisonment, that's what I'm thinking."

Evelyn slowly stood up. "I think I'll die here just from the lack of furniture and ill-kept conditions. This place doesn't appear very clean. I don't know if you've noticed."

Rosa stopped pacing. "Clean?"

"I think I saw a mouse run along the baseboards as they were bringing us to this room."

Rosa's eyes widened. "Baseboards? What baseboards?"

Evelyn tried to remain calm. "If there weren't any baseboards, then what did I see?"

Rosa continued to pace. "Filth! Sludge! You saw filth and sludge, Chancellor Gordon!"

"Goodness. How did we wind up here?"

Rosa rubbed her hands over her tired eyes. "Sasha."

188

"Surely, you can't put this blame all on the doctor, Miss Emanuel."

"Yes, I can. He creates inferior time travel machines. He practices quackery."

"Good God! Do you realize what you just implied?"

Rosa paced the room. "Just be quiet for now, I need to think things through. I have to think of a way to get us out of here."

Evelyn stood straight and gave Rosa a strong stare. "Young woman, have you forgotten who I am?"

Rosa gazed at the ceiling. "I know you're the chancellor of the university."

Evelyn folded her arms in front of her. "Then, don't forget."

"Excuse me, but we're in a life-threatening situation. I'm not at my best right now, forgive me." Rosa continued to stare at the ceiling.

The chancellor walked beside Rosa. "What on earth are you looking at?"

"This ceiling seems to have a trap door of some kind. We either remain here and wait for their death sentence or we try to escape."

"Yes, we must escape but I don't see how we can reach that trap door. How would we get up there?"

"Without Colin and Sasha, this will be tricky."

"Speaking of Colin and the doctor, I'm worried."

Rosa tried to hold back her tears. "I don't want to think about them right now, or I'll be paralyzed."

Evelyn scanned the room. "This room has nothing. It hasn't any furniture, or windows. What can we do?"

"But, it has a trap door on the ceiling. It's our only hope."

"Good God!"

"Bend your knees, so I can sit on your shoulders. I'll have to use my skirt and tie a knot to whack the trap door opened. Hopefully it isn't locked," Rosa said as she unfascine her skirt hooks.

189

Evelyn watched Rosa's skirt fall to the floor. "Good God!"

"Bend low enough so I can ride on your shoulders, Chancellor," Rosa ordered.

Evelyn reluctantly bent her knees. Rosa wrapped her legs around the chancellor's shoulders.

"Ouch! This is very painful. Maybe you're not as light as a feather as you may think."

"Now, stand up, but do it slowly," Rosa instructed.

Rosa was still far below the trap door. She held her skirt, which was twisted into a long rope-like shape with a knot at the end of it. The chancellor winched with discomfort. Rosa stretched her torso as far as it would go and she whacked her knotted skirt at the trap door several times.

"Hurry up! I don't think I can keep you on my shoulders much longer. I feel like I'm going to collapse."

Rosa gave it one hard whack and heard a latching sound. The chancellor lowered her body to let Rosa off of her.

"I can't do this any more, its no use," Evelyn blurted out of breath.

Rosa held her twisted skirt in her hands, when suddenly that latching sound intensified and the trap door fell out of its hinges and crashed to the floor, just skinning the chancellor.

"It worked!" Rosa grinned.

"Now, how are we going to climb out of here?" The chancellor asked.

"I have to stand straight and balance myself on your shoulders," Rosa responded with a nervous jitter.

The chancellor's eyebrows lifted. "Excuse me?"

Rosa's eyes widened. "I will need your skirt as well."

"Pardon?"

"I'll tie both skirts firmly together. I can make a rope out them. I'll have to throw this *skirt-rope* through the opened passage, and hope it links onto something so I can climb up."

"I think your idea is absurd, but I have some hair pins that I can give you. We need to make a hook, so this *skirt-rope* can latch onto something."

Rosa grinned with relief. "I'm glad you're with me, Chancellor Gordon."

# Chapter Twenty

Sasha fell into his reality state when he realized he was sitting on a chair, still naked in a dimly lit room with the tank sitting in front of him. His eyes were wide opened. His hands slowly reached to his face to feel around. "No more mask?" He turned his head to notice Colin sitting on the chair beside him, also naked.

"Mr. Limmerick?"

Colin turned to Sasha. His eyes were glassy and he appeared dazed.

"Mr. Limmerick, you hear me or what?"

"I wish we had clothes on, it's gettin' rather chilly," Colin responded.

"Mr. Limmerick, we survive de-sensory tank, da?"

"I suppose so. Thought we was dead, in fact, I didn't think 'cause I couldn't."

"It was like death. We not know this because we couldn't, da?"

Colin forced a smile. "I suppose. It feels great to be alive, so it does, but I don't know for how long. We're still captive in Soviet Russia, I think."

"We must find our ladies and go from here."

"Aye. The time machine needs to get us back to our time. It's on the submarine or maybe dismantled for all we know."

"Nyet, I am not worried because they say they have much nuclear energy. We can go to 1911 with that. I would like to take some back with us."

"Nuclear energy?"

Rosa tried to stand up, while balancing on the chancellor's delicate shoulders. "I just don't want to fall and break my neck!" Rosa panted with angst and exhaustion.

"I'm holding onto your feet so they don't slip. I'm not the size of Colin, you know, this is killing me. I don't have the physical strength for this."

"It's not as if I weigh a ton, either. Colin always told me that I'm as light as a feather."

"I'm sure you definitely are, but when you're standing on my shoulders, I think otherwise."

Rosa almost stood straight, balanced on the chancellor's shoulders. Both women were wearing their corsets, where Rosa tried to lasso the tied skirts through the ceiling passage. She tried several times, where the hairpins at the end of the knotted part of the twisted skirts did not hook onto anything, Rosa almost fell off of the chancellor, but she managed to stay balanced. She tried to gain momentum with lasso gestures, and the knotted end of the twisted skirts managed to latch onto something on the floor above. Rosa immediately came down from the chancellor. The rope of skirts hung down from the ceiling. Rosa and the chancellor embraced each other with relief. Rosa unlaced her shoes and began to climb. The chancellor watched every move Rosa made. Rosa held the rope of skirts with her hands and latched her delicate legs upward. She hoisted her petite frame up and over through the opening and managed to get herself onto the next floor.

She peered down at the chancellor.

"Don't just stand there, take off your shoes and start climbing!"

"I hope I can. I've never done anything like this before."

"You wanted to be a time traveler."

***

The door swung opened, where Olga entered with one fully armed Soviet guard. She immediately fixed her eyes on the two naked time travelers sitting on chairs.

She grinned when she stared at Colin. "Stand up!"

Colin stood up. "Can we get our clothes back?"

"You speak when you are not spoken to? How dare you!" She stepped up to Colin and smacked him across the face with the back of her *Makarov*. Colin's lip bled.

She had a fixed stare at Colin. "My God."

Colin and Sasha glanced at each other.

"How can this be," Olga said focused on Colin.

"Can what be?" Colin asked.

"So sexy. I have not seen man so sexy before. How can this be?" She ran her tongue over her lips. "I must have you."

"Fetch me clothes, and we'll discuss yer admiration for me further."

"Clothes? Not yet!"

"I don't know what ye want from us. We've done nothin' to any of yez."

She turned her head to Sasha and pointed at him. "It's him!"

Sasha rolled his eyes. *"Shto?"*

"You!" She squinted her eyes when she looked at Sasha.

*"Shto?"*

"You are trader! You make KGB angry because you are trader!"

Olga pointed to Colin. "I will let you live because I want to feel you. I want to suck you. You will live."

She cackled and then she pointed to Sasha. "You will unfortunately have to die!"

Colin's eyes widened. "He did nothin' wrong! You can't do this! It's unethical!"

She laughed. "Unethical? You stupid people who embrace democracy are unethical. You do not give all people equal share!"

Sasha folded his arms in front of himself. "What you do to my Russia?"

"We'll try and help ye as much as we can but I don't think we can. Just tell us what ye need," Colin pleaded.

"Your friend is Russian. He continues to play stupid. In fact, all of you play stupid! He is trader! He must die for this!" She shouted.

She marched over to Sasha and had her guard crack his *Simonov SPP-1* machine gun over Sasha's head. Sasha fell to the ground, but he wasn't completely knocked out. Colin fell beside Sasha.

"This man's head is bleedin', I need a cloth or something to place pressure on the wound. If I was wearin' me clothes, I would use me shirt or something, but yer so against us wearin' anything, I don't know."

"You both will now be thrown outside in middle of Russian winter! Happy January!"

The Soviet guard grabbed Sasha and Colin and pushed them to the exit.

"You!" She shouted at Sasha. "You will die for being trader! You must be loyal to Brezhnev! He is your only God!

The two naked time travelers where pushed outside with the rifle pointing at their backs.

She chuckled. "You will stay out until you die, trader! The British one must stay out but not long enough to die!"

The two time travelers could here her cackle from outside. The heavy iron door shut.

The two men stood in deep snow. Their bare flesh burned from the intense cold temperatures.

Colin tried to jump. "Mate, we need to keep movin'!"

Sasha's head dripped blood in the snow. "Mr. Limmerick, I cannot do as you do. I am losing blood."

Colin tried to hold Sasha up. "Mate! Don't give up! We gotta get outta here, get our wenches, get back to the sub, and activate the time machine back to our time. Mate, we're going to over come this! Surely we will!"

Sasha's body was becoming limp - he slowly sank into the snow. "Mr. Limmerick, I have bleeding head. I not feel good."

Colin noticed Sasha was starting to sink into the snow. "Mate! No! Feck! No!" Colin took Sasha into his arms and threw him over his shoulder. "Mate, I'm gonna save ye! I won't let ye die, I promise!"

Colin's adrenalin got the best of him, where he scurried through the snow with Sasha on his shoulder.

***

Rosa and Evelyn were free from confinement. They both hid behind large cabinets to stay invisible from KGB officials as they walked by. They stayed low and tried not to make a sound. They no longer had their long skirts to lag them down. They whizzed past a window. Rosa noticed somebody running in the snow.

"Colin!" She yelped.

Evelyn ran back to the window. "Did you see Colin?"

The two women peered through the window.

"He's not wearing any clothes and he has Sasha hanging over his shoulder!" Rosa blurted.

Rosa took a longer look. "Sasha is bleeding? Did he die? Why is he so limp over Colin's shoulder?" Tears burst out of her.

Evelyn grabbed Rosa. She placed her hands over Rosa's mouth. "You must stay silent. If we get caught we will definitely die!"

"Our men need clothes. It's freezing out there," Evelyn suggested. "We have to be smart about this, Miss Emanuel."

"I saw blood! What happened?" Rosa's cry was so hard, she was difficult to understand.

"Shh! We have to move fast. We need to get into some kind of closet to fetch garments for Colin who is running around knee-deep in Russian snow!"

"And for Sasha?"

Evelyn's eyes partially closed. "I, I don't know."

They gingerly walked along a dingy Soviet hallway. A Soviet officer passed by at the far intersecting hallway. The two women stopped and remained still. The Soviet officer didn't see them and continued to walk on.

Rosa noticed a door. "What's this?"

"Hopefully it's a closet," Evelyn responded as she fiddled with the doorknob.

"It's locked. It's likely not a closet," Rosa said.

They came across an enclave, which appeared to be a small kitchen area. The two women noticed white linens, neatly folded on top of a rack. They grabbed them all and searched for a staircase or a lift. They heard footsteps approach them. There was a shadow of three men coming their way. They immediately crouched to the floor and covered themselves with two of the linens. They pretended to be an end table. Three Soviet officers walked past them. They were spitting with laughter at each other's Russian jokes. They walked past the women, hidden in linens, until one of the men scurried back and opened the refrigerator. He mumbled to himself in Russian and pulled out a jar of caviar and placed it on Rosa's back, thinking she was an end table. He called out to his cohorts, leaving the jar on top of Rosa and he pranced off.

The two women were silent for a few seconds, too terrified to even move.

"Chancellor, what do I do?" Rosa whispered.

"Do you think the coast is clear?"

"That man put a jar of food on my back, if I move, it will fall to the ground and make noise, not to mention the mess."

"Is it heavy?"

"No, but I don't want to bring attention to us. I'm so scared. Can you see if you can take it off me?"

"I'm too scared that someone will see me."

"Don't you think if we stay like this, someone will eventually realize that we're not furniture?"

Evelyn slowly sat on her knees, where the linen fell off of her. She noticed the caviar jar on Rosa's back where she immediately swiped it.

"Rosa slowly stood up. "Don't place that jar anywhere. It could come in handy."

"Do you like caviar?"

Rosa took a deep breath out of frustration. "No, we could use it as a weapon."

"I see."

They took the linens and found a lift. The chancellor pressed the button.

"Be prepared to run if a bunch of those goons exit this lift," Rosa cautioned.

"Throw that caviar jar at them."

"I think I'll save it for a much rainier day than this," Rosa said clutching the jar in her hands.

The lift reached their floor. The door slid opened – nobody was there. Rosa and Evelyn glanced at each other with relief. They huddled onto the lift and made it to the ground floor. The door slid opened, nobody was there. Rosa held the jar of caviar above her head, just in case. They dashed to what looked like an exit. They felt illiterate, where they couldn't read Russian signage. They made it outside. The snow was deep and the wind howled. They didn't see Colin or Sasha. They jumped through the snow, feeling the cold wetness run up to their knees. They cut through the blistering temperatures and made their way to the other side of the wall. Evelyn scanned everything in front of them until she noticed bloody snow.

"I see blood, you said you noticed that the doctor was bleeding when you looked through the window?"

Rosa squirmed when she saw the snow. "Oh, my God!"

"Stop the crying, you don't know what happened to Dr. Dimitrikov! You have to stop this!"

Rosa saw Colin staggering in the distance. She ran to him as fast as the deep snow would let her.

"Colin!" Please wrap yourself in these linens! It's all we could find!" Rosa called out.

Colin glanced at Rosa and Evelyn, holding Sasha in his arms. "I donno what to do. I haven't any boots. If I get frost-bight, it'll be it, ye know."

"Colin?" Rosa sniffled. "Colin, how's Sasha?"

Colin glanced at Sasha in his arms. "Love, I donno. I just donno. I feckin' donno anymore. I – I just donno."

Rosa placed her face to Sasha's heart. "Colin?"

"Aye, love."

"Colin, what happened?"

"These KGB people were torturin' us. I need boots, that's all I know. I've been bucked into frigid Atlantic waters before, but somehow I survived, love. Somehow I survived. I survived. Don't know how. Just don't know."

"Torture? That's why you haven't any clothes?" Evelyn commented.

"Colin? Is Sasha alive?" Rosa asked with tears streaming down her face.

"Lets see if we can leave the premises. I don't know for sure. I just don't know. I can't really say. I need me boots, that's for sure."

They noticed they were gated in. Colin sat Sasha, lifelessly, in the snow and he wrapped one of the linens around his waste. His feet felt like blocks of ice, so he continued to move, to build up body heat.

"Over there, perhaps, we could climb over that shorter end of the gate," Colin pointed.

"It looks dangerous," commented Evelyn.

"This entire episode is dangerous, Evelyn."

Rosa's eyes were fixed on Sasha. She watched Colin hoist Sasha over his shoulder. They fumbled through the snow and made it to the gate. They noticed two armed Soviet guards in long, grey coats, standing at the other wall. Colin took Rosa, and lifted her over the gate. She fell into a deep cushion of snow. Then he did the same with Evelyn.

"I'm gonna place Sasha over the gate, yez both need to be ready to carefully bring him to yer side," Colin instructed as he lifted Sasha over the gate.

Rosa and Evelyn worked up some body heat as they tried to carefully let Sasha onto the snow. Colin climbed over the gate. He took a few more linens and wrapped his feet with them. "I look ridiculous. I need me clothes."

"I'm so sorry, they did this to you," Evelyn said.

"I'm so sorry, whatever they did to Sasha," Rosa said.

"Look, we need to get out of their sight, now!" Colin cautioned.

They ran without looking back. Gunshots began to fly past them as they ran. They made it past a corner and ducked into a store.

Colin looked at a young woman, perhaps in her early twenties, who apparently worked at the shop. "Um, do ye understand English?" Colin asked.

She stared at Colin's odd style of dress. *"Nyet, ya nye pan-ni-ma-yu."* She shook her head meaning *no*.

Colin glanced at Rosa and Evelyn. "Uh, um, okay, um, I need clothes. Do ye know where I can buy some?"

*"Ya nye pan-ni-ma-yu."*

"I don't understand how we're going to get anywhere in this country," Evelyn snorted.

"We have to try. "Colin, can you sit Sasha down on that chair. I want to see if he's still with us," Rosa asked timidly.

The young female shopkeeper stood beside Colin. She touched his stomach to test how cold he was. She looked up at him and smiled. She left.

Sasha sat, lifelessly, in the chair. Rosa placed her ear to his chest. She gasped. "Oh!"

Evelyn placed her hand on Sasha's face. "He is breathing," she said.

"He's breathing? Thankfully. I thought he was dead," Rosa sighed with relief.

The young shopkeeper handed Colin a pile of men's clothes.

Colin smiled at her and recklessly forced a smaller size of trousers on. He slipped on a sweater and gave the young woman a kiss on the cheek. The chancellor still had some currency buttoned in her pocket. She paid the young women with British money.

Colin placed a snug pair of boots on his feet. He looked at Rosa and took her into his arms.

"These KGB people were terribly upset with Sasha bein' Russian 'n travelin' with British people, who are supposed to be enemies to this Soviet regime, I suppose."

Rosa glanced at the young, female shopkeeper. "She doesn't understand a word we're saying, does she?"

"I don't think so, love. Lets get some clothes on Sasha, I'm hopin' he don't have hypothermia."

"We can save Sasha. Hopefully he doesn't have hypothermia. We need to warm this man up," Rosa instilled.

"Do you think those Soviet people would be searching the streets for us?" Evelyn asked. "I'm getting anguishes to leave Saint Petersburg."

Rosa and Evelyn dressed Sasha. He moved. Rosa smiled. He moved again.

"Sasha we need to return to the submarine, so you can get us back to 1911," Rosa said. "We can see Sasha's doctor friend in 1911. He may need some stitches on his head."

"I could likely activate the time machine if it's still able, but no guarantees to where we'll end up," Colin said.

"Even when Sasha activates the time machine, there's still no guarantees," Rosa commented.

"We just need to look in the direction of The Baltic Sea, I don't think that should be a problem," Colin said.

"I think it's that direction," Rosa pointed. "There's signs that look like they might be pointing to The Baltic Sea, but I don't know because everything is in Russian."

"Good God, I haven't a clue," Evelyn blurted in a state of confusion.

# Chapter Twenty-One

They slid along Saint Petersburg's slushy sidewalks.

"We need to pick up the pace. Those Soviet goons are likely scoutin' the area in search of us, don't ye think?" Colin cautioned.

They turned the corner and saw the harbor before them. Rosa grinned. "I knew it was close by!"

"Shh, love, someone could hear ye speakin' English, which automatically makes us spies to these people. I'd keep everythin quiet. Try to pretend yer Russian," Colin suggested.

Rosa glared at him. "How do I do that?"

"I donno, just don't act foreign."

She peered at him.

"Alright, then, just act like ye know yer away 'round here."

They stood by the peer and stared. The submarine was in the distance.

"Well, there's the submarine, so how do we reach it?" Evelyn asked.

"We need a lifeboat, that's all, but I'd have to ask permission. Just don't speak Russian. Don't know how I'm gonna do this," Colin responded.

"Look, we don't have a lot of time. Even if we have to just take a lifeboat, we'll do it. What happened to the one that initially belonged to the submarine?" Rosa asked.

"I'm not seein' it," Colin answered as he scanned the harbor. He repositioned Sasha over his shoulder. "The minute they realize we're British, they'd automatically shoot at us, dear sweet Jesus, what shall we do?"

Rosa glanced at Sasha. "I don't care what we have to do to get a lifeboat to that submarine, we have to pull through for Sasha. He needs to see a doctor."

Colin gently laid Sasha onto a bench that over looked the pier. He noticed three men, who may have even been fisherman. Colin meandered his way to them. He noticed that one of them just walked off the gangway of his boat. His boat had a lifeboat. Colin stood in front of these men. He smiled at them. They spewed a few sentences to him in Russian. Colin pretended he understood by nodding his head with a smile. Colin was considerably bigger than them. He stepped closer; they stepped away from him. Colin stepped closer to them, so close, that he was in their personal space. They gave Colin a bold stare, however he didn't back off. They raised their voices at him and they appeared alarmed by his presence. One of the men took hold of Colin's long hair and gave a slight tug. They spoke with laughter about the length of Colin's hair, Colin pulled away, where he had some idea of what they were saying.

*"Kto tbi?"* Who are you? One of the more stout men asked.

Colin grinned but was silent.

*"Kto tbi?"* The stout man asked again.

Colin forced a chuckle and pointed to the lifeboat.

The Russian fisherman appeared confused, where they just spoke amongst themselves.

Colin forced a fake chuckle. "Um…um…uh."

The stout man stared at Colin. *"Kto tbi?"*

Colin grabbed the stout man and socked him in the face several times until he fell unconscious. The other two men ran off. Colin stood still for a few seconds. He examined his surroundings. He didn't really notice anyone close enough to cause any trouble. He immediately hopped onto the gangway of that man's boat and took the lifeboat and brought it to his cohorts.

"Colin! What are you doing?" Rosa blurted.

"I fetched us a lifeboat like I said I would."

"No, Colin! Can we take that man's boat instead? I'd much rather be on a boat than a lifeboat."

"Ye want me to steal someone's fishin' vessel?"

"Yes!"

"Oh, shite!" He mumbled under his teeth. He took Sasha and placed him over his shoulder. "I'll get all of yez onto the boat. Rosa, Evelyn and Colin, with Sasha over his shoulder entered the fishing boat.

They entered the gangway. Colin made his way to the wheelhouse and stared into space with a deflated feeling. "Good lord, how primitive this is, this is our future?"

Rosa and Evelyn sat in the galley with Sasha slumped over a chair. Sasha's eyes were opened. Evelyn glanced at Rosa. "What's taking Colin so long to get this vessel started?"

"I don't know. Maybe all the instructions are in Russian."

"A fishing boat would have instructions?"

"How should I know?"

There was a jolt, Rosa and Evelyn looked at each other with some relief on their faces. The boat started to move. The Arctic winds were strong. Colin directed the boat beside the submarine and they stopped.

Rosa glanced at Evelyn. "We don't have far to go."

Colin entered the galley. He placed Sasha over his shoulder. "I'm as close to the submarine as I can possibly go. I'll help both of yez to make that wee jump."

"Stop," Sasha mumbled softly.

Rosa smiled as she stood close to Sasha. "Sasha, are you alright?"

"Nyet."

"Sasha, how do you feel?"

"I feel terrible, what else?"

Colin's eyes widened. "Mate, ye was so limp, we kinda thought we lost ye at some point, ye know."

"I am hurt. My head, it hurts."

"Can ye walk, mate?" Colin gestured as if he was going to carry Sasha.

Sasha pushed Colin away. "Da! Da! Get away from me, Mr. Limmerick! Such terrible motion when you try to carry me. I feel like I will be sick."

Colin and Rosa stood back to watch Sasha upchuck on the floor of the galley.

Evelyn made her way to the deck. Rosa and Colin were silent as they watched Sasha create a large mound of bile on the floor of the galley.

Rosa's eyes were wide but she was silent. Colin glanced at Rosa, then at the mound of bile.

"Sure glad we aren't in *the Atlantic Mermaid* now. Better those mates' boat than mine, wouldn't ye think?"

Rosa was still silent as she gazed at Sasha.

"What?" Sasha said noticing her gaze. "I feel terrible, da?"

"We're as close to the submarine as I can get, I'll help our wenches onto it, but Sasha, I'll help ye onto the sub, if ye need it."

"I not want your help. I will do myself. I feel very sick that is all."

Colin helped the two women to the submarine. Colin took Sasha's arm and directed him onto the large vessel. The two women walked along the deck of the large vessel and noticed strange markings on the floor.

"Colin?" Rosa whimpered.

"Aye?"

"What's all this?"

"Don't know, really. Sasha would be able to answer it better than I.

Sasha made his way to the markings. "I think these could be markings left from time vortex. Maybe. I'm not sure."

"Time vortex markings?" Evelyn expressed.

"Don't quote me. Sasha would know this more."

Colin found the latch, leading to the inner submarine. They climbed down the ladder. It was quiet, not a being in sight. They gingerly walked to the next corridor, still hearing and seeing nobody.

"I'm terrified we're going to get caught either by those Soviets or by the cave lion," Rosa whispered with angst, not watching where she was going and slammed into a hard object. She stubbed her toe. Colin grabbed her and forcefully held his hand against her mouth.

"Whatever ye do, love, don't scream."

Evelyn noticed what Rosa hurt herself on. "My God, you found it, dear girl. You found it."

Rosa took a double take to realize it was the time machine. "Oh my! We found it!"

"Shh!" Gestured Evelyn. "We need to get out of here, now!"

"Mate," Colin glanced at Sasha. "Are ye up to gettin' this thing back in operation?"

"I think I could get us back to 1911," Sasha said as she stepped into the time machine. "It better take us to 1911, I feel too sick to go to other time."

Evelyn smiled at Sasha. "Lets keep our fingers crossed, doctor."

The four of them stepped into the time machine, all standing with their hands on the handles. Sasha still felt uncontrollable nausea, but he tried to focus on the control board. He set the dial above their heads to 1911. "I hope this works."

"I think we need to hurry things along, anyone including that ferocious feline could find us here," cautioned Evelyn.

"I am going as fast as it is possible, beautiful chancellor," Sasha responded.

Rosa stood at the control panel. She gazed at the panel with full concentration. "Sasha pull the lever down. Don't forget to pull the lever down, or we'll end up somewhere other than 1911."

Footsteps echoed beyond the corridor from where they were. "Shite! Mate! Step it up! I think Soviet mariners could be comin' from that direction," yelped Colin.

Rosa's delicate hands started to shake with nerves. "Alright, now the dial is asking what time period or year we want to travel to," she gave a nervous grin as she focused on the spool on the control panel. "Sasha, shouldn't we turn this dial to 1911?" she forced a smile, then she paused. "Sasha, I thought the dial above our heads already did that?

Sasha sighed with exhaustion and discomfort. "Da, we must do it again with spool. Twice will confirm time period, da?"

Colin rubbed his sweaty palms on his trousers. He turned his head to the opposite corridor, when he heard a rolling growl from the cave lion. He didn't yet see it, but its deep loud growl penetrated the corridor. "The cave lion is approaching from this opposite direction."

"Hurry!" urged Evelyn.

Rosa felt herself losing composure. "Yes, twice, Sasha this will make sure it will make the full journey through the time vortex, right?"

The dial above their heads began to spin. Evelyn held the wrought iron handles so tight that droplets of her sweat fell to the floor to form a puddle.

The sound of the echoing footsteps intensified. Colin looked at each corridor. The Soviet mariners entered their path; they were visible. They appeared surprised at the sight of the four time travelers inside the time machine. The large dial above their heads spun faster and faster.

Colin heard the cave lion's roar from behind him.

Sasha did not lift his head; he remained focused on the control panel. "It is done. Our destination is January 29, 1911 -- London, England. It is done!"

Rosa blurted with a tremble in her voice.

The large dial above their heads spun even faster, sweeping debris and clouds of dust into a muster. The machine started to sway. Colin kept his eyes on his surroundings. He noticed from the opposite hallway that the cave lion had appeared. It looked hungry, and it walked with a lope. It crouched and lunged at them. The machine rocked back and forth. It lifted from the ground and back down again. They heard several gunshots. The time machine lifted again. As the time machine lifted from the surface, it swayed more than usual. Hard banging sounds crashed and cracked almost deafening. Sasha held onto the handles, the machine spun centrifugal bouts of nausea through his throbbing head and stomach. Something of great strength tore Sasha's hands off the handles. Sasha yelped and fought whatever was forcing him off the machine. Colin knew something was happening on the time machine, but he couldn't see from all the blinding debris. Sasha felt gnarly fingers with barb-wired type hair on them force his hands off the handles.

"What is this?" Sasha blurted with amazement.

"Mate?" Colin called out to him.

"Sasha?" Rosa also called out. She could hear that something wrong was occurring on the time machine.

Colin perked his ears, where he could hear a struggle of some king was happening beside him. "Good God, what's goin' on here?"

"Sasha! Sasha? What's going on with this machine? Are you well?" Rosa called out, so terrified her voice cracked.

"Sasha!" She forced out again.

The chancellor felt the machine tilt almost on its side. She almost fell off, where she screamed her lungs out.

"Evelyn! Please hold on! This is the roughest ride I've ever been on!" Colin shouted.

Rosa screamed. "Sasha!"

Sasha struggled. The hairy being tore his hands off the handles. Sasha tried with every bit of strength he had to remain on the machine.

"Someone is pushing me off machine! I am too weak to fight!" Sasha screamed.

"Good God!" The chancellor cried out. "Who?"

"Monkey man, he is here on my machine!" Sasha blurted.

"What?" Colin blurted. "Neanderthal's here! Shite!"

209

Colin, Rosa, and Evelyn could hear Sasha struggle. They heard Sasha swearing in Russian. They heard the sounds of the Neanderthal grunting and groaning.

"Shite, mate! Ye gotta try to stay on! I can't really help ye, 'cause I can't really see ye, feck!" Colin.

The time machine swayed from one side to the other. It twirled faster; then, it spun slower. Colin's nausea was worse than ever. He tried not to vomit, but then he could no longer hold it in. The struggle between Sasha and Neanderthal continued. Sasha's injury had taken the best of him, where his strength was not his usual. Colin felt as if he was turning green. He spewed bile into a centrifugal spin of motion. Rosa's long hair caught the floating bile. Evelyn's face was suddenly covered with Colin's vomit.

Sasha yelled, winched, and shouted. His struggle continued until the strong prehistoric primate ripped his hands off the handles. Neanderthal tore at Sasha, where it linked its arms with Sasha's. They both fell off the machine.

The machine jetted upward. The two women screamed.

"Shite!" Colin blurted.

"Colin? What just happened?" Rosa pleaded.

"I donno! We won't know until this thing lands!"

"Sasha!" Rosa called. "Sasha!"

"Mate!"

"Doctor! Please answer!"

# Chapter Twenty-Two

Sasha's eyes opened. He moved his head to one side of the mossy ground to notice that Neanderthal lay beside him, knocked out from their fall from the time machine.

Sasha slowly sat up. His hand reached for the back of his head to notice that the bleeding had stopped. "This is good," he said to himself with a smile. He tried to stand up, but realized he had little energy. He staggered and even tumbled over, when he attempted to stand. He glimpsed at Neanderthal who appeared as if he were asleep.

Sasha rolled onto his front side, where he tried to prop himself up. He managed to stand. He realized how famished he was, where he noticed wild berries close to the ground. He grabbed a bunch and shovelled them into his mouth. He walked around, where he noticed more clusters of berries. He tore them off their thin branches to stuff them into his mouth. He stopped to take a few breaths, and then continued his feeding frenzy. He noticed a small lake beyond the meadow, where he knelt to it and cupped his hands to splash water over his face. He felt good enough to sing a Russian folk song to himself. Droplets of water fell from his face until he felt a strong presence stand behind him. He turned quickly to see Neanderthal standing before him.

"So, it is you, monkey man? You better understand that you are stuck with me until I find way to send us out of here."

Neanderthal shoved Sasha quite hard, where Sasha crashed to the ground. "I not know if you give me gesture like friend or like enemy. I cannot read you. Mr. Limmerick did not come with us. You must learn to be nice to me, even though I hate you."

Neanderthal grunted a few times, then he pulled some branches and moss together to create a bed. He laid on it and fell asleep. Sasha felt relieved.

"I hate that horrible creature. He will likely try to kill me because I know he hate me just as much." Sasha rummaged around the surrounding area, to gather twigs and branches. He scanned the surrounding landscape. "What time period is this? I so lost without time indicator dial."

***

Colin laid flat on the manicured lawn, with the chancellor on top of him. Rosa was on top of the chancellor.

"Good God!" Rosa squealed.

The chancellor's face was against Colin's. "Well, well this has been a gentle landing," she commented.

"Thankfully, yez both are alright."

Rosa fell off of the chancellor. "Go a head, Chancellor of the University! Make a spectacle of yourself, see if I care!"

"My word, you must be jealous," the chancellor snickered to herself. She looked around the grounds. "Are we where I think we are, Colin?"

Colin sat up to notice that they were on the university grounds in downtown London.

"Thankfully!" The chancellor blurted with glee.

Rosa walked around, almost in circles. "Colin?"

"Aye?"

"Colin? Where? Where is?" Rosa panicked.

"Aye, I know. I don't see mate anywhere."

"Colin, what happened? Where's Sasha?"

"Oh, is the doctor not with us?" The chancellor asked.

"He and Neanderthal must have fallen off the time machine. Shite!"

"Oh! What would that mean?" The chancellor asked playing dumb.

Rosa walked in front of the chancellor, kissing her teeth. "What would that mean, you ask? What do you think? We may never see him again. He could even be dead. Does this answer your stupid question?"

The chancellor buried herself in Colin's bicep. "Colin, get this terrible woman away from me. She's horrible!"

Colin sighed with frustration. "This is not the time to exchange unkindness. We need to get Sasha back with us."

"Colin, she's not for you! Stop wasting your time with her!" Shouted Rosa.

"It looks like we're back in our own time period. It must be 1911, don't ye think, ladies?" Colin tried to clarify.

"I must say it's nice to be back in England in 1911. I can smell the sweet aroma of our beautiful roses," the chancellor said.

"I think we need to see if the time machine's indicator can show us where Sasha and Neanderthal are," Colin suggested.

Rosa walked to the time machine and stepped in. "The time indicator is right here and it doesn't seem to be damaged," Rosa called out.

Colin broke away from the chancellor and stepped inside the time machine with Rosa. "I think ye need to turn the dial clockwise just one time. It should tell us where he is," Colin said.

Rosa turned the dial clockwise. She and Colin peered at the dial. "Colin, it says 1911. That's where we are. How can we get information that tells us where Sasha and Neanderthal fell off?"

"Shite. It may not even read such a thing as that, because they fell off."

"Now what do we do?" Rosa asked.

"Do we activate the time machine again?"

"How is that going to find them, Colin?"

Rosa examined Sasha's control board. She noticed a second dial. Not as large in diameter as the first dial they looked at. "Colin, here's another dial. What does it read?"

Colin turned it clockwise. Nothing happened. He turned it counter-clockwise. Nothing happened. Colin and Rosa looked at each other with an expression of despair on their faces.

The chancellor stepped into the time machine. "Colin, I'm sure there must be a way to gather this information of where the doctor is."

Colin turned the dial twice counter-clockwise. Numbers came up.

"Colin, what's it saying?" Rosa blurted in a panicked state.

"Twenty-eight?"

Rosa's face drooped. "Twenty-eight, what?"

"Twenty-eight...hmm. Not sure, really."

The time machine rumbled a few times. The dials made odd sounds. "It's reading 26000 B.C., I think," Colin said.

Rosa's mouth dropped. "They're in prehistoric times again, Colin," she tried to clear her throat. "Wait a minute. Isn't 26,000 B.C. twenty-eight thousand years ago?"

"Aye, it is, love," Colin responded with a smile on his face. "I'm gonna shut this thing down now."

"Why?"

He took her arm. "'Cause we gotta think this through, that's why."

"No, Colin, we waste too much time thinking things through. We must retrieve Sasha at once?"

"Colin is correct about this, Miss Emanuel," Evelyn added.

"He's not correct! We must get Sasha back here with us!"

"Well, Neanderthal is in his correct time period, but Sasha's not."

"Colin, don't you care about Sasha?"

214

"Definitely. We need to figure out how we're gonna bring him to us, don't ye think?"

"We need to set the dials to 26,000 B.C.! There's really nothing to it."

Colin lifted her over his shoulder and stepped off the time machine. "Please, love. We need to pray that Sasha survived his fall from the time machine. If we need to time-travel again, we'll surely do it."

"Excuse me?" The chancellor expressed.

"Aye. Ye heard what I said. Evelyn, I suggest ye stay back for this one. Rosa and I will go."

Evelyn squinted her eyes at Rosa. "Really?"

Rosa grinned at the chancellor.

"I will most certainly not allow you to ride this contraption with this woman, Colin!"

Colin glanced at her. "Ye gotta be kiddin' me. This is not a contraption. It's a time machine. "I think we should push off in the mornin'."

"Sasha can't spend the night in a prehistoric time period, Colin."

"Well, he's done it before."

"You were there. It's just him and Neanderthal."

"Neanderthal should protect him."

"Colin, Neanderthal and Sasha don't really get on well."

"Sasha don't really get on well with me, either."

"I don't like this at all. What if Neanderthal tries to---?"

"Tries to what?"

Rosa's eyes widened with anxiety and stress. "What if Neanderthal tries to eat Sasha?"

"My word!" The chancellor took her hanky to dab her face.

"Alright, love. Have it your way, we'll leave right now."

"Now?" The chancellor blurted.

Colin took Evelyn in his arms. "Ye really need to stay here, Evelyn. I'm sorry."

"I forbid you!"

"Ye can't do that 'cause our mate is in some prehistoric time just now and we really gotta fetch 'im, don't ye think?"

"He's a scientist of time travel, he should know what he's doing, one would think," Evelyn snapped.

"Evelyn, he's a physicist who thinks he's a scientist of time travel. He's not well versed with prehistory or any history for that matter. It's best Rosa and I fetch 'im immediately."

"Colin, I'm so worried. He had such a terrible time in Russia 1970. This has not been a positive experience for him. I wouldn't be able to sleep knowing he's somewhere in a prehistoric time with Neanderthal, who he strongly dislikes," Rosa commented.

"The only thing that concerns me, love, is I haven't a clue how to operate the time machine to get us precisely twenty-eight thousand years into the past. The machine is rarely precise."

Rosa sighed out of frustration. "Look, Colin, I'm here, I'm sure I could get us to where we need to be."

"Really? Then, why hadn't ye done this before when we landed in the time of the ancient Celts and just after The War of The Roses, hmm?"

She started to quiver. "I wasn't experienced enough then."

Colin chuckled and gave her an affectionate hug. "Is that so?"

The chancellor folded her arms in front of her and tapped her foot from frustration. "I really think you should sleep on this, Colin."

"No!" Rosa raised her voice. "No, we shouldn't!"

Colin took Evelyn's hand and brought it to his lips. "I'll be back shortly."

"How can you say that? Time travel does not entail a short time away," the chancellor whimpered.

"Well, I'm glad you're one of the few people who really understands how extensive time travel is."

"Yes, and because I do understand, I forbid you to go!"

Rosa shoved the chancellor. "Wait a minute who are you to forbid a grown man to go anywhere?"

"He is my suitor, therefore, I should have a say in this, shouldn't I?"

"Rosa, I'll meet ye here in an hour," Colin said.

"An hour? No! We must go now!"

"I've gotta get cleaned up, ye know, a change of clothes that are actually me own size would be grand. I think I smell bad too."

Rosa looked around with a hesitated response. "Oh."

The chancellor leaped to Colin and took his arm. "I'll help you scrub your back while you soak in the tub, my love."

"Oh, I see that you won't be meeting me here in an hour," Rosa whimpered.

He placed his hands on Rosa's shoulders. "Look, me word is me word, ye should know it by now, love."

Rosa watched Colin walk toward his flat with the chancellor glued to his arm. She made her way to her residence with her head hung low.

"Hello, Miss Emanuel," a tiny delicate said.

Rosa lifted her head to see Amoli stand before her. "Amoli Sharma."

"You appear so very sad. Is everything alright?"

"You mean with Colin, obviously."

"Well, yes."

"He's just fine. I have to be off soon, though. Too much to do."

"Did you just time travel?"

"Yes."

"What time period did you travel to?"

217

"We just came back from 1970."

"Dr. Dimitrikov must like that year very much. He keeps returning to it."

"Sasha didn't make it back," Rosa spewed out a hacking cry.

"Oh, no! I'm very sorry to hear that. Very sorry!"

"I'm terribly upset Sasha didn't come back with us. He's with Neanderthal stuck in Neanderthal's prehistoric time." She sniffled. "Sasha won't be able to cope in that kind of environment."

"At least he's not alone. He has Neanderthal."

"That's what we're afraid of."

Amoli's eyes widened with fear. "What do you mean?"

"Colin is afraid Neanderthal could eat Sasha."

Amoli's hands slapped over her face. "Oh no! Neanderthal wouldn't do that, would he?"

"We got to know Neanderthal better on this Arctic quest and we discovered Neanderthal can be just horrible at times. He almost killed Colin."

"Oh! How frightening! Where is Colin?"

Rosa's eyes shifted a bit. "Go to his flat. I think he's cleaning up. We're going to clean up and take the time machine to find Sasha."

"You're going to do this again?"

"What choice do we have? We must find Sasha. We won't rest until we do," Rosa stomped off. Amoli stood alone. She noticed the busy carriages whiz by and then she stared at the ground. "Poor Dr. Dimitrikov. I'm so very frightened for him." Amoli glanced at her reflection on a puddle on the road.

"Well hello."

She turned her head to notice Colin standing behind her. She gasped. "Colin!"

"So excited are yez? Don't remember the last time ye ever seemed so glad to me."

She jumped into his arms. "I'm glad to see you, yes I am. I just saw Miss Emanuel."

"Then, she told ye?"

She slowly pulled away from him. "Yes, she told me. I'm so very sorry about Dr. Dimitrikov."

"Well, I suppose we gotta go fetch 'im."

"Maybe I should come with you."

"Oh, yer father will surely hate me more than ever, then."

"I had a special bond with Neanderthal. I'm sure I could get him to calm down."

"Hopefully, all is well with Sasha 'n Neanderthal. I want so badly to believe all is well."

"Where's the chancellor of the university?"

"She went home. She was terribly exhausted. Poor woman. She had never time traveled before. She didn't know what she was getting' herself into."

"Are you still with her?"

Colin paused before he answered. He stared at the pavement and then looked at Amoli.

"I suppose I am." He glanced at the carriages passing by.

"Will she be on this next time travel quest?"

"Definitely not. She can't bear it. It was too much. This was a different quest. We traveled to Russia 1970. Russia will change its name, no doubt. Russia will change. Sasha won't know it anymore."

"How did Dr. Dimitrikov take all this?"

"Not well."

"He always appeared homesick. He really loves Russia."

"Homesick? I don't know about that, but he does somewhat hold respect for Russia, I suppose."

"I cannot imagine returning to India to discover that it changed, including its name."

"Aye, I would feel quite the same about Ireland. Maybe if Ireland ever breaks away from England, and I know in me own heart, it someday will. Who knows? It could be a very different place, includin' its name, don't ye think?"

Amoli sighed and smiled at him.

# Chapter Twenty-Three

Sasha tried to build a fire with dry twigs. Neanderthal knelt down to watch, when suddenly a flame emerged. The prehistoric prime mate stepped back with fear.

"What you do? Why you look like you will run? We must build fire to stay warm and to cook food."

Neanderthal grunted and gingerly sat beside Sasha. "Now, go catch something for us to cook on fire so we not starve to death, da?"

Neanderthal scratched his head and tried to gather what Sasha was telling him.

"Go catch food for us to cook on fire! Go!" Sasha pointed. He watched the ancient prime mate scamper off into the woods. Sasha felt his jacket pockets and pulled out a broken cigarette. "What I do now? My last cigarette and it is broken. I will die this way." Sasha stood up and gingerly walked the surrounding area. He paused to notice there was not a being in sight. "What is this? Crazy time period."

Neanderthal approached him with a slain animal of some kind in his arms. He laid a carcass of a young *Megaloceros giganteous* on the ground before Sasha.

Sasha examined it. "I know what you get."

Neanderthal grunted with excitement.

"You get Mr. Limmerick's favorite research specimen, da?"

*The Neanderthal* reacted as if he had just received justification from Sasha.

"Wait a minute," Sasha said as he walked around the carcass. "You not kill it yourself. It was already dead?"

Neanderthal's excitement dissipated.

"I cannot eat old meat. This is not good. You go kill something yourself. We need fresh meat."

*The Neanderthal* stepped back from Sasha. He appeared distraught.

Colin walked across the campus, behind the Natural History Building. Rosa awaited his return, dressed in a warmer coat. "It took you long enough, Colin."

"I'm here, aren't I?"

Rosa pulled the canvas tarp away from the time machine. They both stepped in and placed their hands on the handles.

Colin pulled the lever down. "It's runnin' now. What's next?" Colin asked with uneasiness in his voice.

Rosa turned the dial on the control board. "Now, you need to turn the bigger dial that's above our heads. You can reach it, I can't."

Colin turned the dial and then looked at the several numbers on the control board. "We need to program this to take us twenty-eight thousand years into the past. How we do that?"

Rosa's eyes widened. "I don't know."

"Ye don't?"

"I haven't a clue."

Colin studied the control board. Um, I think I should turn this spool that's off to the side, maybe?"

"Perhaps."

He turned the spool but it stuck at one set of numbers. He tried to force it along, but it didn't budge. *"Shite."*

"What's the matter?" She asked with a panicked gasp.

"It seems to be stuck. Do ye think it's broken?"

"Broken? It better not be."

The machine was activated, where it began to levitate from the ground. It made a loud sound. Wind encircled around them and carried debris, like a mini tornado.

"Colin!"

"Aye?"

"Don't force it!"

"What?"

"Don't force the dial. It's stuck for a reason."

"Ye think?"

"I do."

"Sweet Jesus!"

"It's stuck because that's where Sasha got bucked off the machine with Neanderthal. Those numbers displayed on the control board are showing the exact year they fell off. Colin, we need to go there, now!"

"I'm so very glad you didn't leave without me!" Amoli blurted as she positioned herself on the time machine.

"Lass! What ye doin'?" Colin asked surprised, as he helped her get a better grip onto the machine.

"Amoli Sharma, what are you doing here?" Rosa asked sternly.

The sound of the activated machine created a wind tunnel of loud noise.

"I'm here to help you find Dr. Dimitrikov. He's in good hands with Neanderthal, I know this for a fact!"

"No Amoli, he's likely not in good hands with Neanderthal. It's likely all is quite dreadful!" Rosa lashed at her.

The machine tipped turbulently into a spinning motion. It plunged into a vortex of time.

The time machine was tipped onto its side. Rosa tried to climb out of it. She noticed Amoli showed some movement.

"Keep moving, Amoli! I want to know that we are all alive!" Rosa blurted.

Amoli wiggled her way to Colin. She tapped him on the face. "Colin, please wake up!"

His eyes opened, where he tried to focus. "Amoli, I can't believe ye came out with us. Why?"

"You know why."

Rosa stood up to dust herself off. "Can we proceed to find Sasha?"

Colin pulled himself away from the time machine and helped Amoli up. She noticed Colin had a continuous gaze on her.

"Is something the matter, Colin?" She asked.

"I think ye got more beautiful," he smiled and blushed at the same time. "Is it possible?"

Amoli giggled.

Rosa rolled her eyes back. "At a time like this, you two are playing games. How absurd!"

"It's been such a long time, since we both have seen each other, that's all."

Rosa appeared anxious. "We must find Sasha, alive? Right?"

"Definitely. First, maybe we should search for any reminisce of them on the ground, footprints, a cigarette butt, somethin', ye know," Colin said.

Amoli went off to examine anything she could find on the ground.

Rosa stepped toward Colin. "Let me get this straight, Colin. You likely let the chancellor of the university into your bathtub, maybe? And, now you are twenty-eight thousand years in the past searching for your research partner and you're exchanging hanky-panky with the little Indian princess? Yes?"

Colin kneeled to the ground to rub his hands along the rough terrain. "Huh? What ye say, love?"

"You heard me."

Colin picked up a cigarette butt. "He's been here."

Rosa tore it from Colin's hand. "He's here! Which direction do we go, though?"

"Surely, we need ourselves more evidence, don't ye think?"

Rosa wore a crazed expression on her face. "We have to find more! No more talking, we must find Sasha!"

Amoli kicked debris around with her feet. She noticed a few strands of blond hair caught on a young fern. "Colin!"

"Did ye find something?"

She ran to Colin, holding the hair strands tightly in her hand. "Look!"

224

Rosa barged between them. "Let me look at it!" She held the blond hairs to the sun. "It has to be his!"

"Hopefully. We got two clues. We should look for one more."

Rosa extended her arm and pointed. "They went that way!"

"One more clue. We don't wanna be walking around in circles."

"You're ridiculous!"

"Am I?"

Amoli nudged Rosa. "This is why Colin will never take you back."

"Good reddens! He's your problem, now!"

"I cannot believe what I'm hearing out of you, Miss Emanuel. Have you lost your mind?"

Colin placed his hand on Amoli's shoulder. "Let her be. She's been through a great deal."

"So have you, I'm sure. Where did you go?"

"The future. We was on an Arctic quest at first."

"How exciting!" Amoli squealed.

"Not exciting at all. It was horrible! I'll never travel through time again!" Rosa blurted.

"Aye, ye will. Surely, ye will."

"Never!"

"Ye just traveled through time, now. We need to find Sasha." Colin started to search for more clues. He examined the scrub, and the grasses. He noticed a button from Sasha's jacket. "Clue, number three! We're good at this."

Amoli clapped her hands and Rosa turned away.

"Which direction shall be walk?"

"Follow me. I think I know how to get to him," Colin said.

Colin led Rosa and Amoli through muddy and soft ground. The relentless winds had Rosa tighten her scarf around her neck.

"Colin, where are you taking us? It's getting so dark. I just hate it here. I'm worried for Sasha," Rosa said, while she trotted to keep up with Colin's pace.

Colin's long hair blew over his face. He turned to Rosa. "Knowing Sasha, he purposely pulled buttons off his jacket to help guide us to him. I'm finding threads, his handkerchief, even cigarettes."

Amoli smiled. "I'm so glad. Hopefully, we will find him soon."

The sound of a drum echoed through the scrub. Colin perked his ears. "Here that, don't yez?"

"Someone is playing a drum?" Rosa questioned.

"It sounds like it," Colin responded. "Hopefully, Sasha is part of the drummin' serenade."

Rosa tried to smile. "Perhaps. Sasha just isn't the musical type. I think that drumming means he's in trouble."

"Maybe he's at a wedding," Amoli suggested.

"A Neanderthal wedding, Amoli?" Rosa responded sarcastically. "How absurd. We're twenty-eight thousand years in the past. I don't think our prehistoric predecessors had matrimonial ceremonies."

Colin casually slid his arm around Amoli's shoulder. "Anything's possible."

"Amoli appeared somewhat uncomfortable, where she gently pulled away from him. "I think we better continue."

The sound of drumming grew louder. Rosa's angst got the best of her, where she didn't seem to mind that her feet were sinking into muck. Her skirt dragged in the mud, which slowed her pace. They came to a cliff and looked beyond, to see a ceremony. There was a fire in the middle of several chanting beings. Rosa noticed Sasha was there, but he was tied up.

"Good God, Colin, do you see Sasha?" Rosa blurted.

"He's tied up? Neanderthal is there, but he's not doin' much, now, is he?"

"Why doesn't Neanderthal untie him?" Amoli asked.

Rosa shoved Amoli in the arm. "Because he's a prehistoric primate, that's why?"

"Oh."

Several male Neanderthals encircled Sasha with an eerie chant.

Sasha rolled his eyes back. "I demand cigarette before you kill me. You must give me that?"

The elder *Neanderthal* looked at Sasha, but did not respond. The drumming stopped. The elder stepped before Sasha and grunted a bit. He examined Sasha. Sasha chuckled to show his disrespect.

"Why's he doin' that for?" Colin blurted, while still in hiding.

"It's as if he wants them to kill him," Rosa responded.

The elder *Neanderthal* blurted something to their Neanderthal friend. They untied Sasha and formed a circle around him. Neanderthal handed Sasha a club.

"This is not cigarette. You not know what I say?"

Neanderthal also had a club.

Colin, Rosa, and Amoli, were still out of sight. "Are they challengin' mate to a duel? Feck this is."

"It's a duel!" Rosa blurted.

"What's a duel?" Amoli asked while she tugged on Colin's sleeve.

"They's challengin' mate to a fight."

"Really?"

"Colin, didn't you have a difficult time staying alive when in a scuffle with a Neanderthal?" Rosa asked in a panic.

"Aye."

"Colin, do something. Sasha will get crushed. Save him."

The circle of Neanderthals hollered and cheered for their relation. Sasha didn't appear frightened. He treated the club as if it were a sword and abruptly smacked *Neanderthal* several times on the head. The circle of prehistoric primates roared and cussed at Sasha. They watched *Neanderthal* drop to the ground.

"He's doin' fine, I'd say, love," Colin commented to Rosa.

Neanderthal, dazed and confused, got himself up and swung the club at Sasha, but Sasha was quick and light on his feet to dodge the blow.

Amoli clapped.

Colin took a strong hold of her wrists. "Lass! Ye can't bring attention to us, or we're dead, ye got that?"

"I'm sorry."

Neanderthal charged his club at Sasha but Sasha intersected it with his club, as he would if he had a sword in his hand. The club fell to the ground. Neanderthal fell to the ground to retrieve it, but Sasha grabbed it quick enough to toss it into the crowd. The Neanderthal-spectators griped and roared. Neanderthal no longer had a weapon. Sasha hacked a few sinister laughs. He circled around the grovelling beast and began to swing his club. The spectators let out high shrieked screams of panic.

"Colin?" Rosa said with little power in her voice.

"Aye."

"What is Sasha doing?"

"Donno, really. Likely the bloke has gone mad, don't ye think?"

"I think all those cigarettes he smokes have given him some kind of brain damage."

"Likely."

"Will Dr. Dimitrikov hurt Neanderthal?" Amoli asked.

"He bloody better not," Colin responded with uneasiness.

Sasha took his club and raised it over Neanderthal's head, while the prehistoric primate was still knelt to the ground.

"I was waiting for this moment, monkey-man. I want to show your friends how much I hate you!"

Colin ran out, past the crowd. He took the club from Sasha and tugged Sasha away from the spectators.

"Mr. Limmerick? What you do here?"

"What ye mean? Ye know we was gonna come for ye, right?"

"Colin, they're coming for us!" Rosa screamed.

Colin took Rosa and Amoli's hand and pulled them away.

"Try not to face them, just keep moving," Colin blurted.

"I know cave we can hide in!" Sasha suggested.

"Sasha! You're such an ass, sometimes! You got the entire clan in such an uproar! They won't stop hunting for us, that's for sure," Rosa blurted.

"What you want me do? Lay down and die for them?"

"Just hold yer tongue, mate! Keep movin', don't look back!"

Sasha led them to the cave he spoke of.

"Sasha, what makes you think they won't find us here?" Rosa asked.

"Mr. Limmerick will barricade opening, da?"

"With what, mate?"

"Great big boulders in this cave. Big strong beast like you can do this, I know."

"Really?"

Colin scanned the cave. He took smaller boulders, one by one and placed them to barricade the cave opening.

"Colin, this won't stop them, they're stronger than you?" Rosa panicked.

Amoli started to cry.

"Look, we need to get ourselves back to the time machine, that's all," Colin panted, as he placed boulders in the opening.

They heard grunting and hissing outside the cave.

"Oh God!" Amoli yelped.

"I'm not gonna let anythin' happen to yez."

"Colin, they're trying to get into the cave!" Rosa raised her voice.

Colin placed his hands on her shoulders and shook her a bit. "Of course they're tryin' to get into the cave! Feck!"

Rosa whimpered. "Do something, Colin. They're trying to get in."

"Aye! I feckin' know this! We've got Sasha's club, and we've got our modern intellect! What else do we need?"

"Luck," she sniffled.

Rosa looked at the barricade. Some of the boulders fell out of place and a long gnarly finger poked through. Rosa's eyes bulged. "Oh God!"

Colin raced to the finger and slammed his foot on it enough to break it. The prehistoric primate belched out a scream.

Sasha cackled a bit. "These monkey man not know how to say, *ouch* yet."

"He would've done that to me, if he had the chance," Colin said with a straight face.

"I hope that wasn't our friend's finger," Amoli commented.

"Who cares whose finger?" Sasha blurted.

Rosa tugged on Amoli's arm. "Are you out of your mind? That prehistoric being who came along on a free ride with us is no friend of ours! Do you know how many times he tried to kill Colin?"

"Oh."

"He's a prehistoric primate, what kind of comradery are you expecting?"

Amoli's eyes were wide and glassy with tears. "Neanderthal has experienced so much with us. I'm very fond of him. I think he is our friend."

Rosa's eyebrows lowered close to her eyes. "Oh, really?"

"I know Colin likes Neanderthal."

Colin forced a smile. "Like?"

Sasha crouched to the ground and sifted his jacket pockets for a cigarette. "I have no more. I will die right now."

"What?" Colin asked with an agitated tone.

"Cigarettes."

"Cigarettes, mate? I see."

"I have none. What I do?"

Colin shook his head with a slight chuckle. "Mate, how'd ye end up in this time period? Ye fell off the time-machine, did ye?"

"Miss Amoli's great monkey friend, push me off. He is evil. I hate him."

"Oh, I thought you fell off the time machine on purpose," Rosa said in a state of confusion.

Sasha sat crouched on the cold ground of the cave. He glared at Rosa and kissed his teeth.

"I still hear those scary sounds of those *Neanderthals* outside the cave," Amoli whispered.

"The more we speak, the more they'll hear us; the more they want to get at us. We should all just sit and not make a sound, eh?" Colin instilled.

Amoli touched the walls of the cave. "It's so cold in here. Are we in the Arctic?"

"Are we in Europe or the Arctic, Sasha?" Rosa asked while she sat herself on a rock.

"I not know. We could be in Russia for all I know."

"Shh…please, lets not speak," Colin repeated.

They were silent. Some time had passed. Amoli found herself pressed against the cave wall and asleep. Colin, Sasha and Rosa remained awake as they watched the cave turn black from the approaching night.

Amoli found herself in a deep shiver. Her eyes opened and she panicked when she could see nothing except blackness. She brought her hands to her face, where she could not see them.

"Well, it looks like our young lass fell asleep despite how froze she is," Colin commented.

"She must be in a deep sleep. I think she's snoring," Rosa commented. "How unfeminine of her."

Colin and Sasha glared at Rosa but remained silent.

Rosa leaned her back against the damp cave wall. She tried to sleep but couldn't. Colin sprawled himself on the uncomfortable cave floor. He stared at the stalactites above his head. His eyes were wide opened.

Sasha sat crouched in the corner and bruited about not having a cigarette to smoke.

Almost an hour had passed until Amoli awoke in a panicked state. "No!" she screamed.

"Lass, we're all here. It's night, now," Colin assured her.

"Colin, please, can I at least hold your hand? It's as if I lost my eyesight. It's so dark in here, now."

"I'll try to get to ye, but I also don't want to injure meself." He slowly and gingerly tried to crawl to her.

"Colin! Hurry up!"

Rosa kissed her teeth. "Would you stop making such a racket? You'll draw them back to us."

"Lass, try not to speak anymore, just make blowing sounds, so I know yer whereabouts."

His hands and knees felt everything beneath him. His large hands slowly made their way to her legs and thighs. "Lass, do ye feel me hands touchin' ye?"

"Yes, I feel better that you're close to me."

"Why is that, Amoli Sharma?" Rosa asked with a curt tone.

"I don't feel so alone and I'm so very cold. Maybe Colin could warm me up."

"Really?"

"Yes."

"Didn't you toss Colin away? Did you forget?" Rosa asked, bighting her lip.

Sasha had fallen asleep where he started to snore.

232

Amoli sighed out of frustration. "I didn't toss Colin away, Miss Emanuel. You're the one who tossed him away."

"Look, yez both gotta keep quiet. We don't need to discuss this."

Rosa stared at Sasha as he snored loudly. "Nothing seems to bother him."

Colin sat closer to Amoli. Amoli felt for Colin's hand and squeezed it.

"Colin, please warm me up. I'm so cold."

"I'll do the best I can."

She fell asleep into his arms.

Time passed and the sun started to rise.

Thin rays of light eventually seeped through the cave barricade. Amoli woke up, coughing profusely.

"Where are we?"

Colin woke up. "We're still in the cave. It must be dawn, already."

Rosa awoke. "I can't stop shivering. Is it ever cold in here."

Sasha remained in his dream state, in a deep snore.

"Alright then, I'll remove the barricade and we gotta make a break for the time- machine," said Colin as he started to remove the boulders.

Rosa shoved Sasha in the shoulder. "Wake up! We need to hurry. We are going to run to the time machine. Wake up!"

"Sasha woke up coughing. "What you want?"

"Lead us to the time-machine."

"We go, now?"

"Yes!"

Sasha slowly stood up. He brushed himself off and smiled at Colin. "Are you ready? We could be chased by monkey man and his clan, da?"

"I'll do what I can. We can't remain in this cave."

"Be ready for disaster, Mr. Limmerick."

"We only know disaster," Colin replied.

Colin removed the last boulder. He poked his head out and saw nothing but foliage. He heard bird and insect sounds, but he saw and heard nothing else. He crawled out of the cave and slowly stood up. He scanned his surroundings with vigil. He took a few deep breaths to ease himself from his fear. The four time travelers stepped out of the cave, wide-eyed and ready for anything. Sasha took the lead where he tried to lead them to the time machine. The stumbled as they cut through the dense scrub. Burrs as well as milkweed caught onto their closes. They continued their quest through clusters of tall coniferous-forested lands. They ducked under hanging vines of foliage and found themselves knee deep in muddy grasslands.

They continued their trek, until they caught glimpse of one of the Neanderthals through the trees.

"Colin, don't look behind you but I just saw a *Neanderthal!*" Rosa informed as she held her skirt up from the running, muck and sludge of the difficult terrain.

"Did ye?" He said, almost out of breath. He turned his head and caught a glimpse of a Neanderthal sounding its bone flute.

"Shite! The wanker did see us, I think. He's lettin' his mates know we're still here! Feck!"

"Oh God!" Rosa screamed.

"Keep runnin'!" Colin instilled.

"I can't keep with you! I'm so tired! I need to catch my breath!" Amoli wailed.

Colin went to her and threw her over his shoulder. He continued to run. "We can't stop, now! Run!"

Sasha couldn't stop coughing. "Why I do this?"

Rosa ignored him and continued to run. "My shoes are so caked in mud that I can barely move them!"

"Mate! Carry Rosa over your shoulders!" Colin suggested.

Sasha continued to cough. "Are you crazy?"

234

They heard several feet pound against the ground. They heard howls and yelling. They looked behind to realize fleets of Neanderthals were trailing behind them.

They came to a lake.

"Colin! What do we do?"

"Swim!"

"I can't swim," Rosa revealed.

"I can. I'll hold ye near me. Ye won't drown."

"I guess Neanderthals weren't good swimmers," Amoli commented as Colin held her and Rosa's hand. They entered the murky lake water.

Colin swam with each woman to the side of him. "They was ancient mariners. They'll likely out swim us."

Amoli pulled away from Colin. "It's alright, I used to swim in India. I can do this. Help Miss Emanuel. I'll be fine."

Sasha swam behind them. "I think they are now in water. They will kill us. Maybe drown us!"

"Shut up for now, mate. Keep swimming! Where the hell is the time machine? Feck!"

"When we finished with lake. It is behind trees. It is so close."

"We didn't get to where we was by swimming. Is there another way to do this?"

"Da, but it is long way. We now have monkey man's tribe after us."

Rosa gasped, every time a lake creature got in her way. "Are we almost there?"

"I can see the other side, don't worry yerself, love."

"*The Neanderthals* are getting really close to us!" Amoli yelped.

The time travelers noticed how the lake became shallow. They were approaching the other side. Long gnarly fingers crept up behind Colin. Overwhelming strength held his head under water.

"Good God!" Rosa blurted. "What's happening? Sasha, help!"

Colin fought with a *Neanderthal* under the murky lake water.

Sasha took Rosa's hand and continued to bring her to the other side of the lake.

Splashing, punching, dunking, thrusting, as well as other gestures of combat occurred under the water. Sasha, Rosa, and Amoli got to the other side. They knew Colin was situated in the lake where he could actually stand on the surface. Another *Neanderthal* approached, where both prehistoric primates tried to pull Colin to the bottom. His size got in the way of their plan. He stood up and punched the other *Neanderthal,* where it fell in the water, lifeless. Colin stood in the knee-deep water, where the other Neanderthal tripped him to make a grand splash back in. Colin splashed and struggled with the feisty young Neanderthal. It tried with all its strength to keep Colin's head under water.

"Sasha!"

"Da! I know!"

"I can't stand here and watch Colin under attack! Do something!"

"I do not have great muscles like Mr. Limmerick and I not have great strength of monkey men. So, I stand here and watch. That is good enough."

Rosa stood in front of Sasha and slapped his face.

"Ouch! Why you do that?"

"Help him!"

"What can I do?" His shoulders were shrugged.

"If you don't help Colin this instant. I swear Dr. Sasha Dimitrikov, I will never speak to you again."

Amoli grinned in the background.

Sasha removed his jacket. "Very good." He caressed Rosa's cheek. "I will do as you wish, beautiful lady."

Colin struggled in the water, splashing and wrestling with the relentless *Neanderthal.* He tried to stand up to take a few breaths, but the *Neanderthal* kept pulling him down. Sasha noticed a rock by the shoreline of the lake.

He picked it up and waded himself into the lake. He approached the violent chaos between the *Neanderthal* and Colin. The prehistoric beast had no inkling that Sasha was standing before him. Colin did get a glimpse as he was then pushed back into the water. *The Neanderthal* tried continuously to bring Colin to the bottom. It was obvious that this creature would stop at nothing. Sasha situated himself directly behind the beast. He was calm and approached the situation as routine. This *Neanderthal* was shorter and stockier than the one they had come to know. Sasha towered over him. Colin forcefully tried to stand up. Sasha raised the rock over the prehistoric prime mate's head. Colin noticed this, but continued his struggle. The rock came crashing over the Neanderthal's head. He instantly fell into the lake.

Sasha extended his hand to Colin. "Mr. Limmerick, take my hand, you must be very tired."

Colin was breathless with overwhelming fatigue. He stood up with Sasha's help. Rosa and Amoli stood at the beach area. Sasha held Colin's arm for support.

Sasha noticed more Neanderthals were still approaching them via the lake. Rosa and Amoli yelped. The four time travelers ran into the dense brush that overlooked the beach area.

Colin's fatigue slowed him down. "Yez all run a head. I can't catch me breath."

Rosa and Amoli took each of his arms.

"Colin! Don't back down now. We're so close to the time-machine," Rosa urged.

"Colin fell to his knees, panting for oxygen.

"Colin! You must get up. Those Neanderthals will destroy you!" Amoli pleaded.

"Mr. Limmerick! No time to catch your breath. We must go!" Sasha shouted as he gathered branches from the ground.

One of the *Neanderthals* forced itself on top of Colin. Rosa and Amoli threw rocks from the ground to try to disable the creature.

Sasha thrust a branch at the beast's face. The Neanderthal appeared agitated from Sasha. It tried to grab the branch but Sasha pulled it back and wacked the creature on the head. It grunted.

Colin stood up and thrust his foot in the prehistoric prime mate's chest, where it fell to the ground. Colin took Amoli and Rosa's hands and dashed into the trees. Sasha stood on guard with the branch in hand. He saw no other beings so he followed his cohorts.

The four time travelers cut through the dense scrub without looking behind them. They ran, jumped over fallen trees, slid down rugged slopes, waded and swam their way through small lakes. They came up to an area of dense mature trees.

"Well, there it is!" Sasha displayed.

"Where what is?" Rosa questioned.

"It is still in-tact. Step in, we will now go!"

Sasha peered down at the control panel for a matter of seconds.

Amoli smiled while she tried to catch her breath.

"Sasha?" Rosa gestured. "Sasha, what's taking so long?" She persisted to ask.

Colin glanced at the control panel. "Mate? Somethin' wrong?"

"It is dial. It is missing."

"What?" Rosa blurted.

Rosa heard a rustling in the bushes. "What's that?"

"It's coming from over there," Amoli pointed.

Their *Neanderthal* cohort appeared.

"No monkey man allowed on time machine. You are forbidden!" Sasha blurted.

"Wait, mate, it's as if he wants to convey somethin' to us," Colin said.

"I think Neanderthal wants to come back with us. Maybe he likes the twentieth century better," Amoli commented.

"Lass, I don't think we can do that. Our time period only suited him at me own expense. I couldn't carry on that way with a prehistoric prime mate in me possession. We came this way to bring him to his own time period. It's gotta be this way."

Neanderthal stood next to Colin. He gestured that he wanted to climb aboard the time machine.

"Ye can't come with us. Ye belong here. Twentieth century London isn't for ye."

The creature grunted and appeared anxious to step into the time machine.

Colin glanced at Amoli, Rosa, and then Sasha. "Mate, what we gonna do?"

"We leave him here! We cannot leave because we not have dial. We are stuck."

Neanderthal leaped up on the time-machine platform and placed his long gnarly fingers on the handles.

"Ye can't be doin' this. Sorry," Colin said as he tried to pry the beast's hands off the handles.

Neanderthal grunted at Colin. He then positioned himself toward the dense brush and vanished.

"I wonder what he's up to?" Rosa said.

"Ye think he's up to somethin'?"

"Most definitely."

"He is up to no good," Sasha blurted.

"Maybe we should look around to see if that dial is layin' around somewhere," Colin suggested.

They stepped off the time machine to scan the surrounding area.

Amoli kneeled crawled on her hands and knees in search of the dial. She ran her hands over the mossy ground but found nothing.

Rosa held her skirt up to step on the muddy ground. "I'm not finding anything. Sasha, what are we going to do? Does this mean we're stuck here?"

"It not mean anything. We must try to find dial, da?"

Then, Neanderthal re-appeared clutching the dial.

Colin stopped his search to gaze at the prehistoric being. "Feck me. What ye got there?"

"Colin? Neanderthal has the dial. Get it from him," Rosa whispered.

Colin stepped closer to Neanderthal, but he stepped back, as Colin got closer.

"Oh," Colin gestured and glanced at Sasha.

Sasha lunged at Neanderthal. "Give that to me!" Neanderthal backed away with a few distressful moans and ran away.

"Good job, Sasha," Rosa said with a sigh of frustration.

"Dr. Dimitrikov, I really think you need to learn some social skills. You wouldn't like if someone charged at you the way you just did with our friend," Amoli commented.

"Friend? Who is friend? Monkey man?"

"Why do you call him that? He is a Neanderthal."

"Who cares?"

"Amoli, don't waste your time with Dr. Dimitrikov," Rosa nudged her in the shoulder.

"Why?"

"Because he's an idiot."

"No name callin'. We now need to find Neanderthal in this vast land of nothingness and get that dial back, don't ye think?"

"Most definitely, but one of us would have to use psychology on him."

"Psychology on monkey man?"

Rosa stepped closer to Sasha. "Look, we're in trouble. We need that dial in order to enter that time vortex, yes?"

"Da, da."

240

"Then, stop acting like a child. You or Colin needs to ease up on Neanderthal. I am in favor of Colin because you're a Neanderthal yourself."

"Oh, how I wish I have cigarette right now."

"I think all that nicotine is eating away at your brain."

Colin stood behind Rosa and caressed her back. "Love, ease up, huh. I should be lookin' for our fine friend just now, shouldn't I?" Colin tipped his head at his cohorts and ventured off into the dense scrub.

"Will Colin be safe?" Amoli asked feeling a bit nervous.

"Of course not," Rosa responded. "Sasha, go with him. He shouldn't be alone."

Sasha sighed out of frustration and stomped off into the brush.

"How can we be safe?" Amoli asked.

"Well, we're with the time machine. If we remain on the platform, it may confuse the other *Neanderthals*. Or, it could even scare them off."

"What if it doesn't?"

"Well, then, it's time to say good-bye."

"Oh."

Colin and Sasha crouched low behind a large tree. They noticed a group of *Neanderthals* sitting with Neanderthal. They appeared to be mesmerized by Sasha's time dial.

Sasha sighed. "Now, what we do?"

"Yer wishin' ye could smoke just now, I'm wishin' I could get hammered with a bottle of whiskey."

"We cannot do either. Female *Neanderthals* don't even look good enough for -- *you know*."

Colin slowly turned his head to Sasha. "For what?"

*"You know."*

"What?"

Sasha nudged Colin in the arm. *"You know."*

Colin's eyes widened. "I think yer fecked in the head to even think that."

"If we had gun. We could shoot them all and then we would have time dial, da?"

"I think if we approach in combat, we'd likely end up badly beaten or dead."

"I think you are right for first time, Mr. Limmerick. We need gun."

"Well, we don't feckin' have a feckin' gun, ye feck head!"

"Maybe I have gun tucked away in time-machine. We should go back and look for it, da?"

"We'd be wastin' our bleedin' time. We need to settle this here 'n now."

Sasha tugged on Colin's jacket. "How you going to settle? Settle what, with those monkey man?"

Colin pulled away from him. "Look, Neanderthal knows us. He may comply in givin' it back to us."

"When has monkey man ever showed compliance? He is terrible!"

"Right, never. He's never been a good mate to any of us. He's rather boorish, likely cause he's a *Neanderthal.*"

"Excuses! Excuses!" Sasha blurted with his arms in the air.

"We gotta be kind to him. He's got his mates with him. We've gotta be careful. No losin' yer temper."

***

Rosa and Amoli sat beside the time machine. They heard constant sounds and calls from unfamiliar beings.

"Miss Emanuel, are you as frightened as I am?"

"Damn right I am."

"Oh," Amoli responded as if Rosa's answer was not what she was looking for.

"I trust Colin will retrieve that time dial and we will return to our time."

"I very much hope so. I keep thinking that something really awful will appear out of the bushes and then what?"

242

"Oh, come on, Amoli. We've experienced far worse. Are you forgetting the dungeons of 1487, those horrible disgusting Celts of 840 AD?"

"Oh, yes, how soon I forget."

"This is nothing."

"I suppose you're right."

They could feel a vibration that came up from the ground. Something heavy and large was approaching. The vibration intensified. Branches snapped with every second that past. Leaves rustled.

Rosa's eyes widened. "Good God! What's that?"

A large hoof appeared before them. Then, gigantic antlers peered through the branches.

"Oh, God!" Rosa blurted.

"What is it?" Amoli panicked.

*"Megaloceros giganteous?"*

"Colin's favorite?" Amoli yelped.

"Shh. Don't move, remain silent," Rosa urged in a whisper.

The beast stepped toward the two women. They were both sitting on the ground beside the time machine. The beast peered at the contraption. It appeared a bit standoffish, and then it gingerly lowered its head to take a sniff at the women.

It's large snout poked at both women's hair. It sniffed. It entangled its snout with their hair. It sniffed.

Amoli was so frightened; she began to shake. Rosa was like a statue. The prehistoric mammal nudged its enormous hoof at Amoli. It pulled away from her and focused more on the time machine. Amoli turned her head, slightly just to catch the beast in her peripheral vision. Rosa glanced at her with a stern look. The beast turned to the two women, where it noticed there was some movement. They remained still and silent.

*Megaloceros giganteous* made its way to the women again and rested its snout on Rosa's head.

Amoli noticed a rather large *Opilione* crawl beside her leg. She stressed in silence as she continued to watch it crawl onto her leg. Rosa still had the large snout of *Megaloceros giganteous* breath in her face. Its large wet tongue slobbered over her hair and face, but Rosa remained like a statue. Amoli watched the large arachnid crawl over her legs. It began to move up toward her breasts. It then, crawled inside the collar of her sari. She kept her eyes on *Megaloceros giganteous*. When the large mammal appeared a bit disinterested, she let out a large scream, jumped up and dashed into the brush. Rosa also tore away from her sitting position and followed Amoli. The large mammal jolted with anxiety and jumped up on its hind legs. It snorted and squealed with fury.

Amoli peeled through the dense forest to make sure the crawling mass of disgust was no longer hanging onto her clothes. Rosa followed, leaping over dense bushes and jumping over puddles.

"Amoli!" Rosa called to her.

"I can't look back, I must keep running!" Amoli responded in frenzy.

"*Megaloceros giganteous* can't chase after us in this dense forest! Why do you think it became extinct?"

Amoli slowed down; then came to a stop. "Oh."

Rosa tried to catch her breath. "Don't be so reactive around here. Those *Neanderthals* are relentless. Please, allow Colin and Sasha obtain the time dial."

"Oh, yes."

The two women found themselves in the midst of a dark, dense forest. They heard animal or bird sounds that weren't familiar to them.

Amoli's eyes widened. "What's that?"

"I don't know. We're twenty-eight thousand years in the past. We could meet up with anything."

"Oh yes."

"I feel as if we're turned around because I haven't got a clue of where Colin and Sasha would be right now," Rosa commented with some concern.

"Should we look for clues on the ground, then?"

"Oh, yes, perhaps. I don't know what good it would do. We really should return to the location of the time machine because at least that's where Colin and Sasha would definitely retreat to."

"Yes, most definitely," Amoli responded as she scanned their surroundings. "Um, which direction is the time machine?"

Rosa looked around. "Maybe that way. Or is it in that direction?" She walked a few steps forward. "I don't know."

"We're lost, aren't we?"

"Maybe. What made you scream?"

"A disgusting spider or I'm not really sure what it was."

"You screamed and brought us here because you saw a spider?"

"It was crawling all over me. You would have screamed as well, Miss Emanuel."

"I don't think I would've. Now we have to face up to the fact that we could be lost in the middle of a prehistoric forest because you saw a spider?"

Amoli began to whimper.

"Tears? There's no time for tears. We must find our way back to the time machine."

Amoli sniffled. "Which way do we go?"

"I don't know."

"Colin! Dr. Dimitrikov! Colin! Dr. Dimitrikov!" Amoli shouted.

Rosa shoved Amoli. "Shut-up!"

"Why?"

"Do you want a clan of *Neanderthals* to find us?"

"No."

"I swear I have no idea what Colin sees in you."

Amoli began to cry.

"I see some of the branches appear a bit broken, maybe the time machine is in that direction," Rosa suggested pointing in front of her.

"And, what if it's not in that direction?"

"Then, I suppose we need to pray."

Colin and Sasha scurried to the Neanderthal settlement. They kept themselves close to the ground. They noticed a small group of females sitting together and making something.

"Well, Mr. Limmerick here is your chance to test your charm with females that are not even human."

"They may not find me alluring at all. It's likely possible, don't ye think?"

Sasha shoved Colin in the arm. "Go! Test your beauty on them! Keep them occupied so I can get time dial."

"Don't be confrontational with them, or you'll blow this, ye understand?"

"Go!"

Colin crouched close to the ground. He sat beside the females and smiled at them. The females glared at him and continued to occupy themselves with making jewelry. Colin soon realized a cordial smile was not going to win them over, so he gently placed his hand over one of the female's hands. She stopped what she was doing and slowly raised her head to look at Colin. She was silent and still.

Colin brushed his fingers along her arm and continued to smile. One of the other females noticed Colin's tweed cap. She removed it and slowly placed it on her head. The other females were enamored by it. They ran their rough hands over his long hair and entangled their long gnarly fingers with it. They began to giggle and sit closer to him. The female who still wore his tweed cap on her head began to fiddle with the gold chain necklaces around his neck. The female *Neanderthals* gathered around his jewelry to admire the bright shiny gold pieces that hung around his neck. They examined him, touched him, and even fondled him. He continued to talk to himself silently with prayers. They also noticed the gold chain bracelets around his thick wrists. He took several deep breaths and tried to remain calm.

Sasha remained crouched to the ground. He noticed that the male *Neanderthals* noticed Colin with their females.

*"I not see time dial? Who has it?"* Sasha asked himself. He then saw their friend, Neanderthal tossing the time dial in the air, like a *Frisbee*. The other *Neanderthals* howled and screeched with glee as the time dial floated through the air.

"Such savages," Sasha whispered to himself. When the time dial glided through the air, Sasha jumped out of nowhere to snatch it; then he dashed into the brush. The male *Neanderthals* reacted by jumping up and down, screeching, and yelling in hysterics.

The female *Neanderthals* around Colin started to react. Their fingers entangled in Colin's hair, where they started pulling at it. Colin tried to pull away from them, but they were too enthralled with his hair. He saw Sasha disappear into the brush.

Colin slowly stood up after he pulled the females away from him. They tried to trip him to the ground. Their great strength overwhelmed him, where he found himself laying flat on his back. Several of them pressed themselves on him and tried to rip the chain necklaces and bracelets from his body. He pulled back and tried to stand up. They pressed their forceful bodies onto him. He tried with every bit of strength to stand up. They noticed the earring in one of his ears. They tugged on it, which caused his ear to bleed. He pushed himself upward, back on his feet. They pressed themselves onto him. His knees buckled a bit. They bore down on him and he was flat on his back again.

"Oh God!" He gasped. "If I knew yez all would fancy me gold this much, I would've removed it first."

They stopped and remained still. They were enamored with Colin's speech. They forced Colin to the ground. He could hear Sasha wailing in the background as the team of male *Neanderthals* chased after him. Colin rolled on the ground with two of the females. He tried to push against them and force them to the ground. It seemed almost impossible, for their strength was unbeatable. His hair had chunks of mud entangled in it. His face was scratched, bloody and bruised. He wrestled with the females until they started to tire. He tried to stand up but their firm grip around his legs wouldn't let up. Against his own conscience, he punched both of them to the ground until they drew blood. He smiled at them, tipped his cap and ran after Sasha.

Colin could see Sasha deep in the brush. "Mate! Mate! Slow down! I can barely keep up with ye!" Colin called out, while he tried to catch his breath.

Sasha continued to run with his time dial in hand, where he ran into Rosa. They both fell to the ground and into a mud puddle.

"Sasha," Rosa murmured underneath Sasha's torso.

"Da?"

"Get off me."

"Oh my God. I find Miss Rosa so beautiful in mud bath."

"Get off of me, please."

"It can be worse. What if Mr. Limmerick was on top of you?" He paused with a grin. "Maybe you want such big muscle boy on you, da?"

"Sasha, please, get off me."

He stood up and helped her up. She smiled at him as she brushed off the debris from her torn dress. "Hello, Sasha."

"You look so beautiful covered in mud. Da, so nice."

"Maybe I'll always wear mud, just for you."

He leaned toward her to kiss her check.

Colin ran to them and panted with exhaustion. "Where's Amoli?"

"She's crouched by that tree," Rosa responded.

Colin gazed at Amoli. "Why? Did something happen?"

"She's being Amoli Sharma, that's all," Rosa responded in a curt tone.

"I need to catch me breath, feelin' winded, so I am. Just had a wrestlin' scuffle with two females."

Sasha grinned. "You have sex with un-humans? Mr. Limmerick, you have sex with anything. They are ugly. Tell me, would you have sex with tree?"

Amoli lifted her head as she rested against a tree. "I heard that!"

Rosa glared at Amoli. "Why should you care anymore? You broke your engagement. Colin is no longer your business."

Colin walked to Amoli to help her up from the ground. "Come, lass, lets be off. There's no time to wait."

Amoli received his hand and stood up. "You slept with *Neanderthals?*"

"This is getting' outta hand, I'd say. The time machine is over there, not far. Lets get there!"

They briskly made their way through the rough prehistoric terrain. "Colin, I think you have sunk very low if you engaged in anything with those females!" Rosa blurted as they continued to make their way to the time machine.

Colin chuckled and shook his head. "It don't really matter if I explain me-self. Yer gonna believe what you wish."

They were vigilant and anxious to be on the time machine. They tore through the last bit of thick forest. The time machine was sighted, still untouched. They ran without looking back. They heard noises, anything from birds to the sounds of the *Neanderthal* clan. They kept running, leaping over brush, fallen logs, long grasses. Colin held his grip with Amoli and Sasha did the same with Rosa. Sasha and Rosa were in front of Colin and Amoli. Sasha grinned as they approached the time machine, with the time disk in hand. He noticed Neanderthal standing inside the time machine. Rosa's eyes widened.

Colin and Amoli were tailed behind them. Colin gasped when he noticed Neanderthal standing in the time machine. Amoli panicked.

Sasha and Rosa stopped running and stood outside the time machine.

Sasha glared at Neanderthal, who was propped up on the machine with his hands on the handles.

"Get out!"

Neanderthal ignored Sasha.

"Get out!"

Rosa tried to calm Sasha. "Sasha, please."

"You hear me! Get out of my machine! You stay here where you belong. Get out!"

"Sasha, please. If you persist, you run the risk of making matters worse," Rosa placed her hand on Sasha's shoulder.

"I can take this wild beast no more! He has caused so much disruption for us. I will not calm myself! I hate him!"

Amoli stood outside of the time machine with Colin beside her.

"Look, Dr. Dimitrikov, Neanderthal is starting to cry. Look what you did," Amoli said with empathy in her voice.

"I not care!"

"Sasha, please. At least don't raise your voice," Rosa insisted while stroking Sasha's arm.

"Don't care! I hate this thing!"

Neanderthal pouted hard and loud."

"I don't think this is very helpful, Dr. Dimitrikov. I don't think Neanderthal meant to take the time machine in the first place," Amoli added. "I suppose he made a mistake. Everyone makes mistakes."

"Are you kidding me, Miss Amoli? This is no mistake. I want him away from us, now!"

Colin sighed out of frustration.

"Does it bother you, Mr. Limmerick, that you had so much beatings from this *thing?*"

Colin paused. "Does it bother me? Aye, supposin' it does. However, ye need to understand we've be been dealin' with a prehistoric creature. Ye can't expect 'im to understand things the way we do."

"I see where this is going. I see it. I see it. You natural history people expect me to feel sorry for this *thing?*"

"Sasha, please keep your voice down," Rosa urged.

Sasha snapped away from Rosa. "Don't you tell me! Get off my time machine! Now!"

Neanderthal lunged at Sasha and forcefully pushed him into the mud.

Sasha struggled to pull himself out of the deep, moist mud. "That's it! You must pay for this, monkey man!"

Colin helped Sasha up. "Mate, mate, calm yerself. Yer gonna draw too much attention in this direction."

Neanderthal stepped off the time machine and tugged Sasha away from Colin. He lifted Sasha above his head with vengeance in his expression.

"What is this?" Sasha squealed.

Rosa and Amoli panicked and screamed.

Neanderthal threw Sasha to the ground. He was buried in in liquid mud.

Rosa screamed as she ran to Sasha's aid.

Neanderthal screeched and panicked. Colin stood in front of the excitable prime mate. "Mate, calm yer-self. Sasha is just a tad miffed 'is all. No worries."

Neanderthal yelped loudly and ignored Colin.

"What ye doin'?" Colin asked with some concern.

Neanderthal continued to howl and call.

Colin glanced at Rosa who was helping Sasha out of the mud. He then looked at Amoli, who appeared terrified.

"Um, *I-I* think Neanderthal is *c*-callin' his mates," Colin stumbled on his words.

The mayhem intensified. Rosa tried to wipe the caked mud away Sasha's eyes so he could have his vision. Amoli whimpered and panicked. They could hear the sounds of the Neanderthal clan approach them.

"What's are those noises?" Amoli asked.

"He's callin' his mates, I think, lass," Colin stepped closer to her. "He's callin' his mates, aye so he is." Colin could see them through the trees.

"Colin, what do we do?" Rosa asked with a desperate whimper.

Colin pulled Amoli onto the time machine. "Lets go!" He motioned to Sasha and Rosa. "Lets go!"

Sasha slipped his way onto the time machine, with Rosa by his side.

Sasha was entombed in mud, that he was almost undistinguishable. "I cannot touch anything, my hands have so much muck on them. Rosa!"

"What?"

The Neanderthals appeared from behind the trees.

"Rosa, listen to me. Do as I say you! Da?"

The Neanderthals dashed to their friend, who was making the commotion.

"Turn time dial forward. Do it five times. It should read twentieth century. It must read year 1900."

Rosa turned the dial forward five times. "I don't see 1900, Sasha! Now what?"

"You not in twentieth century yet. You are at end of nineteenth. Turn some more!"

"Oh, yes. I see it."

*"Da! Khorosho!* Press button beside it to hold it at 1900."

The Neanderthals started to climb onto the time machine.

"Colin, they're here with us! What do we do?" Amoli started to cry.

"Now, you must go to other smaller dial on other end of panel. You must go to number eleven. Done?"

"Done!" Rosa responded with sweat dripping off her face.

One of the older bigger *Neanderthals* grabbed Amoli and tore her off the time machine. "Colin!" She gasped. "No!"

"Shite! Wait, mate. Not yet!"

Colin jumped off the time machine and landed a punch across the *Neanderthal's* face. It grabbed Colin and thrust him to the ground. Amoli noticed a rock beside her foot. She grabbed it with both hands to realize it was too heavy to throw.

She watched Colin wallow in the mud with the prehistoric creature. She took the rock and brought it to the beast's head and smashed the rock onto its face. The *Neanderthal* fell lifelessly in the mud.

"Mr. Limmerick, you now must move big dial above to 1900 and then use spool on side. Move it eleven times. Do it! Come! Get back on time machine. Do it!"

Colin struggled to lift his body from the liquid mud. Other *Neanderthals* got in his way. He had little reserves but managed to take Amoli's hand and struggled to leap back on board the time machine. He turned the large dial above their heads. *The Neanderthals* tried to leap onto the time machine; it hovered above ground, where the movement made it difficult.

The time machine made a noise, Sasha sighed with relief when he heard that sound. The machine slightly lifted from the ground. It tilted a bit and lifted higher. Their friend, Neanderthal jumped on.

"Get off!" Sasha yelled.

Neanderthal shoved Sasha. Sasha shoved him back. Colin grabbed hold of Neanderthal's wrist. "It stops right there, shouldn't it?"

Neanderthal grinned at Colin with a guilty stare. Colin glared back at the prehistoric prime mate with sternness in his expression.

"Ye can no longer hang about with us. It's time ye be in yer own time, don't ye think?"

Neanderthal grunted and scowled at Colin. Outraged and sensing rejection, he punched Colin in the belly, enough to knock his wind out.

Rosa gasped and quickly grabbed hold of Colin's jacket sleeve. Colin's hands left the handles. "Don't let go or you'll get flicked into the time vortex! Breathe! Breathe!"

Colin gasped as he tried to catch his breath.

"Don't let go of handles, Mr. Limmerick. Stay on machine!"

The time machine lifted with a vortex of wind and debris mustered around it. Colin tried to tear Neanderthal's gnarly fingers away from the handles. Neanderthal resisted. He snorted he even slobbered on Colin.

"I'm knackered, cold, in pain and fed-up with yer *shite!* Get off this time machine ye wanker!" Colin blurted with a deep throaty voice. He managed to kick their prehistoric friend off the machine while the machine levitated further from the ground.

"Oh God!" Amoli screamed.

Rosa was silent.

The time machine plunged into the vortex of time.

# Chapter Twenty-Four

The time machine, tipped on its side, smoldered a little with the four time travelers encased in it. Amoli's eyes were opened. Paralyzed from fear, she was afraid to move. Her hair was tangled and caught on part of the large dial. Her sari was torn and her nose was bloody. Her faint whimper turned into a cry. Rosa, who lay beside her tried to sit up.

"Why are you crying for? You are well aware Amoli Sharma of how hideous time travel can be."

"I can't move," Amoli whimpered.

"Good God, I hope you didn't damage your back. Try to move," Rosa urged.

"I-I can't."

"Oh, no! Try!"

"I can't."

Rosa crawled to her. She grabbed hold of Amoli's shoulder. "You can move your arm. So, get up!"

"My hair is caught in something. Every time I try to move, I just can't."

Sasha up. "What so much commotion?"

"Sasha help me untangle Amoli's hair from the time dial," Rosa asked.

"Da, I will do." Sasha crawled to Amoli, where he managed to trace where in the dial her hair was caught. She winched a few times and even yelped.

Colin slowly sat up to Amoli's wincing and crying. "Lord Jesus! What's gone on?"

"Relax, Colin, Amoli just got her hair caught in the time dial. It's really knotted up too," Rosa replied.

"Oh, poor lass. If I can get meself up. I'll surely come to yer rescue." He tried to hoist himself up. He was muddy, his clothes were torn, he was bloody, and he had two black eyes.

"Perhaps I can be of assistance to you my fine gentleman," a feminine voice said.

He looked up and saw the chancellor standing before him. "Evelyn, It's brilliant to see ye, 'cause this confirms that we's definitely in England."

Amoli's whimpers stopped.

"Colin, my dear, you really do look awful. Can I ring my physician to aid you?"

She extended her delicate hand to him for help. "Please, I can't imagine touchin' ye just now. I'm lookin' me very worst."

"I see your prehistoric beast is no longer with you."

Colin looked around as he finally stood up. "He's not here, is he?"

Sasha cackled in the background. "It was like getting rid of rodent problem. I not want to see that *thing* again."

"Lets just hope we don't see any of those creatures from the other side of the time vortex again," Colin responded.

"Excuse me!" Amoli blurted. "My hair is still caught in the dial!"

Colin made his way to Amoli and kneeled down beside her.

"Who is this?" The chancellor asked.

"You know who I am and I know who you are!" Amoli blurted.

Colin tried to free her hair from the dial. "I don't think I can free ye, lass, unless
I cut yer hair from it."

"No!" Amoli's crying began again.

"I won't cut off much, lass. I'll try to be careful."

"Her hair is knotted inside the dial. I think you will definitely have to cut more hair than you think. Hair grows back, by the way," the chancellor added with a curt tone.

Colin stood up and stepped closely to the chancellor. "Evelyn, I don't think ye'd fancy the idea of yer hair gettin' cut now, would ye?"

"Did she just time travel with you?" The chancellor asked.

"She did," Colin responded.

"I thought you both were no longer speaking?"

Sasha stood up and smiled. "I will go into university and get knife."

Amoli's crying intensified.

Rosa ran after Sasha. "Let me come with you!"

"Where did you go with her?"

"We dropped off Neanderthal to his own time period. I feel like a coach driver." Colin grinned with a slight chuckle.

"I don't think this is one bit amusin.'"

"Look at me, Evelyn, do I look like I just got back from a festivity?"

"Please get yourself cleaned up. Your clothes are torn."

"Was ye at least bit worried 'bout me?"

"Of course I was. But, I would like to know why this young woman was with you on this time travel expedition?"

"Amoli knew Neanderthal. She was fond of 'im, too."

"Really?"

"Aye, that she was."

Evelyn threw her hands in the air. "Colin, clean up, we need to make a dinner party tonight."

Amoli's eyes widened.

"I'm not feelin' well. I'd like to go to bed, really."

"A close friend of mine is unveiling his new piano concerto. You would just love it."

"Surely, I would, but I'm afraid I can't attend."

"I already informed him that I would attend this occasion with you."

"Yer actin' as if yer friend knows me. It wouldn't make a difference if I was with ye or not, don't ye think?"

Amoli remained on the ground, entangled in the time machine with her hair still knotted up with the time dial. She sighed a few times with a whimper.

"Colin, I must say I am getting quite cross with this behavior. I love you and I want the world to know this."

Colin chuckled as he stared at the ground. "I really can't attend, as I already told ye. Sorry, Evelyn."

She stepped closer to him. "If you weren't so dirty I would embrace you right now."

"Aye, so I do look rather disgustin'."

Amoli sighed. "What's taking Dr. Dimitrikov so long with the knife? I'd like to be freed from this contraption."

"Good question, lass." Colin turned his head to notice Sasha and Rosa walk toward them in the distance. "Here they come, thankfully."

Sasha kneeled beside Amoli and chopped a lock of hair from her head. "You are now free, Miss Amoli."

Amoli immediately sat up to look at the hair Sasha had cut. She started to cry. "No!"

"Mate, couldn't ye let me do it? I would've done it more subtle than that."

"Her hair was caught, what can I do about it, but cut it off. Da?"

The chancellor walked to Amoli. "Hair grows back."

Amoli held her lock of hair in her hands and cried uncontrollably.

Rosa stood away from them and pretended to be interested in a rose bush.

Colin took Amoli in his arms. "Lass, I'm so sorry."

The chancellor cussed under her breath. "What am I seeing? So, Colin, this is the man you are?"

Colin looked at the chancellor. "Come again?"

"You heard me! You are my suitor and this is how you treat me?"

258

"We just came back from a turbulent time of twenty-eight thousand years ago. We ran into a clan of *Neanderthals*. They were brutal to us."

"Brutal?" Evelyn began to pace. "Any different than our future time with Russia's KGB?"

Colin took a deep breath and stared at the ground. "I would say no different, than Russia in 1970. I would say every time travel expedition has been rather awful."

"I think so, Colin," Rosa interjected.

"I second motion. All are terrible," Sasha added. "But, Mr. Limmerick like to play God. He get what he ask for, da?"

"So tell me this, my dearest, tell me why you continue these escapades?" Evelyn asked.

"Sasha's right, I've been playin' God, and when that happens, all else fails," Colin responded, feeling deflated.

Evelyn continued to pace. "Colin, you are addicted to time travel. Do you know that?"

"I'm addicted to a lot of things, but time travel isn't one of them."

Evelyn stopped her pacing. "You're not addicted to anything else, my love, except time travel."

Rosa sighed out of frustration. "I think since we just time-traveled again, we should clean up and get some rest."

"Lovely idea, love," Colin responded with each of his hands on Rosa and Amoli's shoulders.

"Colin," Evelyn said.

"Aye."

"When should I expect you tonight?"

Colin hesitated. "Eight."

Evelyn walked off.

Rosa glared at Colin. "You showed her."

Colin gently pushed Rosa and Amoli forward. "Come, lets get some rest. I've got some time before I pick up Evelyn."

"Now, what I do?" Sasha asked as he lagged behind.

"Do? Pick up your broken time machine and drag it back to the lab in the Natural History Building," Rosa responded.

There was a knock on Colin's door. He was in the shower and didn't hear it. The knock intensified. He still didn't hear it. He turned off the water and stepped out of his tub. He dried himself off and heard the knock. He wrapped his towel around his bottom half and answered the door.

Rosa stood in the doorway and stepped into Colin's flat. "Colin, we need to talk."

She sat herself down on the sofa.

"Uh, can I offer ye somethin'? I don't have much, 'cause I was time travelin'. Ye know how it is, don't ye?"

"Colin, now that we can think clearly, we need to make sure there was nothing else that escaped through the time vortex," she blurted with concern in her voice.

"Can I get meself dressed before ye go any further?"

"Well, I know you're off to take the chancellor of the university to that dinner party. Then, you will be off to your fishing boat."

"So, is that a *no*?"

"*No?*"

"Aye. Shall I get some clothes on?"

"Well, Colin, whenever I see you, it's quite natural for you to be parading around half naked."

He chuckled as he sat closely beside her on the sofa. She inched herself away from him.

"Colin aren't you taking a very expensive woman out tonight? Why are you sitting so close to me?"

"'Cause I think ye came here to see me half naked, that's why."

She abruptly stood up. "I did no such thing!"

He continued to sit on the sofa and tried to towel dry his hair.

"Well I suppose I should be leaving."

"Love, please calm yourself. We've been through so much together."

"What is that supposed to mean?"

"Calm yerself and sit a bit. I haven't any tea to offer ye."

"I didn't come here for tea. You need to get yourself ready for the chancellor's festivity. I should leave now."

"I don't really have loads of time, aye that's true, but ye can still sit a bit while I get dressed."

"I think you need to see me to the door."

He escorted her to the door. He took her hands and held them in his. "I will see Evelyn tonight 'cause I suppose I have some commitment to her. I suppose."

"Do you, Colin?"

He bent down to kiss Rosa's cheek. "Thanks for comin' over, love."

She left.

Later that night, after the dinner party, Colin took Evelyn home with one of the finest carriages in the city. He arrived to his building and noticed someone standing at the entrance. The moon was bright, almost like a lantern, where Colin had trouble defining who it was.

"Hello Colin," a tiny feminine voice said.

He squinted his eyes and stepped closer. "Lass? It's rather late for ye to be out, isn't it?"

"Are you just getting back from the chancellor's dinner party?"

"Aye, so I am."

"Was it nice?"

Colin stepped very close to her. "Most definitely."

"Oh."

"So tell me, lass. Is yer father setting up some huge Hindu wedding with some fine bloke from India? C'mon, ye can tell me."

"Why?"

"Why what?"

"Why are you with her?"

261

"Why am I with Evelyn? She's a fine wench, I think."

Amoli turned away from him. "I see."

"I don't really like her."

"Ye'd have to get to know her, that's all."

"Why would I do that?"

"Donno, really."

"I need to change me clothes, so I can get the last train to Fishguard."

"So, now you're off to your ship. You see!"

"See what, lass?"

"I broke our engagement because you're always running here and there. Can't you stay put?"

He ran his hands along her shoulders. "I'm not the prince yer father would like ye to marry. I'm just a workin' class fisherman."

"Who also attends university. How strange."

He chuckled as he tried to take her hand. She pulled away.

"Why ye shy from me?"

"I must go home, now."

"Please, let me walk you home. It's dark."

"My aunt is waiting for me across the street. I must go," she smiled at him as he watched her cross the street.

# Chapter Twenty-Five

It was almost 3:00 AM Colin reeled in the catch of herring. He gazed at the sea, where he could hear his crew's snores from down in the hull.

"Captin, I'm turnin' in. Ya think ya can do one more catch tonight, or are yaz gonna call it as well?" Eddy asked holding a lantern in his hand.

Colin sighed as he took a swig of whiskey. "One more, I think."

Eddy laughed. "Oh, Captain, you are a human machine. Will ya ever quit even for some shut-eye?"

"They's bitin' tonight. One more. I have to."

Eddy threw his hands in the air. "Ya just amaze me, Captain. How ya keep goin' about that way, I donno."

"One more, I think. If I drop to the floor, then ye know it wasn't meant to be."

"Did you get some rest on the train at least?"

"I did."

"Glad to hear it. See yaz in the mornin'."

Colin smiled as he watched Eddy leave the deck. The captain lowered the net into the water and climbed his way to the wheelhouse to steer the boat to the most fruitful location.

"I can see 'im splashin' about. This is the where I'll surely park."

He stared at the dark straight, almost in a trance and he gulped his last drop of whiskey. He stumbled to the galley and turned on the radio in search of his favorite Irish love songs.

"John McCormick! He's a grand new singer, I must say. Don't think anyone even knows 'im outside of Ireland."

*The Star of The County Down* started to play on the radio. The radio reception was almost un-definable. He opened another bottle of whiskey and took a swig and began to sing along:

*Near Banbridge Town,*
*in the County Down, one morning last July.*
*From a boreen green came a sweet Colleen*
*and she smiled as she passed me by.*
*She looked so sweet from her two bare feet to the crown of her black-black hair*
*Such a winsome elf, I pinched myself to be sure I was really there.*
*Oh from Bantry Bay up to Derry Quay,*
*And from Gallway to Dublin town.*
*No maid I've seen like the sweet Colleen,*
*that I met in the County Down.*
*As she onward sped,*
*I shook me head,*
*And I gazed with a feeling rare*
*And I said, says I, to a passer by*
*"Who's the maid with the black-black hair?"*
*Oh, she smiled at me and with pride says he,*
*"That's the gem of all Ireland's crown.*
*Young Amoli Sharma from the banks of India*
*She's the star of the County Down*

He staggered to the deck and flopped in the chair beside the large crank, used to pull in the net with the next catch. He continued to sing a disjointed version of *Star of the County Down*. He drank his whiskey as he sprawled himself on the chair. He pulled out his wallet, where a photo of Amoli fell to the planked floor. He picked up the photo and kissed it. "She still fancies me, I know it. We'll marry someday soon, surely we will." He was beyond exhaustion. His head fell forward into his chest and he began to snore.

"L-Limmerick!"

Colin opened one eye. "Huh?"

"L-Limmerick! Wake up!" a familiar female voice blurted with a Russian accent.

Colin opened his eyes. "Pardon? Who goes there?"

"You can open eyes, now! I am here! I finally find you, L-Limmerick!

He took a few deep breaths, and tried to ignore the voice.

"Get up, L-Limmerick! You better do what I say!"

He was still sprawled on the chair.

"I must say, I like the way you sit on chair. Such a tiny-tiny chair with such impressive, majestic man spread out and hanging out everywhere."

Colin finally focused on who was standing in front of him. He abruptly sat up to see Olga standing before him, holding a gun.

"Olga?"

"Are you glad to see me?"

He hesitated to respond. "Not at all."

"You know, I am so angry with you."

He was silent.

"You never say me how much you like my tits."

He almost choked on his saliva. "If ye put the gun away, I'd be glad to tell ye."

www.ingramcontent.com/pod-product-compliance
Lightning Source LLC
Chambersburg PA
CBHW010832250626
47157CB00010B/3255